YOU
ME
HER

BOOKS BY SUE WATSON

Psychological Thrillers
Our Little Lies
The Woman Next Door
The Empty Nest
The Sister-in-Law
First Date
The Forever Home
The New Wife
The Resort
The Nursery
The Wedding Day
The Lodge
Wife, Mother, Liar
His First Wife
Wanting Daisy Dead

Romantic Comedies

Love and Lies Series
Love, Lies and Lemon Cake
Love, Lies and Wedding Cake

The Ice-Cream Café Series
Ella's Ice Cream Summer
Curves, Kisses and Chocolate Ice-Cream

Standalones
Snow Angels, Secrets and Christmas Cake
Summer Flings and Dancing Dreams
Bella's Christmas Bake Off
The Christmas Cake Cafe
Snow flakes, Iced Cakes and Second Chances
We'll Always Have Paris

SUE WATSON

YOU
ME
HER

**GRAND
CENTRAL**

New York Boston

This book is a work of fiction. Names, characters, places, and incidents are the product of the author's imagination or are used fictitiously. Any resemblance to actual events, locales, or persons, living or dead, is coincidental.

Copyright © 2024 by Sue Watson

Hachette Book Group supports the right to free expression and the value of copyright. The purpose of copyright is to encourage writers and artists to produce the creative works that enrich our culture.

The scanning, uploading, and distribution of this book without permission is a theft of the author's intellectual property. If you would like permission to use material from the book (other than for review purposes), please contact permissions@hbgusa.com. Thank you for your support of the author's rights.

Grand Central Publishing
Hachette Book Group
1290 Avenue of the Americas, New York, NY 10104
grandcentralpublishing.com
@grandcentralpub

Originally published in 2024 by Bookouture, an imprint of Storyfire Ltd.

First Grand Central Publishing Edition: March 2026

Grand Central Publishing is a division of Hachette Book Group, Inc. The Grand Central Publishing name and logo is a registered trademark of Hachette Book Group, Inc.

The publisher is not responsible for websites (or their content) that are not owned by the publisher.

The Hachette Speakers Bureau provides a wide range of authors for speaking events. To find out more, go to hachettespeakersbureau.com or email HachetteSpeakers@hbgusa.com.

Grand Central Publishing books may be purchased in bulk for business, educational, or promotional use. For information, please contact your local bookseller or the Hachette Book Group Special Markets Department at special.markets@hbgusa.com.

LCCN: 2025939179

ISBN 9781538774953 (trade paperback)

Printed in the United States of America

CW

10 9 8 7 6 5 4 3 2 1

*For Louise Bagley, for always being there,
and always making me laugh!*

PROLOGUE

I sit by the pool and dip my toes into the cold water—it nips at my flesh, catches my breath, and reminds me it can never be trusted. After a blistering summer, autumn's now creeping around the garden, and I watch the breeze scurry across the surface of the pool as I remember that first night in our beautiful new home. Things were so different: we sat under a melting orange sun making plans over chilled wine, our hearts full of hope and the implicit promise of happy ever after.

But nothing is ever quite what it seems, and storm clouds can gather quickly. A summer of chilled wine and sunshine can turn so dark and cold, it makes us shiver, even in the heat. If only I'd known what was behind the door of our beautiful new home, I would never have come here. But then in life we never know what's waiting for us, and life can change in seconds, on a drive, on the beach, or inside our home.

I wrap my robe around me as I walk back to the house, where I close all the curtains and lock every door.

ONE

It's all so perfect: the evening is warm, the wine cold, the sunset slowly melting into the sea. My husband, Tom, has cooked the most wonderful dinner, and we're sitting on the patio of our new home overlooking the sea off the coast of Cornwall.

"To new beginnings," he says, raising his glass to mine. I catch the glimmer of excitement in his eyes as he reaches out across the table to squeeze my hand.

It's early June and the promise of summer stretches out before us, a shimmering carpet of sand and sunshine, our little family reunited at last.

I smile and sip my wine. *It doesn't get any better than this.*

"You've surpassed yourself," I say. "This house is perfect—you've worked so hard, Tom. I could see the potential when we bought it, but I never imagined you'd make such a difference in only eight months."

He beams, pleased that I'm happy.

"Yeah, it's been tough, especially with you and Sam in Manchester, but we're nearly there."

"Nearly there? It's perfect."

"I think we need a new kitchen..." He's leaning back in his

chair, looking behind him into the house through the huge glass doors.

"The kitchen is *fine*, Tom, I'm happy with this one." I join his gaze—the previous owners had good taste and I have no problem with the well-made cupboards in cream and the island topped with a golden-brown wood worktop.

"Don't you think it's a little old-fashioned?" he asks.

I smile at this. "No, Mr. Perfect, I *don't*. You always want more, don't you?" I chuckle. "Okay, it might not be a trendy, shiny, space-age kitchen, but it's lovely and fully functioning. *And* it can't be more than ten years old—it would be a crime to rip it out and replace it."

"I can show you some plans I've had made?"

"Tom," I say in a quiet voice, "you've spent the best part of a year here tearing down walls and . . . Let's just stop a moment and enjoy it. We don't need anything else, it's all good. I've waited so long for this, just this," I murmur, glancing around the gorgeous patio, my eyes resting on Tom, my husband, the love of my life.

This afternoon, after months apart, I made the six-hour drive from Manchester to our dream home in Cornwall. Sam, our four-year-old, was with me—he slept most of the way but woke as we stopped, yelling, "Daddy!" as soon as he saw Tom waiting anxiously on the doorstep. I could see the relief on Tom's face as he saw the car approach, and when I pulled up, he walked to the car, opened the door, and lifted Sam gently into his arms.

"Welcome home," he said, holding our son with one arm and reaching the other out to me as I stepped from the car. We were both relieved to be together after so many long months, and we stood for a while holding each other.

"I can't wait to take a proper look around tomorrow," I say now. I've seen the five lovely bedrooms, the kitchen that opens out onto a huge patio, and the sitting room in shades of green he'd shown me over FaceTime. It was frustrating being stuck in Manchester selling the apartment while Tom wandered furniture showrooms in Cornwall, but he's done a great job.

"I just want this place to be perfect," he's saying. "I don't want you to ever regret leaving Manchester."

"I won't. It was my decision to move here too, love. I may take a little while to get used to it though, it feels so unreal." Then, with a jolt, I remember why we're here, how we came to afford such a stunning house. We bought it with the inheritance from my father.

"It feels bittersweet though; if I had a choice, I'd rather Dad was still with us," I say.

"Me too," he replies, reaching again for my hand. "I've thought about him a lot while I've been here."

"It's four years since we lost him, but it still feels like yesterday." I feel tears prickle my eyes, and I try to smile through them. "I mustn't spoil this."

"Darling, he was your father, you're *allowed* to cry."

"I know, I just feel so guilty. All the money he left. It's lovely, but it makes me feel sad. He rattled around in that big old house up north, patching it up, refusing to turn on the heating, and now we're here . . ." I can't finish. The guilt chokes me.

"This isn't somewhere I ever dreamed of living," I say after a moment, gesturing toward the garden. I'm excited about the gorgeous green lawn for Sam to play on, and the prospect of that garden bursting into life. But it's bittersweet, and I can't help but compare this to Dad's frugal existence in our old family home. By the time he died, the house had increased dramatically in value, and along with some good investments, it added up to more money than I'd ever imagined. We've moved very fast from our little urban apartment in Manchester to this whitewashed house on a Cornish cliff, and all while still coming to terms with his death.

My husband is looking into my face, concerned.

"Don't worry, I'm happy, and I know I'll love it here, it's just that . . . I'm finding it hard to reconcile what we have with the life Dad lived."

Tom nods vigorously. "I feel the same. I wish he could be here to enjoy it with us. I mean, just look at it all."

We both look around at the patio, the Indian stone flooring, the seamless glass balustrade overlooking the beach. Tom has chosen the very best materials, pored over brochures, studied the intricacy of wallpapers, the hues of different paint colors and stone floorings. This place is a credit to him, to his talent.

"For a man whose career is in finance, you certainly have a decorator's eye," I say admiringly.

"I told you the day we saw this house that I'd turn it into our dream home. I promised it would be perfect, and I haven't compromised on anything," he says with a smile.

I return his smile, but not for the first time I wonder if we can *afford* the best. Most of the inheritance has gone into this house, and I earn very little as a freelance journalist, just the odd commissioned article here and there.

"I never thought I would stay anywhere like this, let alone *own* it," he says, lighting the candles on the table. "There, I've turbo-charged the romance," he adds with a smile.

I've never seen him so happy, and I know I can be happy here too, I just need time.

"I'm excited about the garden for Sam; he finally has somewhere to play," I add, thinking about the tiny apartment we've just left—no garden, just a small park several streets away. "It suits you being here," I say, considering his relaxed manner, light tan, and slimmer physique.

"Yeah, I love it here, I just want you to feel the same."

"I do," I reply. How could I not love it here? Tom's slaved over everything: the bedroom walls that go from duck egg to palest sky, the gentle move to bluey greens and the deep-green velvet sofas in the lounge. From the curated wall in the master bedroom covered in photos of us to the hand-painted clouds on our little boy's bedroom ceiling, this house has been a labor of love for Tom. "I never knew you had such a talent for interior design. The house feels so unique... It's really *stylish*—are you sure you didn't have some help?"

"All my own work. Glad you like it. I'm happy that you're happy," he says, squeezing my hand.

I try hard to smile, but despite it being so lovely here, I'll need time to get used to living so close to the sea. I'll always struggle with the past, but Tom's determination to make everything right is a comfort. This is his love language—he doesn't buy me expensive gifts or make grand gestures; Tom fixes pipes and takes out the trash cans. And now, with our newfound wealth, he is making our dream home for me.

We sit in silence for a while, both with our own thoughts tucked away, visible only to ourselves.

"We did the right thing, didn't we, Tom?" I ask, knowing he'll come through because in moments of self-doubt, my husband's always there with reassuring words.

He takes a breath; he knows the drill. "Rachel, you *know* we did. You are doing exactly what your dad wanted you to do. He said, 'Move on, stop living in the past, make new memories and a new life.'"

"I know, but living by the sea... Is *this* what he meant?"

"Yes, I'm sure it is, and I promise I will do everything in my power to make you and Sam happy here. I've been excited about my family coming home. After all you've been through, you deserve happiness, Rachel."

"What would I have done without you?" I murmur. "You've helped to erase the bad memories."

"We'll never *erase* them, Rachel, we just have to carefully weave them into your past so they don't affect your present. You can never erase what happened."

He moves his chair next to mine so he can put his arm around me, and we both look out at the view. "It's ours, all ours," he says, in almost a whisper.

"Yeah, thanks to my dad and... and you, of course."

"Yes, cheers, Roger." He raises his glass to the sky. "My honorary dad. Miss him every day."

"Here's to us, and to just being here." I push all the pain back into the past as I lift my glass with one hand while reaching out to Tom with the other. Our fingers brush, and I feel secure. I've missed him, my safe harbor. I'm almost home—I just don't feel it, not yet.

I gaze out again to drink in that sunset. I should relax, enjoy the moment and stop worrying. I repeat my silent mantra to quiet the thoughts racing through my head: *Nothing bad is going to happen.*

"Rachel, there's no need to feel guilty for living your life," he says gently, "so stop punishing yourself for something that wasn't your fault, wasn't *anyone's* fault."

I take a deep breath and try to gain a perspective on this. "You're right, there's no such thing as *too* happy, and I have to forgive myself and take some of that happiness. Just because everything is perfect, doesn't mean something horrible is just around the corner waiting for me. Does it?"

"Exactly. This is your time, you have to put everything behind you now."

"Yep, this is our happy ever after." We clink glasses, and as we do, something catches my eye behind him.

"Look at that, you can see the clouds passing the sun," I say, watching the shadows move through the glass onto the big white expanse of kitchen wall.

"What? But there aren't any clouds," he says, turning to look at the wall, alarm in his voice.

I look up at the sky, and he's right—it's cloudless. So why are shadows moving across the wall?

The hairs on the back of my neck prickle. "Tom, is someone in the kitchen?"

TWO

"Hello, is anybody there?" We are sitting outside, and the voice is coming from *inside*. It's a woman's voice, and the implied intimacy suggests it's someone we know. But this isn't a voice I recognize.

Tom stands up quickly, almost knocking his plate from the table, but he pushes it back and turns away from me, toward the kitchen.

"Hello?" the voice repeats, a faint quiver of uncertainty now edging around the softness.

"Hello? Who's there?" my husband asks. He looks back at me and shrugs as he walks toward the bifold glass doors that separate the kitchen from the patio. But before he reaches them, the woman emerges. She's smiling, but I feel really uneasy—has this stranger just let herself into our home?

"Hey," she says to Tom, who looks as surprised as I feel.

The woman and I are now both staring at each other.

"Oh, I just realized," she says, flustered, looking from me to Tom, "you're Mrs. Frazer! I had no idea you were here."

"You scared us walking in like that; we have a doorbell, Chloe," Tom says, without smiling.

She looks uncomfortable. "Sorry, I have the keys you gave

me," she says, clutching them in one hand. "I didn't know you were... here."

Tom glances over at me. "Chloe," he says, "this is Rachel, my wife."

"Hi..." I start, as she quickly recovers herself and moves across the patio toward me, arms outstretched. She's younger than me, mid-thirties perhaps. She has mid-length blond hair and delicate features; she's pretty in a fragile way.

"*Rachel!* So you are *Mrs.* Frazer?" She's now embracing me. I still haven't a clue who Chloe is.

"Oh God, you must think I'm *awful* just marching in like this, but I was dropping this off." She opens her large bag and takes out several sheets of yellow paper. "I didn't think you'd moved in yet—your husband said it wasn't until next week. I brought these for you." She turns to Tom, who takes the stash of yellow paper from her.

"Invoices," Tom says, turning to me. "Chloe works for the estate agents we bought the house from."

"Chloe, Chloe Mason." She steps back a little to look at me.

"Oh, I see, that's why you have the keys?" It makes sense now.

"Rachel, you are just as pretty, if not prettier, in the flesh," she remarks.

"In the *flesh?*" I smile enquiringly.

"Yeah, I've seen photographs of you around the house."

"I hate having my photo taken. Tom's always taking pictures..."

"Well, I can see why. You're *gorgeous*. I love that photo of you in the red dress. You look like a film star."

"Well, you're very kind, but I don't think I do. I'm not even sure I remember a red dress," I reply, slightly uncomfortable at her oddly intimate remark.

"Trust me, you look fabulous. Red is definitely your color," she says enthusiastically.

"Thank you," I reply, trying to remember the dress, the occasion. I can't decide if she's genuine or trying a little too hard.

"Chloe has been really good, she let me into the house to measure everything before the contracts had been signed," Tom says, breaking the silence. "That's probably illegal, right?" he asks her, half-smiling.

She giggles. "All the best things are!"

"Well, I'm grateful—we both are," he says, approaching me, slipping his arm around my waist.

"We haven't offered you a drink," I say.

She places her hand flat on her chest apologetically. "Thank you, Rachel, but I couldn't gate-crash your romantic evening. I won't interrupt you a minute longer." She gestures at the empty plates on the table while making no attempt to move.

She continues to stand there, smiling at both of us, and after a few awkward seconds, I say, "As our estate agent, it's only right you stay for a celebratory drink."

I look at Tom as I pass him to go into the kitchen for an extra glass. I expect him to join in, ask her to stay, reassure her that she isn't interrupting anything and is welcome here, but he doesn't. He just stands there like he's unaware of the conversation.

"Tom," I say, widening my eyes at him.

He suddenly seems to realize what I'm trying to communicate and shrugs with indifference. He's exhausted and I feel the same, but we can't be rude. Tom manages another half smile as he takes our two empty plates from the table and pulls out a seat for her.

"We opened a bottle of white. Is that okay?" I ask, lifting the bottle.

"That would be lovely, thank you."

"I love your top by the way," she says. "Such a lovely shade of pink, really suits you. Where did you get it from?"

"Bought it on holiday a few years ago, Santorini—it's lovely and cool on a warm night like this."

"Oh, I'd love to go to Santorini, I've never been. Are you going away this summer?"

I shake my head. "No, we want to spend the summer here, and besides, we've spent enough money moving in. We can't afford a holiday. You?"

"I was hoping to go to Italy but it's fallen through."

"Oh, I'm sorry, what happened?"

"My boyfriend dumped me."

"No. I'm so sorry."

"I thought he was the one. I thought we'd be married, have kids, you know?"

I see the glint of tears; she seems so vulnerable and I suddenly want to hug her. "When did it happen? How long had you been together?" I ask, then pause, realizing I'm firing questions at her; probably the last thing she needs. "Sorry, I ask too many questions. It comes with the job, I'm afraid—I was trained to ask questions."

"Are you a *spy*?" she asks in all seriousness.

"No, I'm a journalist. Always looking for the story!" I smile apologetically.

"Oh wow! How interesting. I don't mind, you can ask what you like. We were together almost a year and he ended it last week." She pauses, and I think she's going to cry, but she manages to hold it back. "It isn't just the person you miss; it's the plans you had, isn't it?" She looks at me as a child would look at an adult, and I see her pain. "Not to mention the tickets we bought for concerts and the holiday in Italy I've had to cancel and lose the deposit on."

"Oh no, that's salt in the wound."

"Yeah, serves me right for trying to surprise him with a holiday. Turns out he had a bigger surprise for me."

"And no warning?"

"No warning at all—one minute everything was wonderful, then suddenly he decided it wasn't working."

She suddenly smiles, lifts her glass and, clinking it against mine, says, "Here's to singles holidays!"

I echo this and glance over at Tom, who's slumped on a chair, seemingly indifferent to our conversation. I think he's waiting politely for her to leave, but I feel a bit sorry for her. I remember my last breakup years ago, and the loneliness was the worst.

"We're just about to have dessert if you'd like to join us?" I ask.

"Oh, I wouldn't *dream* of it—this is your first night together here, isn't it?"

"It's the first of many. Stay a while—it's nothing elaborate, I just made a fruit salad." I stand up and start to make my way to the kitchen.

"Okay, if you're sure?" she calls after me.

"You sit down, Rachel, I'll get it," Tom says, already past me and disappearing inside.

"Tom, don't forget the cream," I call, about to sit back down, but when he doesn't respond, I glance at Chloe and straighten back up. "Sorry, even if he heard me, he won't be able to find it in the fridge. I'll be back in a tick."

She smiles sympathetically, obviously recognizing the well-worn female conspiracy that men can't do anything in the home, while I kick myself for being such a cliché. It isn't even true—Tom is perfectly capable in the kitchen; in fact, he's a better cook than I am. The only reason I need to help is because I've stuffed the fridge full of food with the online shop I panic-ordered yesterday. Anyone other than me would need a GPS to find cream and a bowl of fruit salad in the yogurt/cheese/butter mountain I've created.

"Men," she says, rolling her eyes.

I can't help myself—I mirror the eye roll, feeling the need to bond with this woman. I've left all my female friends in Manchester, and I'm already missing them.

"Cream," I say to myself, walking into the kitchen. I'm trying to recall where exactly in the fridge I may have pushed it. It's lovely to be entertaining, even if it is only one guest. I enjoy the hostess "performance" of gathering together elements for dessert, making small talk, and grabbing extra plates. Once I've served the dessert, I'll put some music on. I've missed entertaining our friends and imagine having a dinner party here. This house is perfect for entertaining, and this is a mini-rehearsal for dinners in the summer once we've made new friends. Perhaps Chloe will come along then too?

Tom's supposed to be collecting the fruit salad, but he seems to be staring into the open fridge absently. I smile to myself; perhaps my rather sexist acknowledgment to Chloe was right after all, and this *is* too difficult for him?

"What are you doing, love?" I ask.

He doesn't answer.

"You okay?" I rest my hand on his back.

"What? Oh, er, sorry yes, I'm fine. Just trying to remember what I came in for."

I chuckle at this. "That makes two of us with brain fog." I smile and push past him gently, reaching into the fridge for the bowl of fruit. "Chloe seems nice," I whisper.

"I was looking forward to an evening with *you*," he replies without taking his eyes off the back of the fridge.

"I know, me too, but I felt I should ask her to stay . . . She seems sad."

"Let's hope she doesn't stay too long," he replies a little too loudly.

"Shhh, Tom, she'll *hear* you."

"Can I do anything to help?" she calls from outside.

"No, thanks," I reply brightly, ignoring my husband's mood.

"Her timing is definitely off," he's muttering.

"It's not ideal . . . but . . ."

"She knows it's your first night here; she shouldn't have turned up unannounced."

"I'm not sure she did—she said she thought I was coming next week, which originally I was. Perhaps she hoped to get you on your own?" I suggest. I'm joking, but I'm also on alert. She came to drop the papers off, but I wonder if she hoped to see Tom and not me?

"I don't trust her," he says, "and you shouldn't either."

"Why?"

He doesn't reply. He just stands in front of me, shaking his head.

This alarms me slightly. "I don't understand—why don't you trust her?"

"I just don't. You can't tell her *anything*," he adds, trying to push past me.

"Tom," I hiss, "just tell me why."

"Because she's dangerous."

THREE

"What do you mean she's *dangerous*?" I whisper, but Tom continues to walk away, back onto the patio, leaving me confused and uneasy in the kitchen.

What the hell is he talking about? I peer out at her on the patio, relaxed in her chair at the table, the soft candlelight on the patio table warming her pale skin, a little breeze fluttering the hem of her dress. *Dangerous?* She was dumped by her boyfriend last week, seems to be permanently close to tears, and she's wearing a dress in pink cotton sprigged with roses. I don't see danger.

I find the cream, grab three spoons, and head back outside.

"Just going to the bathroom," Tom says as I step onto the patio. My heart sinks as he leaves us alone; I'm not scared, but I do feel slightly paranoid now.

Don't tell her anything. What the hell did he mean by that?

I feel uneasy and I'm sure she's picked up on it as she tries too hard to resuscitate our earlier conversation.

"Where's Sam?" she asks.

"Asleep," I reply. After Tom saying she's dangerous and not to tell her anything, I'm feeling paranoid.

"So do you like the work your husband's done on the house?"

she asks as I push the jug toward her on the table, urging her to help herself.

"Yeah, I hardly recognize the place." I feel like we're on slightly safer ground now, and pour her a glass of wine, smiling blandly. "I mean, he isn't a builder or anything," I say, trying to keep the conversation light while feeling tongue-tied, unsure of what I'm *not* supposed to say.

"No, I know, he's a banker," she says in a monotone voice. "I knew him when he worked for UKB."

"Oh, UK Bank?" I look up just as Tom reemerges through the patio doors. "I didn't realize you two were colleagues." *Why didn't Tom mention this before?*

"I wouldn't call us *colleagues*, exactly." Chloe looks uncomfortable now; she probably assumed I knew. "Tom was a big boss, I was just a minion."

"I hope I didn't come over as the big boss?" Tom says.

"No, to the contrary," she replies quickly, then turns to me. "I used to get my asset-based lending figures all mixed up, but Tom was always so patient."

He smiles. "Yeah, I *do* remember that—your math took some detangling."

"My line manager used to lose it, but Tom didn't. You were so patient with me," she says, looking at him.

"I don't miss that place," he says, without meeting her gaze. "It was the best thing I did, leaving there."

"It was a difficult decision to leave," I explain to Chloe.

"I lost my job not long after you'd gone," she continues. "I'm still angry about it."

"But you have a good job at the estate agents?" I ask, feeling the need to offer some consolation—and change the subject.

She shrugs and glances at Tom. "Do you have work now?" she asks him.

He nods. "Yeah, it worked out for me. I've had time to work on the house and I've got some consultancy work coming up soon."

"Yes," I murmur, still surprised that he'd never mentioned knowing our estate agent from a previous life.

"I love the color scheme," she says, changing the subject, which is very intuitive of her. She's obviously picked up on Tom's reluctance to discuss his departure from the bank.

"Me too, it was all Tom. I can't take any credit."

"Thanks, but Rachel, you're underplaying your own role in FaceTiming the decorating." He smiles, taking my hand.

"You are both too cute," Chloe says admiringly.

"Can you be cute over forty?" I ask, feeling myself blush.

"There you go again, putting yourself down," Tom says, caressing my hand reassuringly.

"I think she was talking about you actually, Tom," Chloe quips, and we both laugh at this. She's funny, and I can't help but warm to her.

"Dessert," I say, spooning some fruit into a bowl and handing it to her, before doing the same for Tom.

"So, you two are both used to living in the city—do you think you'll be happy here?" she asks.

"Absolutely, I love it," Tom is quick to enthuse. "I liked this area when I worked here, even though it was just a few weeks at a time; it really grew on me."

"Yes, Tom's always wanted this—after working here he'd come home to Manchester complaining about the air quality and noisy traffic."

"I've been here all my life—can't imagine myself anywhere else," she says, finishing her fruit and pushing the bowl away.

I don't offer coffee as I usually would because I know Tom's tired, and it would be nice to have some time together just the two of us after so long apart. But Chloe seems to be enjoying our company and starts telling me about the nearby shops, the good restaurants, the tourist traps to avoid. She is a fountain of knowledge and would be useful to me as a journalist in a new patch; besides, she's pleasant company, despite what Tom said about her.

Chloe doesn't outstay her welcome, and makes a move to go. "Thanks so much, guys, I'll leave you both to enjoy your romantic reunion. Dessert was delicious, Rachel, and your house is fabulous. I just know you're both going to be happy here," she says.

"I'm sorry, it's been a long day, neither of us is great company tonight," I say as we walk her to the door.

"Nonsense, you've both been so kind inviting me for dessert. I feel like I sprang myself on you. Apologies again for turning up unannounced."

We say goodbye, and after we've waved her off we go back inside, arm in arm.

"Why didn't you say you and Chloe worked together?" I ask.

"No reason, it's pretty insignificant. And we didn't work together, we just happened to work for the same company."

"Yeah, but you were very patient with her asset-based lending figures," I tease.

He rolls his eyes. "Mmm, I don't *actually* remember that. I don't remember *her*."

"But you remembered she's dangerous?"

"Yeah, just rumors about her making trouble for people, stirring things, telling lies. I heard she really kicked off when she was let go."

"Really? What was she fired for?"

"Some trouble with a bloke at work, I don't really know the details."

"Oh dear."

"She's one of those people who wheedles their way in, wants to know everyone's business, and tells lies."

"No. Really?" I reply, sitting down at the table where the empty fruit dishes are attracting wasps. They hover over and around us, all wanting to settle on the sticky dishes and the jug of sweet cream. I try to ignore them.

"Well, she had me fooled. She seems funny, and friendly and—"

"So are psychopaths—that's how they reel you in." He waves his arm in the air angrily at a lazy wasp.

I laugh at this. "Tom, she is not a psychopath. I didn't see any malice, just friendliness and warmth. I think you've spent far too long on your own. You might remember, I wrote the article 'Ten Ways to Spot a Psychopath' last year for a magazine, and I promise you, from what I saw tonight, Chloe doesn't match the profile."

He's half smiling. "She is, I tell you."

"Stop being so dramatic!" I am laughing now. "You can't just label someone you hardly know as a psychopath."

"I'm telling you she is *crazy*!" He whirls his finger around his head, but by now he's laughing at himself as he wraps his hand in a napkin.

"What are you doing . . . ?" I ask as he suddenly brings down his fist on an unsuspecting wasp. The heavy thump on the table makes me jump.

"God, Tom," I snap, my nerves now jangling. "You're the only psycho around here—you didn't have to *kill* it." I curl my lip at the squashed insect on the table.

"Either that or get stung. Have you ever been stung by a wasp?" he mutters, standing up and using the napkin to pick up the dead wasp.

"Yes, and it didn't kill me," I say, disgusted as he wraps the napkin shroud-like around the smashed body.

Watching this makes me shudder, but I resist saying anything more as he moves into the kitchen with the napkin. Just as he disappears, his phone pings, and I absentmindedly look over to see who's texted. My stomach jolts: it's Chloe's name on the screen.

FOUR

I feel my mouth go dry as I pick up the phone. I look but can't see the words—only Tom can open the text.

"Was that my phone?" he asks casually as he walks back onto the patio, wiping his hands on a tea towel.

I put the phone down, feeling a little guilty that I was looking. I wouldn't like it if he was checking my phone. "Yeah, looks like Chloe texted you."

"Chloe? She only just left, what does she want?" he mutters, picking up the rest of the dishes and taking them through without even glancing at his phone.

"Don't you want to see it?" I ask. I know I do, but Tom's clearly in no rush to find out. I hear him stacking the dishwasher before eventually wandering back outside.

He finally takes the phone from the table and holds it up to his face to open it.

"I'm surprised you have a dangerous woman's number saved in your phone," I remark, jokingly.

"She's our estate agent, that's why I have her number," he replies absently. Then his eyes leave the phone and settle on me. He smiles slowly, almost flirtatiously. "You jealous, Rachel?"

"Do I need to be?"

"Well, I'm a good-looking guy, I've been all on my own here, and I'm catnip to the ladies." He winks at me before returning to his phone.

"Luckily for you, Chloe's not my type, but I have her number saved because she's our estate agent."

"She *was* our estate agent. How much aftercare is she giving you?" I'm joking, but I'm also thinking that texting him just minutes after she left, and holding on to our keys, is something more than "estate agent aftercare."

He's looking into his phone. "She says, 'Your wife is lovely,'" he reads, with a puzzled look on his face.

"Why would she text you to say that?" My mind is beginning to conjure up all kinds of reasons why she'd do it, and none of them good.

"God knows why," he replies dismissively.

"Let me see." I reach for his phone.

"Don't you believe me?" He's holding it to his chest defensively.

"Yes, of *course*," I lie. "I just wanted to see if there's an emoji or some kind of context I'm missing."

He slowly hands me his phone, and I'm bracing myself for what is in front of me. But it's exactly as he said—no emoji, no kiss, just: "Your wife is lovely."

"Told you she's mad."

"*Dangerous*, you said, so now she's mad too?"

He seems irritated. "Isn't that message enough for you? It's proof she's a troublemaker. She spreads gossip."

"How could that message stir up trouble?"

"Look at us: you're being jealous and paranoid, and I'm being defensive." He's holding his hands in the air.

"I'm not being jealous and—"

"We are arguing, Rachel. It's exactly what she wants us to do."

"Why?"

"It's what she *does*!" His voice is edged with irritation.

"She let herself in tonight, so why did you give her our house keys if you don't trust her?" I ask. His words aren't matching his actions.

"I gave the keys to the estate agents and she works there. They have a set to let the builder or the real estate lawyer in if I'm not here."

"But the building work has been done... We don't need them to be let in?"

He sighs. "I wasn't going to say anything, wanted it to be a surprise, but I asked a local builder for an estimate for a new kitchen."

My heart sinks. "Why? Tom, I've told you, we don't *need* a new kitchen, and we can't afford one."

"I wanted to surprise you."

"Well, I'm sorry, it wouldn't be a surprise, it would distress me. We can't afford it."

"I'm sorry, you're right, I just got carried away. I've loved working on this house, but the only part I haven't changed is the kitchen."

"Can we just take a pause, see how your work goes, see how much freelance work I get?"

"I'm the guy who works for banks, and yet you're the one who's better with money. The irony isn't lost on me," he says with a smile.

"I want to make a go of it here, but obviously it's been a huge move, and I still feel nervous about living by the sea."

"Of course, and I'm grateful you moved here for me—I haven't forgotten that, but I wouldn't even have suggested it if I didn't think we could be happy. If only you could let go of the past, for your own sake as much as mine and Sam's," he says gently.

"I can't," I mutter through tight lips. "I'm scared."

He sighs and, resting his arm around my shoulders, leans in, his breath on my face now. Irrationally, it reminds me of water engulfing my face, sucking me in.

"What are you scared of, Rachel?" he asks softly.

I just glare at the table, my mouth glued shut, unable to respond.

When I do reply, it's low and quiet, almost a growl. "You know *exactly* what I'm scared of."

Despite the fears still swirling in my head, we go to bed, where we hold on to each other in the night, and I try to forget.

The next morning, I wake in our beautiful bedroom, the sun is shining, and I'm feeling positive and ready to take on the world. It's a very different world to the one we left behind in our cramped little apartment in Manchester, and I love our big new house. It's light and airy, the walls are freshly painted, and the massive bed we bought for the master bedroom feels like the height of luxury. But opening my eyes to see Tom lying next to me is the best part of being here.

"Morning," he says huskily, opening his eyes. "It's good to have you home."

"Home," I echo. It doesn't yet feel like home, but I'm sure it soon will.

I'd hated the idea of living by the sea: I'm terrified of water. I don't swim, so it isn't the obvious choice. But I know how much Tom wants this, and I also owe it to Sam to live an outdoor life away from the grimy city. I mustn't let the past stop me embracing this wonderful future, but in truth, it does—and yesterday, when my best friend Rosa called me as I packed the last things in the car, it hit me. I was leaving my hometown and would have given anything to stay in cold, wet Manchester. It was my home, but now I have to make this place like home.

I get out of bed, kiss a sleepy Tom on the head, and walk through the hall to Sam's dinosaur-themed bedroom. It's Sam's first morning at preschool, and I've never felt so nervous.

"Where's Daddy?" are his first words.

I sense a little anxiety after months apart. "He's here, darling, he's just getting up. Remember I told you that Daddy was here making our house special? Well, now we're here *with* him, and this morning you're starting preschool—you're a big boy now."

I see a flicker of uncertainty in his face: he has no comprehension of preschool. He's an only child whose first eighteen months were in lockdown, so I'm concerned about how he'll fare among children he doesn't know.

A little while later, as the three of us eat breakfast, I say under my breath to Tom, "Are we doing the right thing sending him today?"

To Sam's delight, we're breakfasting on jam and toast using a cardboard box as a makeshift table. Along with some other furniture, we're waiting for the real kitchen table to arrive, and our crockery is still limited as there are still so many boxes to unpack from the apartment move.

"We could wait a few weeks, let him settle in... He seems so young," I continue.

"I know, love, but another week, another month, it's never going to be easy. He needs to mix with other kids. It'll be good for him, get him ready for school," Tom insists quietly.

Sam looks up. "What's *school*?" he asks, despite us having gone over and over the whole concept of preschool for weeks now.

"I've told you darling, it's a place with lots of friends and nice people who teach you things. Remember it's preschool first, then regular school is for when you're an even bigger boy," I say, stroking his hair, finding it hard to imagine this little one leaving the house, let alone going to school. I want to put my arms around him, keep him with me forever.

"But today, Daddy's taking you to preschool. It's great fun—you'll meet lots of new friends and play games and—"

"Presuhskool?" He stutters on the word. It's adorable. "Is Daddy coming too?"

I glance at Tom, who immediately reassures him. "Of course, but I don't think you'll want me to stay. You'll be with your new friends and you're way too cool for Dad to hang around, buddy," he adds with an affectionate smile.

Sam's bottom lip quivers, so I step in. "But Daddy and I will *both* come and collect you later on, when you've finished playing with your new friends."

This seems to placate him enough to go back to his toast, but he's now nibbling at it suspiciously, not with his usual gusto.

"Come on then, mate," Tom enthuses, "let's go to preschool!"

Together, we stand from the table and make our way to the front hall.

"I won't be long," Tom says as I offer him a light jacket for Sam. "He doesn't need a jacket. It's *June*, Rachel." His forehead's screwed up with doubt.

"The sea air can be chilly," I reply. I'm not arguing with Tom; I want Sam to wear it. "It's Cornwall, not Florida. Sam feels the cold." I'm still holding the jacket out to him.

He takes it, sighs, and rolls the jacket under his arm. "When I get back I'll give you the full tour," he says.

"Great! I can't wait to see the garden. I might have a wander out there now."

"*Don't* go into the *walled* garden," he says firmly.

"Why?" I'm intrigued.

He just shakes his head slowly.

I can't work out the expression on his face—is he teasing me? We've been apart for so long I feel like I need to get to know him all over again.

"The walled garden is a surprise—I want to be the one to show it to you."

"What have you done with it?" I shade my eyes, turn to look through the window, and my heart lifts. I can see what looks like an arched doorway in the wall.

"I told you it's a surprise."

I didn't notice the doorway last night in the dusk, and as we'd been busy getting Sam to bed and entertaining Chloe, I hadn't even ventured down into the garden.

"Did you put that door in?" I point to the archway, freshly created to look integral and aged like it had always been in the beautiful old wall.

He gives a slow smile without looking at me.

From what I remember, inside the walled garden was just wasteland; I'm dying to know what he's done in there. He sent me photos of everything in the house as it was finished, but never the garden.

"I assumed you hadn't even started on the walled garden yet," I say.

He shrugs, amusement in his eyes.

"Why are you being so mysterious?" I can't take the smile off my face.

"I told you, it's a surprise."

"It's a *surprise*, Mummy," Sam parrots in the same voice, and we both instinctively smile at him.

"Come on, bud, we're going to be late," he says, taking Sam's hand as they walk toward the door.

"Is it a secret garden?" I ask, childlike for Tom's amusement.

"Be patient, I'll be back soon," he replies softly, like he's talking to Sam. He knows that as a child, my favorite book was *The Secret Garden*, and I wouldn't be surprised if the garden he helped design has echoes of this.

"Say goodbye to Mummy," Tom's now saying to Sam, and my stomach turns over.

From the day he was born, he's only ever been with me or Tom, we've both been taken away with work, but never at the same time. Today is the first day he won't be with either of us. I tell myself preschool will be good for him, but as they leave, I feel like I'm being torn part. I try to hold back the tears stinging my eyes, but my smile becomes a grimace. I desperately want to go with them, take Sam in and be with him until I can't anymore. But I can't... I mustn't pass my anxiety on to Sam, and it's best that I stay home on the first day. This is the right thing to do, and as Tom said, I may be triggered and get upset at the preschool, and that would unsettle Sam. I can barely hold the tears back now as I bend down in the doorway to kiss my little boy's chubby cheek.

"Bye, baby, have a lovely time," I say, feigning brightness as I tickle him.

Sam giggles. "Again, Mummy, tickle me."

This goes on for a few seconds until Tom says, "Come on now, Sam. Big boys don't get tickled by their mummies."

"Tom, he's *four*!" I exclaim, feeling a little stung.

He doesn't answer, which is probably just as well. My anxiety levels are through the roof, and if challenged, I might cry in front of Sam just as they're leaving, and that isn't in the parenting books.

I watch them walk down the driveway to the preschool, Sam's tiny hand in Tom's. They have the same skinny build, the same gait to their walk, and as they disappear into the late-spring sunshine my stomach twists with dread.

FIVE

With Sam and Tom on their way to preschool, the house is quiet, and I'm compelled to open the big glass doors that lead to the patio and step outside. I think about Dad now, and how it's thanks to his money that we live somewhere so beautiful and our son will have a better life. I just hope I can live a better life here too, and leave my demons behind, as Dad would have wanted.

I remind myself that whatever happens, we *have* done the right thing for us as a family by moving here from the poky little apartment up north. We were saving for something bigger, but then just before Covid hit, I discovered I was pregnant with Sam. Suddenly plunged into lockdown, I was scared and pregnant, worried about the baby and about my dad, who lived alone. What should have been a happy time, with Tom and me going for baby scans hand in hand, or my friends throwing a baby shower, was just isolation and worry. And then my dad got sick with Covid and was rushed into the hospital when I was eight months pregnant.

It was one of the worst times of my life: I couldn't see my dad, I went to antenatal appointments alone, and no one threw any baby showers. We adhered to the rules, staying in our bubble, good citizens being considerate of our lives and the lives of others.

I gave birth in the hospital without my husband, and my dad died without family around him, only a nurse holding his hand. He couldn't be with his daughter, never got to meet his newborn grandchild, and I couldn't give him a funeral.

I take the steps down to the garden and wander out onto the lawn, eyeing the walled garden beyond. The house was originally built on three different levels, and the architect has enhanced this by putting our master bedroom downstairs, the kitchen and living area mid-level, plus more bedrooms upstairs. This means we can walk out of our bedroom into a small garden area, which leads on to the walled garden. It also means we can access the bedroom from the garden, which is why I made sure to lock it from inside this morning. So why is it open now?

I walk cautiously toward the half-open door. There's no way in to the garden other than through the house, or perhaps over a wall? I look around—the walls are high; no one could get in without me seeing them. Could they?

I tentatively open the door wider. "Hello?" I call, knowing if anyone answers, I will probably faint with shock. I walk farther into the bedroom, suddenly realizing how vulnerable we are sleeping on the ground floor like this. I wander around now more confidently, opening wardrobes, checking the en suite, and carefully looking behind frosted glass, into the shower. Nothing. I return to the bedroom, where the photos above our headboard calm me: happy times, the two of us, and then later happy times, the three of us. I see the one Chloe must have been talking about, of me in a glitzy red dress—it was taken at a journalism awards evening. I'd won the best newcomer award in my region and I was elated—I can see the sparkle in my eyes. Chloe's right—that red dress looked good on me. I was about twenty-five and life hadn't touched me yet. I never realized how attractive I was back then. *We never do, do we?*

I look at the photo of my little boy in blue plastic sandals, standing on the beach, his face looking into the sunshine, his open smile. I reach for the box on top of the wardrobe, where I placed it yesterday, my precious cargo brought from Manchester. I sit down on the bed and open the box slowly. Reaching in, I run my fingers over the sandals, shiny blue plastic, cold to the touch. I warm them lovingly in my hands, remembering how tiny he was. A stripey T-shirt sits folded in the box too, along with some photos and a furry little dog he used to hold and chew as a baby. My box of baby souvenirs... How quickly time goes by.

After a few minutes, I replace the memories in the box, put it back on top of the wardrobe and turn to leave. But to my surprise, the French doors are now closed. I am convinced I left them open, thinking that if someone had got in here, I'd need to escape quickly. *Perhaps it was the wind?* I tell myself, knowing that today there is no wind, not even the slightest flutter. I have this compulsion to leave, to get out of the bedroom and be outside, so I walk quickly to the doors and open them. As I do, I glance back at the old me on the wall, the red dress, the sparkling eyes, and wonder if that was as good as it gets.

I walk back out into the garden, making sure to close the doors, and wonder fleetingly when Chloe saw that photo of me, and why she was in my bedroom.

I'm tired, I've been away from my husband for months, and moving into a new home, I'm bound to feel a little insecure. Chloe may have used the en suite when she was here letting the builder in; she may have even used the French doors to go into the garden. It's a downstairs bedroom—people have far more innocent reasons to access it than if it were upstairs, so I push the thoughts from my head, to return to another day. For now, I have other things to do, like see what Tom's done in the walled garden. My heart skips a little in anticipation.

It was the walled garden that captured my heart when we first viewed the property almost a year ago. In my mind's eye I imagined transforming the wasteland within into a bright green lawn for Sam to run around, hiding in the little nooks and crannies of the walls. I remember that day so clearly: Tom and I just looked at each other, and I could tell by his face this was it.

"We *have* to have that house," he said on the drive back up north.

I wasn't quite as excited as he was—the house was almost a million pounds, and I didn't want to blow *all* my inheritance on it. Dad had worked hard all his life, and as he grew older, he stayed alone in a big old house with damp on the walls and leaky plumbing just so he'd have something to leave me. I never expected it to be worth so much, but there was a lot of land, and along with some investments it was just over a million. Due to problems with probate, it had taken a long time for the money to land in my bank account, and until it did, I wasn't prepared to make any plans. I was concerned that legal fees and inheritance tax would eat it all up, and only when I could see it in black-and-white was I prepared to spend it.

So, once I knew exactly what we had, I sold Dad's house, put the apartment up for sale, and bought this one. The process has taken years, but it gave me time to adapt to the idea of a new life in a different location. Tom is more of a risk-taker than me, and while he popped open the champagne and made plans, I felt sick and nervous. I just had a bad feeling but couldn't put my finger on it. Then a week later, Tom lost his job at the bank. I knew then I should have trusted my gut, but I'd been swept along, and I wanted the same as Tom: a new life with fresh air and a garden for Sam.

Tom was simply told that the bank was cutting back on staff—and his role was now redundant. Looks like something similar happened to Chloe, but they'd fired her. *I wonder why?*

Tom's been ages, and I'm concerned he may have been delayed because Sam didn't want to be left. So, I text him.

Is Sam okay? Will you be long?

In the few minutes it takes him to get back to me, my imagination moves fast. I go from worrying about Sam's attachment issues to something far worse. I catastrophize over everything, particularly when it comes to the safety of my loved ones. And Sam is my heart. My phone suddenly pings, making me jump, and I anxiously open Tom's text.

He's fine, back soon.

Typically of Tom, he doesn't elaborate. I'm dying to know every little detail of my child's arrival at preschool for the first time. I want to know what he said, how he seemed, if he made friends with the other children.

Tom chose the preschool since he was down here already and able to visit the place, meet the teachers, check out the facilities. But I'm going to take Sam tomorrow. I'll be fine, I *want* to be there for him, and I need to see it for myself. Then I'll wave goodbye knowing he's fine—but will he be fine? When will I ever be able to relax and be a good mother again?

I distract myself by turning around and looking back at the remodeled white exterior of our house. Our home. It's beautiful, and I'm very lucky. This place, this house, this garden could *save* me. It's entirely possible that I could be happy and safe here, and able to finally move on from everything. *Nothing bad is going to happen.*

I stand at the wall and breathe in the heady fragrance of old roses: deep, sweet, almost cloying. I close my eyes and try to see beyond my fear of change, my sense of loss. Sam will finally be able to play outside, run around, make noise, and invite all his little friends over. We could have his birthday parties in the walled garden, play loud party games, have wonderful, messy picnics, all behind that solid, safe wall. It's going to be magical, and I can't wait to see what Tom has done.

The garden wall is too high for me to look over, but I try to imagine what's behind. I'm compelled to rip open the door and just run inside, but I promised Tom I would wait, and like an impatient child faced with a wrapped birthday gift, I stand on one leg, then the other, longing for my husband to return and open the door.

Tom's taking forever, and I'm losing my willpower—it wouldn't do any harm to take a peek, would it? But just as I reach for the handle of the door, I hear his voice and I spring back, surprised.

"*Rachel*"—his warning is playful—"don't you *dare* go in there without me." He's shaking his head but smiling as he makes his way down the garden toward me.

"Were you watching me, Tom?" I ask playfully.

His face is pretend angry, just as it is for Sam when he does something cheeky.

"Okay, I was going to just peek through the door—you've been *ages*, I couldn't wait a minute longer."

He's still looking at me like a cross teacher.

"Anyway, how was Sam? He didn't cry, did he?"

"No, he was *fine*."

He gently moves me aside and walks to the doorway, standing in front of it, arms folded, guarding the entrance to my garden.

"Let me see!" I plead playfully.

"I'm not sure you deserve to see—you promised not to look."

"I didn't actually *open* the door." I'm beaming, enjoying this exchange.

He starts laughing and grasps my waist, pulling me to him, his arms around me, his kisses warm and urgent, just like last night. I melt into his chest, the white linen shirt cool against my face and neck. We've missed each other. I want him, but at the same time I can't delay this a moment longer, and I pull away gently. "Can I look now?"

He rolls his eyes and achingly slowly starts to open the door, then he stops. "Remember what this looked like before?"

"Yes," I reply impatiently.

"Well, when we cleared the ground, moved all the dying shrubs and garden detritus, there was something underneath."

"What?"

"Something really special."

I can't even begin to guess what wonderful treasures were hidden here, and I want to see for myself. I'm imagining a small children's play area, festoon lighting, beautiful planting, and little nooks and crannies for garden games. I've also hinted at a little train for Sam to play on, or a tractor, and a chessboard, a *giant* chessboard—I can barely contain myself.

Eventually, he pushes open the door with a shove.

Standing behind him, I hold my breath as the door springs open. I can't see any planting, none of my favorite powder-blue hydrangeas or white roses that Tom knows I love. As we walk through the arch, it all looks surprisingly flat, and I'm confused by what I'm looking at. I can't quite make it out, even as I walk farther into the sunlit space. I see nothing of my secret garden, no trees, no undulating lawn with a stone statue of a little girl in the center, no ups and downs, light and shade, places to hide, corners to read, or warm spots for cats to lie.

I stand in the entrance, shocked at what seems like an empty space in front of me. The wall's been plastered on the inside, smooth and white, and arty garden furniture is dotted around: bright, flamingo-pink parasols against black sun loungers all in a retro 1930s style. In the middle of this is a huge, dark blue rectangle.

I can't speak. My beautiful, imagined secret garden has been razed to the ground.

Tom then presses a switch on the wall, and the huge rectangle starts to move. Slowly it slides along the ground, and what's beneath is revealed, inch by inch. Disappointment stabs me in the chest as I realize with horror what I'm looking at.

What now fills the beautiful, green space I'd imagined, the secret garden of my dreams, is the one thing I can never live with. A huge, glittering, *terrifying* swimming pool.

SIX

"This was here the whole time," Tom's saying, "underneath all that rubbish—the foundations of a pool, can you believe it?"

Tears fill my eyes as I stare into what, to me, seems like a watery grave. I can barely comprehend what I'm seeing.

The past rushes up and overwhelms me like a wave. *A flash of frantic splashing, a child's screams.*

"I felt like I'd found buried treasure," he says, gazing at it like it's a lover.

I can't speak. Surely he knows how distressing this is for me?

But he's so enchanted, so seduced by the turquoise tiles, the state-of-the-art cover; he's now showing me the pool lights, illuminating the tiles which in turn illuminate the water.

"At the flick of a switch..." He's just talking, talking, oblivious to my feelings, oblivious to my fear. He simply assumes I love it as much as he does. It's like he can't even see me.

Eventually he drags his eyes from the bright blue to look at me, and his expression fades.

"Why, Tom?" I hear myself say. "Why?"

He doesn't seem to hear me. He bends down, mesmerized, plunging his hand into the pool, swirling it around. The water is now lapping up the sides, licking its lips, waiting, waiting. Why would my husband *do* something like this?

I can't bear to be here with him.

Like a frightened child, I run away, back through the arch, slamming the door behind me. I make my way through the garden, and all the time Tom's calling out, "Rachel, stop!" He's yelling louder now, his footsteps thudding quickly behind me as he runs to catch up.

I run up the steps to the patio and am marching toward the open glass doors into the kitchen when he catches up with me.

"Rachel, what's the matter?" He grabs my arm and I turn to look at him, his face a picture of hurt and confusion.

I lean against the kitchen island, panting, unable to formulate my words, breathless from running and from the burning in my chest.

Only after a few minutes can I utter anything. "Why would you... *do* that?" I ask, tears now streaming down my face. "I thought it was a garden, a beautiful garden for Sam to play in, for us all to enjoy... and you've *ruined* it. You've turned it into something *horrible*."

"Darling, I'm so sorry, I misjudged this terribly. I had no idea this would upset you so much." He seems genuinely incredulous.

"But surely you *knew* I'd be upset?"

He's shaking his head. "I'm an idiot, an *idiot*. I thought I could help you to overcome your fears. I thought if you had this beautiful pool in your secret garden, you could learn to live with what happened, see Sam swim, know he's safe."

I look at him for too long, grasping for the words. "I gave up the life I knew, where I felt safe, to come here for you. I will struggle, but I'm trying so hard. But that... that... Tom, you filled the garden with a *swimming pool*?" I say in disbelief. "Is this some kind of sick joke?"

He flushes with anger or embarrassment or something. "Look, I know you don't swim, but... I really thought if I made it beautiful, chose something stylish, the pink parasols, the black loungers." He pauses, then remembers something. "Then there's the bright turquoise mosaic in the pool itself... If you look closely, you can see our initials, TRS—me, you, and Sam..." His voice fades—he knows there's no point in trying to persuade me.

"Jesus!" is all I can muster.

He takes a breath. "I can see how you might feel it's blind of me, but it's quite the opposite... I thought... I *really* thought I could turn your fear into something else, something beautiful."

I'm shaking my head in amazement.

He moves closer, putting both his arms around me. He's trying to make me feel better but his attempts to soothe me just reignite my resentment, making me want to break free of him. I push him away with such force I almost knock him to the floor. The look on his face is pure hurt and fear, and immediately I hate myself. How could I do this to the man I love?

"I'm so, so sorry, I got it wrong, I got it so wrong." He sounds wretched, which makes me feel even worse.

He keeps his distance now, his head down, his arms either side, like a rag doll. I realize in that moment that my pain is so infectious, it hurts the people I love almost as much as it hurts me. We both stand in silence for a long time, me leaning against the kitchen island, Tom propped against the fridge, like two fighters exhausted but still in the ring, both reluctant for a second round.

"I know you can't swim, but I thought we could—"

"No, I *can't* swim," I reply, still desperately trying to keep a lid on the pressure cooker in my chest, "so why fill my garden with a swimming pool?"

He's looking at me like he doesn't know me, or doesn't want to. "Because it's not just about *you*," he murmurs quietly. "What about Sam?"

"Exactly. He can't swim either, and what if he goes near that pool..." I can't even finish the sentence.

"And *why* can't he swim?" he says gently. "Because *you* won't let him."

"I will, I just need time," I say, aware that Tom is right; I'm hindering my son, holding him back with my own fears. I haven't been able to let him out of my sight since the day he was born.

"Have you thought about seeing a therapist?" Tom asks.

I sigh deeply. *Not this again.* "I've told you, there's no point. I know why I feel this way, and the last thing I want to do is to re-live it all again and again on a loop for someone else to analyze. I analyze it myself every single hour of every single day, Tom."

"You talk in your sleep too. You're haunted, Rachel, and you always will be until you get some help," he says. "I naively thought, as you refuse any kind of support from outside, that I might be able to help by building the pool."

I soften at this. "I know it comes from a good place, love—you see my hurt and always try to fix it, but some things just can't be fixed."

"I just think that it might help you to face your fears head-on," he says, tenderly, reaching out and touching my cheek.

"You might be right, but when I do eventually face my fears, I have to do it on my terms, in a safe space."

"That's exactly what I'm saying: this is your home, and you can learn to swim. Sam can enjoy the water and we can all be together in that safe space with you. But if you really don't think you'll ever be able to do that, then I'll have it demolished. We can pave over it, Rachel, so let me know what you want to do, eh?"

I agree to think about it, but deep down I can't imagine a time when I'll feel strong enough to go in the water. As for Sam, I can't hold him back, nor should I, but I'm just not ready yet.

"I need to send some emails," I say. "I had some ideas about articles I could write."

"Okay," he says slowly. I think we both know I'm lying, that I just want to have some time alone. My head is full—how can I sleep with that in the garden, just feet away from my child? How can I even live with it while I'm awake? I'll be constantly worrying that Sam or someone else will fall in.

It suddenly dawns on me that I haven't seen a bill for the swimming pool; it would presumably have been paid for through my bank account, from Dad's money.

"Before I go, there's just one more thing," I say. "How much did it cost?"

"The pool?" he asks, clearly stalling.

"The pool," I repeat, my heart beating fast now. I can't begin to imagine how much a swimming pool costs. But I doubt very much it was in our budget.

"I got a good price, used local people..."

I wait, looking at him, my mouth dry.

"How much, Tom?"

"About sixty thousand."

"No. No. You haven't spent all that money?"

"I had it built to help you." He flushes. "And it will add value to the property, it's a good investment," he insists, desperate to justify this massive amount of money.

I just lean on the kitchen counter, unwilling to look at him, unable to take it in.

"You keep telling me how the money is for *both* of us, but it isn't really, is it?" he adds resignedly.

"I know Dad left it to me, but as far as I'm concerned it belongs to both of us—but the issue here is that the money is finite. We've burned through nearly all the inheritance on this house."

"Since the money, you've changed—you've become so controlling, and it's affecting our marriage," he snaps.

"I agree, the money has changed the dynamic between us, but that's because we both have differing perspectives. I want to conserve it—you now do consultancy work and don't have a salary, and so far my writing brings in very little and I'm starting again here, in a new place with new people. I can't write stuff for my old editor because it's a Manchester paper, Manchester news."

"So now it's my fault because I have no job and you gave everything up to come here?"

I want to say yes, but that wouldn't be fair.

"Tom, I'm not upset because we don't have regular incomes. I'm upset because we're spending what little money we have left after the house spend. And you keep making big decisions that affect *me*, both emotionally and financially. You've obliterated our garden and replaced it with something we can't afford that I don't even want . . ." I hear my voice shaking with emotion.

"Something *you* don't want? Is that it, Rachel?" His voice is calm but jagged with hurt and resentment.

"I'm not upset because I don't *want* it—I'm upset because I'm fucking terrified of it!" I yell. "*And* you've spent all our money on it!"

"*Your* money, it's *your* money. Your dad's stipulations around his inheritance were very clear: he said my name couldn't be on the bank account. Do you have any idea how that makes me feel?"

"I'm sorry he did that. I hate that he was so specific about me being in control of the money, but he was confused. Ignore the trustee—it's *our* money."

"I can't ignore it. I need your permission, your signature, to do anything! I can't even buy you a birthday gift, or surprise you with flowers or chocolates, or pay for dinner, because it needs your signature. And honestly, I don't care about the money—what really hurts is that your dad must have hated me."

"Oh, Tom, don't be silly. You have a credit card, you can use it."

"But you know everything I'm spending on it, and every large purchase has to be signed off by you."

"I didn't ask for that, it was Dad's stipulation—I'd change it if I could but I can't."

"It just hurts," he says, "and it's humiliating."

"I know, love. He was just confused in his last few months. He always said you were the son he never had."

"Yeah, well, turns out I wasn't. He didn't trust me, and neither do you!"

SEVEN

Tom and I each retreat to separate parts of the house for the rest of the day, both of us locked in our separate resentment and sense of injustice. It's only when I look at my watch and realize it's almost time to collect Sam that I leave my office and seek Tom out. He's sitting on the patio, scrolling through his phone, and I ask if he's coming with me for Sam.

"Yes, of course," he replies. He seems quiet, hurt, but so am I, and I refuse to comfort him. Besides, I still have some questions.

"Tom, where did you get the money to pay for the pool?" I ask.

He looks defeated.

"There's nothing in the monthly bank statement, no invoices?"

His eyes are damp. "I haven't paid for it yet..."

"You are kidding me, right?"

He shakes his head.

"So how are we going to pay for it? I told you weeks ago that Dad's money was running out, so why did you go ahead?"

"I thought there was enough left to pay for it."

"Yeah, we have a little still in the bank, but that's to eat and pay the bills. Don't you get it, Tom?" I can't believe we've come to this. Only a few months ago I was planning to give some of the money to a children's charity, and now we have nothing.

"It's all very well buying a house as an investment, but to sink every single penny we have into it, when neither of us has work, is insane. I can't believe we've got ourselves into this position."

He doesn't respond—how can he? He knows I'm right. He's been foolhardy, drunk on the sums of money in the bank, but he's been spending like we have more.

I'm aware that we now need to rush to collect Sam from preschool on time, and now is not the moment to push this conversation further.

We walk silently to the preschool, both angry, both holding on to our own perspectives on this as people do. When we arrive, we conceal our stalemate from the other parents, nodding and smiling during the pickup. My enthusiasm for making new friends in this new life is, for now, on hold. I'm finding it difficult to take my mind off the vast amount of money we still owe for the massive tank of water in our garden.

"Did you have a lovely day at your new preschool?" I ask Sam as we walk home, Tom and I either side of him, each holding a hand.

He nods. He seems okay, but doesn't say much. I hoped that perhaps being with other kids might stimulate him, but while the other little boys came tearing out of the class roaring loudly, our little boy walked neatly toward us and waited sensibly while I put on his jacket.

"He's been such a good boy. He's very quiet, isn't he?" the schoolteacher remarked before we left.

"He's always been like that. I think he's probably going to be studious rather than boisterous," I said, feeling like I was apologizing for my son's good behavior.

How I wish he'd roar and shriek and give me reason to tell him to calm down and be good, but sadly my child is perfect. Too perfect. I wonder if perhaps he's been affected by lockdown in an apartment with only his parents for the first eighteen months of his life.

We stop for ice cream on the way home, and by the time we reach the house things have thawed a little between Tom and me. So, when Tom holds me back slightly as we walk into the house and says under his breath, "Can we show Sam the pool?" I nod in reluctant agreement. Tom is visibly excited, and I realize that as much as I hate this, and am crippled by the fear, I have to go along with this for Sam.

"We have a *surprise* for you," Tom says, smiling conspiratorially at me while pulling Sam's hand and walking on ahead. He guides our son outside, along the lawn, and toward the arched doorway in the wall, where Tom stands a moment. Sam looks at him, patiently waiting for the surprise, but Tom pretends to have trouble opening the door. I can't help but smile as he flails around then swings open the door pantomime-style for our son, who's giggling at his dad's one-man farce. I follow them through, smiling nervously as they get closer to the water, then I can't help myself—I speed up and grab Sam's hand. Keeping the rictus grin on my face, I try not to allow fear to paralyze me. I mustn't pass on my anxiety to Sam—he *can't* know. I see Tom glancing over, checking I'm okay, then he winks at me and suddenly rips off his T-shirt.

"It's a swimming pool, Sam!" he announces, jumping in with a loud splash.

Sam's mouth is wide-open. He's so shocked, he tightens his grip on my hand and pushes into my legs for safety.

"Where's Daddy gone?" he asks, mirroring my own pain.

"He's there, darling." I point at Tom, trying to quell my anger at his ridiculous and rather alarming way of introducing his son to the pool. He's now a dark shape moving just under the surface. "There's Daddy," I say, my voice hoarse with fear.

"Daddy! Daddy!" Sam calls him, and eventually Tom emerges, smiling.

"What do you think, mate?" he asks, swimming to the edge.

Sam takes a step forward, but my instinct is to pull him back.

"Come on, are you getting in?" Tom's holding out his arms to Sam, who's unsure.

Despite my attempts to hide my feelings, I'm now rigid with fear and unable to encourage him. Sam's obviously somehow picked up on this and he's clutching my legs as I stand there paralyzed.

"Mummy, help Sam get into the pool with Daddy?" Tom asks, waist-deep in murderous water.

"I... I think he just wants... wants to *watch* for now." My voice croaks with terror. I don't know how to hide it, how to stop it. *Nothing bad is going to happen.*

"I don't want to go in the water, Mummy, don't make me." His little face is looking up at me beseechingly.

Every fiber of my body is screaming no, but I look from my little boy to my husband's hopeful face, and I can't believe it as I hear myself say, "Come on, Sam, Daddy's in there waiting. It's perfectly safe." I lie.

Tom looks relieved and smiles at me gratefully, but Sam is still clutching at my legs, refusing to even look in Tom's direction.

"Come on, mate, it's great fun," Tom calls.

I kneel down next to Sam, hoping that if we do it in stages, we'll both be able to cope. I know Tom would rather rip off the bandage and throw him in, but he also knows I would probably have a heart attack if he did that.

"Come on, darling, take off your T-shirt and you can go in the water with Daddy," I say gently. But as soon as I say this, he clamps down his arms so I can't take it off, his little body stiff with tension and absolute refusal.

"I can't force him, Tom," I say, turning to him hopelessly. "I also think he should have a life jacket on."

"I'm here, I can hold him. He needs to learn without a life jacket! You're passing on your fears..." he starts, irritated.

"I'm *not*!" I respond through gritted teeth.

He raises his arms in the water like he's done, then points his finger at me. "This is your doing!" With that, he swims away from us, right to the other end of the pool, as Sam and I stay standing at the side.

Sam's chin begins to tremble. "Why is Daddy cross?"

I can't stand this a minute longer. "He isn't cross, darling, he's swimming, and if you'd like to swim, you can go in the water too."

He shakes his head vigorously.

"Okay, if you don't want to, you don't have to go in."

"I want to go inside." He seems upset, his bottom lip protruding. I don't want to make a scene; it will be detrimental to any future visits here, so without saying a word to Tom, I walk Sam back up to the house.

Later, when Sam's in bed, Tom cooks supper and we sit together outside, eating risotto, without speaking. As usual, I'm the one who has to break the silence.

"Sorry about today," I say, "but I don't think we should force it with Sam."

Tom looks hurt. "No, *I'm* sorry, I was impatient," he says softly. "I've been planning this for weeks, and I wanted to share it with you both, but I went about it all wrong. Now instead of making you happy, I've upset you. I stupidly expected you and Sam to jump in, but you're scared, you need time. I've been an insensitive idiot."

"No, no, you haven't. I need to move on, to try and overcome all the fear, but it sits here," I say, thumping my chest. "You were right last night when you said I need to let go. You love to swim and, understandably, you want your son to enjoy it too."

"I do, but not if it's going to make you unhappy. Let's give it some time, and if you can't live with the pool, we'll fill it with concrete and put some grass down, okay?"

Relief rushes through me like a wave. I'd do that this minute if I could, but I know that wouldn't be fair. I also know that Tom's convinced I'll grow to love it as much as he does, but he couldn't be more wrong.

I say, "I'm sure Sam will come to love it. You have to be patient with both of us—he's his mother's son too, and as much as he'd love to be like his dad, I think he's also cautious like me. He probably isn't a natural swimmer like you."

"Perhaps, but now we live near the sea, it's more dangerous for him *not* to learn to swim."

Tom's tried so hard; I need to offer something. "Perhaps if we book an instructor to teach him, with arm bands and everything, that might help?" I say tentatively.

"Sounds good. I just want him to be able to swim—it's a life skill. I wish *you'd* learn too," he adds wistfully.

I smile stiffly. "Maybe one day. Just let me book someone, and let's take it from there?" I suggest, but Tom's off on one of his fantasies.

"Just imagine it, all three of us together in that pool," he says, trying to sell me his dream. But it isn't that easy. I can't just flip a switch and turn off the past—if only.

"We could all do early-morning swims when the sun's just up, and the water's still cold," he's saying, his eyes glittering at the prospect. "And night swimming, when the world's asleep, and it's just us and a big moon—it's magical, Rachel."

"You make it sound lovely," I murmur, feeling guilty. How can I object to my son enjoying that? My fears are *my* fears; they shouldn't inform the life of my child and affect how we function as a family. Tom's always loved diving and snorkeling and talks lyrically about what it's like under the ocean, the plant life, the beautiful fish, the endless blue. The irony is, what gives him so much pleasure causes so much agony for me.

I put down my knife and fork, abandoning the risotto, unable to eat any more.

"I see all the possibilities that the pool offers, but the fact is, I don't *trust* water. I know what it's capable of."

"You make it sound like something sinister."

"To me it is." My life has been shaped by water, and in my nightmares I'm always drowning.

"This time it's different: nothing bad is going to happen." He smiles, squeezes my hand, and picks up the plates to take through to the kitchen.

"I'm just going to check on Sam," he says, leaving me looking out at the wall that surrounds the pool. Is it keeping us out or locking us in? The bricks are solid, rough to the touch; the gnarled, twisty ivy clings to the stone, slithering around the soft, pink roses. As dusk descends, I gaze for a long time and wonder if the ivy is strangling the roses, until Tom returns from checking on Sam.

"Is he okay?" I smile, but he just gives me a funny look.

"What?"

Tom doesn't sit down but stands by the table, distracted. "Yeah, he's fine, saying mad things, you know. He probably just had a dream."

"Why, what did he say?" I smile expectantly, waiting for some hilarious anecdote about our four-year-old.

"He said that just now, he looked through the window and someone was in the pool waving to him."

EIGHT

Fear blooms in my chest as we both turn our heads to look over at the wall, but we can't see the pool from here. I stand up, and we both instinctively walk slowly down to the garden. When we get there, Tom opens the door slowly, and I hold my breath. I'm so tense my flesh feels tender to the touch. Tom leads the way, and in the heavy silence I hear something in the water. It's too dark to see, but I grip Tom, and we listen to the weight of water as something moves through it.

"What is it?" I whisper.

He doesn't respond. We both stand waiting in the darkness, for whatever or whoever it is to reveal itself.

"Wait here," he mouths into my ear so quietly I can barely hear him. "I'm going to turn the pool lights on." I can barely see him as he moves quickly to the other side of the rectangle, toward the switches.

It's now almost dark, and I feel alone and scared so close to the water. I see Tom's shadowy figure—he seems to be having a problem with the lights.

I'm clutching my phone. "Tom," I call, "shall I phone the police?"

But just at that moment, Tom hits the lights. I whimper slightly to see the water is moving, like an aftershock. Something has broken the surface tension on the pool's fluorescent surface.

Tom walks back to me, reacting immediately to the terror on my face, gently putting his arm around my shoulders.

"No one's here. Sam probably just had a dream," he says softly, but our eyes are drawn to the still-moving water. I can see it's shaken him a little too.

"Yes, no one can get in," I agree. "They'd need to come through the house to get to the pool." I'm aware I'm saying this to comfort myself as much as Tom.

As we walk back to the house, my old friend anxiety is slowly wrapping its arms tightly around me.

"Yeah, Sam just had a dream," he's murmuring.

"And he saw the pool today for the first time, so it must be playing on his mind," I add. "But it's creeped me out a bit, you know, the idea of someone waving from the pool. At night..." I open my eyes wide in mock-terror, but it's actually real, and he knows it.

Reaching the patio, we both sit in silence at the table for a few moments, until Tom speaks.

"Well, I guess our kid has an imagination?"

"Yes, he certainly does," I reply uncertainly.

Hearing about Sam's nightmare has sent me back to the place I fear most. It's a place where bad memories lurk in the sea caves and danger lies in wait beneath the navy blue glitter of dark ocean... or swimming pool.

Tom pours us both another glass of wine, and I see it's the one Rosa bought us as a housewarming gift. This makes me feel homesick for my friend, and the place I lived all my life.

"You okay?" Tom asks, picking up on my melancholy.

"Yeah, I'm fine, just thinking... I'm going to miss Manchester, and Rosa."

He shrugs. "I'm sure you'll find another Rosa."

There's an edge to his voice, which often appears when I mention her.

"Don't be mean, Tom!"

"Sorry, I don't mean to be. I just don't understand what someone like you sees in someone like *her*."

"Really? She was the nurse who held my father's hand as he died because I couldn't be there," I say. "She is one of a kind, and I hope she'll always be in my life."

"I'm not saying she's awful, I just sometimes think she's a bit... full of herself."

I'm not sure where he gets this from. He just doesn't like her, they don't gel, but he doesn't know why, so "full of herself" is all he can come up with.

I haven't known Rosa that long, but it feels like we've been friends forever. She was the one who called me during lockdown to break it to me that Dad had passed away. Knowing how devastated I was, she kept in touch over the following weeks by phone, and when lockdown lifted, I asked if I could buy her lunch. I just wanted to meet her and thank her and ask her about Dad in his final days. She told me how much he loved me, and how he'd shared memories of Mum, and that was it: the beginning of many lunches and a friendship that I treasure. Rosa is a positive thing to come from something terrible. Rosa left the health care service after Covid and found work as a nurse in a private hospital in Ireland, but we texted or called every day while she was there, and she's back in England now. I can't wait to see her.

"I know you don't like her. I realized early on that you guys will never be friends. You're both very different. You don't have to be her friend, just be nice. Please?"

"Okay, I guess we have one thing in common: we both love you," he offers with a wink.

"Yeah, and she can always come and stay when you go away on a consulting job. You won't have to pretend to like her if you aren't here."

"I guess I'll have to make some calls about the next job. I'll have to go back to real life sometime, won't I?" he says. "I hate the banking world, wish I could stay here and mess around with bricks and paint."

"I know, love, but now we've spent all this money on a house, you need to get out there and keep me in the manner to which I've become accustomed," I joke. I'm trying to keep things light, but I'm genuinely worried now I know the pool has taken the last little bit of money we had left. "I'd hate for us to have to sell this place after all the work you've done," I say.

"Are you threatening to take my toys off me?" His eyes are laughing, but this remark makes me feel bad.

I reach out, touch his arm. "No. I wish there was an alternative."

I write features, do the odd interview whenever I can for whatever money, but being here is going to make it harder to find stories. A journalist's biggest asset is contacts; I had them by the bucketload in Manchester, but now I'm going to have to think differently. I keep telling myself I'll make friends, and I hope they can lead to stories and new contacts. But in the meantime, Sam's my priority.

"For the first time in a long time, I enjoyed what I was doing with this house. I enjoyed working with the builders, using my imagination, managing people instead of money. I suppose that's why I went ahead with the pool. I just want to keep going, you know?" He gives a mirthless chuckle at this, and I see the pain in his eyes.

I lean in and kiss him. "I know, and I know you did it all for me, even the pool."

"Do you forgive me?"

"Of course. This place is wonderful. You've fixed it like you fixed me," I add, remembering the wreck of a person I was when we first met.

He takes a long breath. "Thanks, that means a lot." His face is tender, his eyes damp. "I'm just glad I haven't disappointed you. I really wanted this place to be right, you know? And the pool—"

I lift my hand to stop him. "It will be fine, I just need time," I say, not wanting to get into it again.

He stands up and wanders back into the house, leaving me alone to gaze out onto the darkening patio. It's at times like this I'd just like him to sit with me. He doesn't have to solve the problem or even talk about it—I just need him to be there. I sometimes doubt that Tom really understands what I went through all those years ago. If he did, he wouldn't have put a swimming pool in our garden.

I sit for a little while, the eerie glow from the pool lights hovering just above the wall like a mist, and then I hear it. A splash. My heart is jumping and, too scared to go down into the garden on my own, I call for Tom. When he doesn't immediately appear, I run to the edge of the patio to see if anyone's out there, and I stand there a long time, listening. But after a while, there's only silence and I begin to question whether I really heard a splash, or if I'm just so overwrought I imagined it. So in the end, I tell myself it was nothing, go inside, and lock the doors behind me.

NINE

We've been in Cornwall a couple of weeks now, and we're all settling in. I'm working on a new feature about child poverty, and had to spend a few days in London talking to children's charities. It was hell being away from Sam, and Tom too, but I had to do face-to-face interviews. I stayed in a budget hotel and called them on FaceTime, envying their days of playing football in the garden, and having pizza takeaways and ice cream for tea.

"I hate being away from you guys," I said.

"But darling we are fine, take as long as you need, I know how important this is to you," Tom said. "Besides, it's good for Sam and me to bond after being apart for so long. You go and do those probing interviews, I'm proud of you."

Tom had always been supportive of my career, but there had been times when he seemed to see my work as an inconvenience. In the past he'd objected when I'd had to go away, but now he relished time alone with our son; being a dad had changed him for the better.

Back home in Cornwall I continued to work on the article, but when I contacted the local social services about this, the man

I spoke to seemed bemused. "Child poverty? You live in that big house, don't you?"

The implication being: *What do you know about child poverty?* People around here simply assume we're wealthy and this is our second home. It's upsetting, because the irony is I've never had a lot of money, and now that we've plowed almost all the inheritance into the house, money is tighter than ever.

I'm made aware of this again today as we sit in the beer garden of the local pub, where Tom is greeted by locals as "the man from the big house." I find it a bit embarrassing, but Tom isn't bothered. I think he likes it—he has this glow about him that he never had in Manchester. It's probably down to being outdoors more and having a tan, but he's also happier. I want to embrace this life, be happy, too.

"Hey guys, how lovely to see you . . . Tom, you finally brought Rachel to the pub?"

I look up to see Chloe, the estate agent. "Hello," I say, pleased to see a familiar face.

"And this must be Sam?" she says, perching on the edge of the bench I'm sitting on.

Sam is busy with a small collection of Lego pieces and doesn't look up.

"Sam, say hi. This is Daddy's friend Chloe," I say.

"Hello," he mutters, still not looking up.

"Hey, I'm not just Tom's friend—I hope I'm going to be yours too?" she says, glancing over at Tom with a smile.

"I hope so too, of course," I say with a chuckle. "Sam, say hello to *our* friend." But Sam is too engrossed in his Legos to respond again, so I leave it.

"So, you're settling in?" she asks.

"I am, life is just so different here. Tom's taken to it really well, haven't you?" I ask.

He smiles awkwardly, still not comfortable around her, but I'm glad of someone to talk to other than Tom, so I expand on this.

"Where we used to jump in the car, we now walk everywhere, including taking Sam to preschool. But Tom and Sam do a lot more walking than me—they go for long walks along the beach together."

"Do they? How lovely for Sam. I don't suppose he's used to water, is he?"

I flinch slightly. "What do you mean?"

She suddenly seems flustered, like she knows. "Oh, nothing, no reason, just that—well, Manchester isn't known for its ocean, is it?"

We both smile at this, and I give her the benefit of the doubt.

Not long after that, she wanders off with her drink, saying she has to find her friend.

"See, she's quite nosey," Tom remarks quietly.

"Who's nosey?" Sam asks absently while clicking together his Lego pieces.

"No one, nosey!" I say, touching his nose.

"I don't know how Sam does it," I remark the next day as Tom and Sam return home after one of their epic walks. "You guys left at two, and it's now five—you haven't been walking for three hours, surely?" I ask, walking into the hall to greet them, flour all over my apron.

"Well, this one had a few piggybacks." Tom chuckles, ruffling our son's hair. "And we *might* have gone to the café for lemonade and cake," he adds in an elaborately guilty voice for Sam's benefit.

"Oh, really?" I reply. "That was a bit cheeky going for cake without me."

"And yemonade, Mummy, we had yemonade. You can come next time... you really can." He nods vigorously, his eyes wide as he tries his four-year-old best to reassure me. My heart tilts a little.

"Yemonade, eh?" I glance at Tom and we smile at our little one's adorable problem pronouncing the letter *L*.

We are both still smiling at this when Tom's phone rings, and he takes it on the patio, only to return a few minutes later. "I've been offered two weeks' freelance work for a financial institution in Scotland. If it goes well, it could be regular work."

"Oh... great. When?"

"I've agreed to go up there first thing," he tells me.

"What? That's short notice."

"Yeah, well, the sooner I do it, the sooner I get paid."

"Yes, fair enough." I'm so relieved. I have a tiny bit left from the inheritance, but I really do want to keep that for a rainy day. It will be good for Tom to get out there again—the role of house-husband doesn't sit well with him, and after making a couple of risottos and doing one load of laundry, he's pretty much done with the role of Stepford husband.

"With me away you can get on with work," he offers, "especially while Sam's in preschool."

"Yes, I will. I just wish you could work from home."

"Me too, but I have no choice. I have to be there in person. And my priority is to earn the money to pay for the pool," he says, pointedly.

"Tom! I think your priority is to earn money to support us, not pay for the pool."

"It still has to be paid for," he snaps.

"You should have thought of that when you were planning to build a bloody pool we can't afford."

"How many times do I have to remind you this is an investment, and a pool like that puts thousands on a property? It's like a hotel pool, Rachel."

"But this *isn't* a hotel, or an *investment*—it's our home, and I never wanted a pool anyway!"

He just stands there, his head down, like a child being told off. I hate how we've become. I'm the mother figure in all this, the cross teacher, the one who pours cold water on everything.

He stands up, walks wordlessly to the door, then turns around.

"I hate what you've become—I hate what *we've* become."

"Me too!" I instinctively snap back.

He stares at me like he doesn't know who I am, and that hurts.

"I'm going to my office. I have to prepare for work, and I have an early start in the morning," he says, defeated.

I wash our mugs and wipe down the kitchen surfaces with vigor, attempting to channel my anger and frustration. Tom's right, I've changed. I'm actually scared of the amount of money Dad left me, and I've done what I feared the most: spent almost all of it.

We were so much happier in that little apartment, when we had nothing. There was no money to spend or fight about. *The root of all evil.*

Later, I go upstairs and open the door to Sam's bedroom to check on him. His dinosaur nightlight on the bedside table is on, so I walk over to turn it off. As I do this, something jolts in my head. I distinctly remember turning the light off and leaving the room dark when I put him to bed earlier. I feel a little uneasy and glance around the room. Then it occurs to me that Tom may have turned the light back on when he went into his office. I lean over to check it—perhaps it's faulty? But as I do so, I see Sam is awake, staring up at the ceiling. I say his name quietly, but he doesn't move. His eyes are wide open and I'm terrified. Reaching out, I touch his face gently, keen not to make him jump.

"Darling?" I say, but no response. "Sam?" This time I speak louder and he suddenly comes to life and turns to look at me. His face is expressionless. I feel a chill go through me.

"Darling, are you okay?" I ask, sitting on the bed.

He nods slowly and turns to me, and what he says chills me to the bone. "Mummy, has she gone now?"

TEN

I look around my son's bedroom in abject terror. "Has *who* gone, darling?" I hear myself ask, trying hard not to reveal the fear in my voice.

Sam just turns over and goes back to sleep. Was he dreaming again? Possibly? Probably? Did "she" turn his light on? I suddenly feel like there's someone else in the room, watching. Looking intently into the shadowy corners, I'm haunted by the idea that this might not be my son's imagination, that it might be real.

I can't leave him in here alone, and I don't want to wake him, so I lie under a duvet on the floor beside his bed. I stay there until light seeps through the windows, and I'm relieved when my watch tells me it's 6:30 a.m., and officially morning. I check Sam again—he's sleeping soundly and seems fine, so I leave him and go to tell Tom, who doesn't seem bothered that I never came to bed last night. But when I go downstairs to our room, our bed is empty. Has he already gone to Scotland without saying goodbye?

I go back upstairs and hear snoring coming from the spare bedroom, which hurts my heart. Tom's never done that before, even when we've had a row, but I guess we never had the luxury of spare bedrooms before. Perhaps this is what Tom was talking about last night, when he said I'd changed? Perhaps the money has changed both of us? Being able to afford extra bedrooms means more space to be alone... Is this just one of the ways money will tear us apart?

I want to tell him about Sam, share my concerns, but I'm too proud to knock, too angry with him for not sleeping in our bed, for not missing me in the night and coming to find me. So pride takes me back downstairs to our bedroom, where I realize I'm still in yesterday's clothes, and I shower and dress, unsure of myself, my child, and my husband. Was Sam dreaming? Am I overthinking this? Has Tom had enough of me? Am I imagining things?

I'm easily scared, anxious, uncertain of everything and everyone. Did I turn Sam's lamp off last night and simply not remember? I'm doubting myself all the time, and Tom's probably right—it's the money. I feel like a lottery winner who can't handle a life that doesn't fit me anymore, like a coat that's too big, too expensive. I caress the silk sheets, stare at the perfectly painted aubergine wall and long for the shabby old life that I loved, that fit me. Who'd have thought that money could bring so much beauty but so much unhappiness?

An hour later, I wake Sam, who smiles and seems fine. "Morning, sweetie," I say as he sits up in bed, hair ruffled, a surprised look on his face.

He just nods.

"Hey, last night I came in to see you and I think you were dreaming," I say brightly. "Do you remember?"

He looks at me, puzzled.

"You said, 'Has she gone now?' Was that a dream?" I realize this is a big ask for a four-year-old, but worth a try before he forgets.

To my dismay, he just shrugs.

"Oh, I just wondered if you'd been dreaming, like you did before about seeing someone in the pool?"

He shakes his head quite vigorously, like he doesn't want to talk about it.

"Hey, big boy," I say lightly, "can you turn your triceratops light on now?"

He again gives me a puzzled look and shakes his head.

"You still can't get the switch to click on or off?"

He reaches toward it, fiddles with the switch for a while then, abandoning it, says, "No," with a sigh.

"You'll be able to do it soon," I say, hiding my disappointment. I lay out his clothes for the day, and as I leave Sam in his room to dress, I hear Tom brushing his teeth in the family bathroom. He hasn't even gone into our en suite.

I stand in the hallway, the door half-open, watching him. My instinct is to say, "Don't go, stay here with us, we can work out the money." I know Sam will miss him, and I'm now uneasy about being alone here after last night. I'm sure it's nothing but this is a big house, and I don't have anyone to call on if something should happen. I feel like I need Tom here with us.

I lean into the doorway and say instead, "You slept in the spare room last night? That escalated quickly." I keep my tone light, like I'm joking.

He takes the toothbrush from his mouth, rinses it, then pats his face with aftershave as he says, "I just needed an early night, didn't want to be disturbed when you came up to bed. I have a long journey and this contract involves a lot of work by the sound of it," he says without turning away from the bathroom mirror.

I move into the bathroom, and once I'm close to him, breathing in his aftershave, I say quietly, "I'm a bit worried about Sam."

"Oh?" He stops immediately and turns to look at me. "Why?"

I tell him what Sam said, and about the light being on. "I just keep thinking, is he *really* dreaming? Or am I going mad or..." I hesitate. "Is someone watching us?"

A frown forms on his forehead. "I really don't think…" Doubt creeps across his face. "You should have woken me. Was Sam feverish?"

"No. If he was feverish, I *would* have woken you. He seemed fine, but I stayed with him just in case."

He considers this a moment. "And he's okay this morning?"

"Yeah, he seems fine, but that's what bothers me. If he is fine, then perhaps he wasn't dreaming, so what is he *seeing?*"

He touches my forehead. "Are you sure it isn't *you* who's feverish?" He's smiling.

"No, but I could be going slightly mad," I joke. "It's probably a subconscious thing—it'll be the first time I've been here alone, and I'm feeling a bit insecure, worrying about every little thing. It's sending my imagination into overdrive."

"I think it might be, love." He's looking down into my face, concerned. "I'm sorry about yesterday—it's not good for me to leave and just lock myself in my office after us arguing."

"I've forgotten about it already," I lie. "I hope you have too. It isn't important, but Sam is, and I'm worried."

He leans against the basin. "I know you're concerned because he had that convulsion, but it was two years ago, and he's had nothing like it since. Remember the doctor reassured us at the time that it was fairly common and nothing to worry about."

"Yeah, but she also told us to keep an eye on him."

"I know, and we do. You're a good mum, Rachel. You look out for him."

"I just get so scared, Tom."

He puts both arms around me. "I understand, but you mustn't let it fill your head with crazy ideas that stop you seeing the *evidence*. You fear the worst; it takes over and before you know it, we're in a hospital waiting room while Sam's being tested for something he doesn't have." He kisses my forehead. "Remember when you thought he'd stopped breathing and called an ambulance? And when you saw bruises and thought he had leukemia, and the time when you rushed him into the ER with suspected meningitis." He looks down at me, touches my chin and gently lifts my face to his. "It was just an allergic reaction," he says, kissing me softly on the lips.

"I know, I worry, overreact, and—"

"Hey, nothing wrong with being cautious, especially where little kids are concerned. Just don't get carried away." He turns back to the mirror and runs his hands through his hair.

I stand on tiptoe and kiss the back of his neck. "I'll miss you."

"I'll miss you more."

With that, I go in to see Sam, who needs my help with his socks, and we wander together downstairs for breakfast. When I reach the bottom of the stairs, something makes me turn around and look back.

"What is it, Mummy?" I hear a tinge of anxiety in my little boy's voice.

"Nothing, darling," I say, forcing a smile.

I hope I'm right.

ELEVEN

I'm scooping eggs onto Sam's plate when Tom appears in the kitchen, and after switching on the kettle, he turns to me. "Don't forget Sam's swimming lesson is at three o'clock on Wednesday."

"Swimming?"

"Swimming?" Sam echoes through a mouthful of scrambled eggs.

"You *asked* me to book swimming lessons," he says, which isn't exactly how I remember it.

"I *suggested* we do that, but you didn't tell me you'd booked one for Wednesday," I say quietly.

"Sorry, I thought I'd mentioned it."

"Tom, can you just come out onto the patio? I need you to move the chairs," I say to get him outside where Sam can't hear us.

"I don't remember you telling me, but either way—after what happened last night do you think it's safe for him to swim? I think he should see a doctor first." I'm trying so hard not to be an anxious mother, but Tom knows why I'm like this; surely he understands what I'm going through?

He takes a deep breath. "Rachel, we've talked about this. He awoke from a dream and said something that didn't make sense.

He wasn't having a fit or hallucinating—you probably woke him up when you walked in and disturbed him."

I don't answer. It's a perfectly logical explanation, which I prefer to my own ridiculous fear that someone was in his room.

"So, the swimming instructor is coming over at three on Wednesday. If you want to book him in to see the doctor before then, you can, but it isn't necessary."

"A doctor's appointment before Wednesday? Two days away? Good luck with that," I reply grudgingly, then I return to the anxiety building in my chest. "Is he a proper swimming instructor?" I ask.

"No, he's someone I met at a bus stop, said he likes kids in swimwear." He smiles at his own joke, but I'm not laughing.

"Tom?"

"Of *course* he is—he teaches at the public swimming pool."

"Can't he teach Sam at the public swimming pool?"

"Not when we have our own beautiful pool," he says proudly.

"It's just that sitting alone watching my son in six feet of water with a stranger is the stuff of nightmares."

He smiles at me and slips an arm around my shoulders. "It will be *fine*. The instructor's name is Chris and he sounds perfect for Sam. He's young and strong and fun and ... Actually, thinking about it, he sounds perfect for you too. Though a bloke like that alone in a walled garden with my wife while I'm away is the stuff of *my* nightmares," he jokes.

"Trust me, that will be the last thing on my mind. I'll have my heart in my mouth watching Sam." I know he's trying to make light of this, but I'm dreading it so much I feel sick.

He smiles at me indulgently as he grabs my hand, and we walk back into the house. He pours himself a coffee and sits down next to our son, who's finishing his breakfast with one hand and holding his iPad with the other. "Hey, mate, Mum says you woke up in the night. Were you dreaming again?"

Sam shrugs—he's obviously forgotten.

"You feeling okay, no headache or anything?" Tom asks, casually. He's good at this; where I am intense, Tom plays laid-back dad and Sam just tells him.

"No, I don't have any headachings." He carries on eating his scrambled eggs.

"Good. Tell Mummy if you don't feel well, won't you, mate?" Tom takes out his phone and drinks his coffee.

I realize I need to chill.

"Come on, Sam, time for school," I say, slipping into autopilot. I don't know what I'm dreading the most: Tom leaving or Sam's swimming lesson.

"Isn't Daddy taking me?" he asks, disappointed.

"Sorry, Sam, Daddy has to go away for a little while, but I'll be back in two weeks—Mummy will count the days with you," Tom says.

Sam's face crumples. "Why are you going away?" he wails.

"Well, I need to go and make some money to pay for your swimming pool."

I feel extremely guilt-tripped. It's as if I've made such a fuss about the money he *has* to go. But the simple truth is that he's spent money we don't have, so if he wants to keep and maintain the pool, he'll need to earn the money.

"Swimming pool," Sam murmurs under his breath.

"Daddy's arranged for someone to come here and teach you to swim," Tom says, as Sam looks up at him, rapt.

Sam's now been in the pool a handful of times with Tom, who says he's enjoying the water and gaining confidence. But still, I swallow hard—the arrival of the instructor is going to be straight in at the deep end for me, almost literally.

I walk Tom to the doorway and we hug.

"Love you," he whispers, and we kiss goodbye.

"Love you too. We'll miss you," I say, suddenly feeling empty.

"You'll be fine, darling. Me not being around will give you a chance to write those features."

I nod, smile, and give him a little wave as he goes to leave.

I collect Sam from preschool just after lunch and am greeted by a teacher, who assures me in a sing-song voice that Sam has been "super good today."

"Super," I say, echoing her word. She goes on to tell me that he's played with all the dinosaurs, which is nice to know. But what I really want to know is if he has played with any kids.

"We had a game of hide-and-seek," she says, turning to Sam, "and you got super excited, didn't you?" As she talks, she gives Sam a little squeeze, which makes my son giggle. I'm never quite sure of the teacher's "super excited" reports of his mornings—are they real, or perhaps more about preschool PR?

"That sounds great, erm"—I look at her name badge—"Iris. So, he's been playing with the other children?" I ask hopefully, because despite seeming to enjoy preschool, he still doesn't mingle much as far as I can tell.

"Yes, he's been playing with the others." She looks around to locate a child. "He loves playing with Emily, don't you, Sam?"

Sam nods, and my heart lifts a little—perhaps he's just different from the boys currently attempting to take each other's heads from their bodies? A little reticence may not be a bad thing, I conclude, as two boys steamroll into my legs while roaring fiercely at each other.

"Had a good morning, darling?" I ask Sam as we walk out of the building. "What games did you play with Emily?"

"We played dead, and we went to heaven, like her daddy."

This jolts me slightly. "Oh, I'm sorry about that. Poor Emily."

"Emily says everyone dies. She says *you're* going to die, but you aren't, are you, Mummy?"

"Well, I will *one* day," I reply, not quite ready for this big conversation but taking a shot at it. "Hopefully it will be a long, long time before that happens."

"Will you be a hundred?"

"I hope so. That would be nice." I wonder if I should add some more reassurance, but he seems happy with that, and before I can add anything, I see a face I recognize.

Chloe.

She turns and spots me instantly, and I give a little wave. Waving back, she immediately abandons the group of mums she's been talking to. She's now marching over with her child, smiling broadly.

"Hey, Rachel! How lovely to see you guys here—hello, Sam!" She looks down at my son, who smiles back shyly.

"Good to see you too," I reply. I look down at the little girl holding her hand and see that it's Emily, Sam's new friend.

"And this is Emily?" I say. "Apparently Sam and Emily are friends."

"Yes, Emily talks about him all the time!" She seems as pleased as I am that her daughter has a friend. "I haven't seen you here before—your husband usually collects Sam?"

"It depends. I work from home, so we fit around that."

"Ah I see, my sister usually brings Emily on her way in to work."

"Oh, looks like you and I have missed each other. But Tom's away for a couple of weeks now, so I'll be doing both runs."

"Lovely! I was thinking, perhaps Sam would like to come and play with Emily one day after school?" Chloe says, looking at them both.

The children immediately jump up and down—it's good to see Sam so animated.

"Shall we make a date?" Chloe looks up at me, smiling.

I hear Tom's voice—*She's dangerous*—but I can't say no to her; that would be rude.

"Mummy, Mummy, yes . . . a date!" Sam's clamoring, and so is Emily.

"Pleeease," she's saying, "playdate?"

I have no choice. "That sounds good." I try to hide the uncertainty in my voice and not think about Tom's reaction to this.

"So tomorrow?"

"Oh, I don't know . . ." I start.

"Mummy, YES!" Sam's jumping up and down. I'm delighted, but Tom's warning that Chloe is dangerous echoes around my mind.

"Come on, Rachel, we can't let the kids down. The weather's lovely—we can all sit in the garden, and I'll make a picnic." She turns to the children. "Shall we have a picnic tomorrow, kids?"

There's now so much excitement I can't possibly say no. And even if I refuse tomorrow, what about the next day and the day after that? I can't keep disappointing the children. I'm so pleased that Sam has a friend, it would be wrong to deny him this chance.

"Yes, thank you, Chloe, that would be lovely," I hear myself say. This is followed by whoops of excitement from Sam and Emily.

I manage to convince myself it will be good for Sam. I like Chloe, Tom isn't here to approve or disapprove, and as I don't have any friends here yet and she has a child the same age, what harm would it do?

"We can walk a little with you," she offers as we wander through the school gates and walk down the road. "How are you enjoying life here? It must be very different from Manchester," she says.

"Yes, it is. I love it here, but I miss my friends. I haven't really had a chance to meet many people here yet."

"Well, let me be your *first* friend," she says, turning to me, smiling warmly.

"Thank you," I reply. "Actually, I'm working on an idea for a feature in the area, and as you are born and bred here, I'd love to pick your brains tomorrow?"

"It would be a pleasure. I can share the dark secrets from the underbelly of the village," she says with a giggle.

"That's *exactly* what I'm after," I joke.

We walk on a little farther until we get to the corner of their road.

"This is us," Chloe says.

"Okay, well, we'll see you tomorrow."

Chloe's beaming and the two kids are still holding hands and walking on ahead. Emily is a little taller and a few months older than Sam, and in her way, she's looking after him. Watching them melts my heart. Chloe nudges me, and we both smile at them. "She's a nurturer, our Emily," she says. "Don't you ever worry about Sam while she's around, she'll be his big sister."

I'm comforted by this, and I know I have to encourage this friendship for Sam's sake. "Sam, come to Mummy, and say goodbye to Emily. We're going to her house tomorrow after preschool."

When we wave goodbye on the corner, and Chloe and Emily set off down their road, I'm filled with a cautious optimism. If Tom's right and she's a troublemaker, I'll pick up on it tomorrow and steer clear, but if I don't get any bad vibes, then that's the last time I listen to Tom for friendship advice. If he complains about me seeing her, I'll point out that he's the one who wants me to be happy and settle here. In my opinion she's a really nice, friendly woman, and at the moment, I need a friend. I might just keep this prospective friendship to myself for now, but I'm sure Tom's got her wrong. Chloe isn't dangerous—if I thought for a minute she was, I wouldn't be taking Sam to her house for a playdate tomorrow, would I?

TWELVE

The minute we get home from preschool, the landline is ringing, and I run inside and grab it.

"Hey." It's Tom, and his voice sounds soft. "I'm missing you already."

"I knew you would, I'm pretty special," I tease.

"You sure are. How's our boy?"

I turn on the speaker so we can all talk.

"Daddy's on the phone, baby," I say to Sam, who yells, "Dad-deee!" This is so loud, and unexpected, I ask Sam to turn down his volume.

"He's fine," Tom's saying, laughing at the reception.

Sam tells Tom all about the revered train set at preschool while I get him a drink.

"When I get back will you show me the train?" Tom's asking.

"I think we'd have to ask Miss Johnson first." Sam delivers this with great consideration and seriousness.

"I'm sure if you ask her, she'll let me see it," Tom replies.

"She *might*, but you aren't a schoolkid like me. So, who knows?" He holds out both hands and shrugs, and it's messy and uncoordinated. And melts my heart.

"Sam can't make any promises, Daddy," I interject. "I guess you need to see what Miss Johnson says," I offer.

"*Exactyee.*" Sam hasn't used this word before, and he still hasn't mastered the *L*; he obviously picked it up at preschool, and he says the word slowly, enjoying how it feels, like a first taste of ice cream. I love watching my child grow.

"So, Sam had a good morning at preschool, and he has a friend, don't you, Sam?" I say.

"A friend? Oh that's *good*." I hear the relief that matches mine in his voice. "So what's his name?"

"Emily," Sam mutters. He's playing with one of his toys and is a little distracted.

"That's a funny name for a boy," Tom jokes.

"She's not a boy, Dad, stop being a *dick*!"

I'm shocked and do a double take. I can tell from Tom's silence that he's surprised too. I was aware that being at preschool would extend his vocabulary, but I didn't expect *that*.

"Sam, that's not very nice, please don't say that." I frown at him.

He looks up from his tyrannosaurus truck. "Why?"

"Sam, who uses words like that to you?" I ask.

He shakes his head vigorously.

"Apparently unwilling to share any more of his personal life with his parents," Tom says.

"And there's me thinking the kids around here are nice."

"Probably one of the schoolteachers," Tom jokes. "That Iris is a foul-mouth."

"What did Daddy say?" Sam asks.

"Nothing, darling, grown-up talk," I reply. "We have to be careful," I say, quietly now. We then make kissing noises at Tom and he's gone, and I think we both feel a little lost.

That night, I ask Sam again who says "the naughty words."

"My friends."

"Emily?" I ask, because that's the only friend he has, and to my disappointment, he nods.

"I think you should tell her next time that it isn't very nice."

"She told me she heard her mummy say it." He opens his mouth in comic shock.

"Oh dear—perhaps I should tell her mummy not to, because it's not nice."

"Is Emily's mummy your friend?"

"Yes, I think she will be, but friends have to get to know each other first. She was sort of Daddy's friend and now she's mine too. It's okay to have more than one friend," I say, wanting him to understand that friendship doesn't just revolve around one person. As delighted as I am that he has a best friend, I hope he'll also make friends with the other kids. But as he falls asleep mumbling about dinosaurs, I think for now the message is lost on him.

Back downstairs, I call Rosa and tell her all about Sam's extended vocabulary.

"I guess this is all about him growing up," she says. "I've not seen him for ages."

Rosa didn't come to the apartment much when Tom was there. After he came to Cornwall, she stayed over sometimes, but she only saw Sam fleetingly as he'd always been in bed by the time she'd finished her nursing shift.

"I find it really hard to imagine Sam saying anything other than goo-goo, let alone *dick*."

"Do you have to say that word with such relish?" I ask with a giggle.

"Don't like the feel of it on the tongue, then?" she jokes.

"Please stop."

"Dick, dick, dick," she sings down the phone.

"Thank you. I wonder why I ever thought that calling you would help." As always she's made me smile and put things into perspective. It's funny. It's what kids do.

"I think you dealt with it really well," she says. Just then Tom calls, so I say goodbye to Rosa and pick up his call.

"You okay?" he asks.

"I'm good, but missing you."

"Me too."

"Have the company put you up in a nice hotel?"

"Yeah, it's not exactly The Waldorf, but I'm only here two weeks, and the money's good, so not complaining."

He sounds positive; it's probably good for him to work again.

"I saw Chloe today," I say. I wasn't going to mention it, but I felt conflicted. I don't want silly secrets from Tom. I don't want to deceive him.

"Chloe?" He sounds confused.

"Yeah, the estate agent?"

"Oh, *her.*"

My heart sinks. "She seems really nice, Tom. I think she's harmless, you know."

"I told you she's a gossip—you can't trust anything she says, she has a weird relationship with the truth. Please don't get caught up in her web, Rachel, she can be very beguiling."

"I agree, she seems so warm and friendly, I find it hard to understand why you say she's *dangerous?*"

"She is, trust me, and part of her danger is because, as you say, she appears warm and friendly. But she isn't, she's nosey and gossipy and it bothers me that as an estate agent she gets to root around people's homes and get knee-deep in their business."

I scoff at this. "I'm sure she's got better things to do, and you're the one who *gave* her the keys, Tom."

"I told you, before the contracts were exchanged, she broke some rules for me, and let me in to take measurements. It saved us a lot of time and money, and I thought she was okay then, and was happy for her to have keys to let the workmen in and out. I just didn't expect her to turn up unannounced the other evening."

"I was surprised too, but she explained it was because she thought no one was in and she was dropping off some documents. If you feel so strongly, let's get the keys back off her?"

"Yes, good idea."

"I don't mind asking her."

"It might be better if I just get in touch with the agents? If you ask and she takes offense, it could lead to trouble. You have to be careful of someone like Chloe."

He's still so against her, I decide he doesn't have to know I'm taking Sam for a playdate tomorrow. It would only worry him, and besides, I'm a grown-up who can make my own judgments about people. If I see any red flags, I'll keep my distance.

We chat some more, and I tell him about the feature I'm writing.

"That sounds great, I have good work news too," he announces. "They want me back for some more consulting over the summer. I will have to go back about a week after I'm home, then there may be more weeks on and off. Do you mind?"

"No, not at all," I reply, relieved. "You've obviously impressed them."

This means some money will be coming in to pay the bills. We'd never survive on the occasional article I get commissioned to write.

"Oh, before you go," I say. "If you call me tomorrow afternoon and I don't answer, I thought I'd take Sam out, buy him some new T-shirts." I'm surprised at my own cunning, but we do what we must. Sam is desperate to go to tea at Emily's and I won't disappoint him just because Tom won't think it's a good idea.

"Sounds good, but Sam hates clothes shopping—remember the tantrum last time?"

"Oh God, yeah." I recall the shouting and screaming in Marks and Spencer when I wanted him to try shorts on. "But this time I have a plan to bribe him with a milkshake or ice cream or both!"

I put down the phone, sure that Chloe is fine, and trustworthy.

Tom's a man's man: he doesn't seem to get women, particularly ones he doesn't know very well. I think that makes him uncomfortable around them. He's the same with Rosa—he doesn't understand our friendship, and that's fair enough. I think about the keys, and it occurs to me that Chloe may not be the only one with access to the keys to our house. They might be left at the estate agents, or they could have been left with the builders, and someone seeing a set of keys to a house like this might decide to get themselves a set cut. Thinking about it, so many people could have had access to that spare set of keys—Tom was stupid to just hand them to the estate agents. I'm not waiting for him to call them; I'll ask Chloe next time I see her if she has them and get them back.

I sit in the kitchen, knowing I could write or watch TV or read, but it's too quiet, and the shadows are drawing in around me. I stare out of the huge, glass bifold doors, which by day are filled with a view of the patio and garden. But now, when I look out, all I see is a reflection of me, alone in the semi-darkness, and as I stare, I feel my heart contract.

Did someone just run across the patio?

I literally can't move with fright. Even my breathing has stopped. I'm holding my breath for fear I might make a noise and alert them. If someone's out there and I see them, that means they can see me. Alone. Eventually, when I'm able to move, I grab a knife from the rack and move toward the glass. I'm holding it tightly as I unlock the door, turn on the patio lights and slowly, cautiously step out into the night.

Standing on the patio, I know if anyone comes near me, I will use this knife, I will plunge it into them and have no remorse. This is my home, my child is sleeping inside, and nothing and no one will ever harm him while I'm here. I move slowly onto the patio, and just as I'm about to turn around and walk back in, I see it. I can't believe my eyes: an orange beach towel that I've never seen before is lying across the sofa on the far side of the patio.

What the hell?

Looking around me, I walk slowly toward the sofa. The towel looks so alien to me: I've never seen it before. Cringing, I reach out tentatively and touch it with just my fingertips. A jolt of fear runs through me. It's damp!

Has someone been swimming in the pool? Are they still here?

THIRTEEN

Leaving the towel, I immediately run inside, lock the doors, and call the police. "You found a towel on your patio?" the woman says, in a voice that suggests she has far more serious things to be dealing with.

"Look, I know it doesn't sound serious, but my son thinks he saw someone in the pool the other evening."

"Pool? You have a pool?" Envy, or even hate, simmers on the line, that same tone as the social worker I spoke to about writing an article about child poverty. I'm beginning to think we could be the target of locals who simply think we're here to drive up property prices.

"Yes, we have a pool," I reply, wanting to apologize for the unnecessary swimming pool in my garden. I feel shame at the sheer decadence of this when there are children in the world with no food to eat.

She logs my call and says to call again if I should have any concerns, but I can tell by her monotone that she doesn't mean it.

I put the phone down, realizing how pointless it is to call the police, and so I call Tom, who doesn't pick up. He's probably asleep after the long journey today. So I double-check all the doors, turn out the lights, and go to bed.

Having stayed awake all night thinking about it, I decide in the morning I'll put the towel in a carrier bag and keep it as evidence if anything else should happen. I speak briefly to Tom, who at first seems horrified and then tones it down so as not to escalate my fears, which are probably quite apparent.

"It's probably local kids who decided to do a midnight swim—the downside of having our own pool," he says. "You did right to call the police though."

I put the phone down, my worries alleviated slightly, and go to wake Sam, who's excited about preschool and going to Emily's house. I try to focus on this: it's something nice and innocent and Chloe doesn't seem to have an issue with us living here. Hell, she sold us the house!

Once downstairs, I go straight out onto the patio to retrieve the alien towel, but to my dismay it's gone. "Damn it," I murmur under my breath. Now the police won't believe me, and I wonder fleetingly if Tom will doubt me too. Then I start to question myself. I was tired and scared and . . . No, I definitely saw it, I touched it.

Didn't I?

"Hey, Rachel!" Chloe is waiting outside the school with Emily that afternoon. I still feel a little guilty about not telling Tom I'm spending time with her, but I want to make up my own mind who I choose to be friends with. Besides, after last night's discovery on the patio, I need all the friends I can get—this place is starting to feel creepy.

"I offered to grab Sam, but of course Iris says that's not allowed." She rolls her eyes.

"It's fair enough—at least we know they won't hand our kids

over to anyone," I say, and her face drops slightly. "Not that you're *anyone*," I add quickly. She smiles, happiness restored.

"I'll just get him. I want to ask Iris how he's been anyway."

Iris is surrounded by children waiting to be collected, including Sam—according to Iris, he's had a "super busy" morning.

I thank her and take his hand to join Chloe and an excited Emily, who are waiting for us in the playground.

"Sam, Sam, you're coming to my house," she's saying and, grabbing his hand, she whisks him on ahead. Within seconds they are laughing, and Sam is happy again.

As we take the short walk through the village to Chloe's, she's like a tour guide. "That's the best deli—they make their own sourdough. And Wilkinson's, the butcher, does really lean mince and great sausages."

"That's good to know, I need some local knowledge," I say, taking it all in.

"Ah, local knowledge, that's something quite different." She chuckles. "Freddie Wilkinson, the butcher, is a real ladies' man, so watch yourself in there; he's had plenty of affairs, that one. Marina, who runs the deli—she's Spanish, I think—has a thing for younger men. She's in her fifties now, but I heard that years ago she had this big fling with a bloke who was still in college! Then there's the vicar—"

"Stop! Not the vicar?" I say in an outraged voice.

She laughs at this. "He's *gorgeous*."

"Oh wow, perhaps I'll find religion here too? Who'd have thought this sleepy little Cornish village had so much going on?"

"That's the thing, Rachel, people get bored living in a sleepy village—and bored people do crazy shit."

I smile to myself as she chats away—no proof, just scandal and rumor. So *this* is why Tom thinks she's dangerous and a gossip! She was probably filling him in on the butcher's prime cuts and the deli-owner's predilection for young blood throughout our house purchase. But her lurid tales of lust under the shop counter are harmless, and it's clear she loves the retelling and she's very amusing. As we pass the estate agents, where she works, I'm intrigued to know if she has any juicy gossip about anyone there.

"No, I don't—all a bit boring, I'm afraid," she says.

"That's a shame." I slow down a little to look at the property porn in the window.

"Come on, guys, let's get a move on," she calls to the kids, increasing her speed, and they walk in front of her. And when I turn around, she's moved on quite a way down the road. I have to jog a little to catch them all up.

"How long have you worked at the estate agents?" I ask.

"I'm not there anymore. I left ages ago," she says dismissively.

But now I'm intrigued. Is she being deliberately vague? "Oh, when did you leave?"

"Just recently. I was freelance, they just stopped using me."

"Oh, it's just that you still have the keys for our house?" This feels a little suspicious to me, and Tom's doubts about her are now refreshed in my mind.

"Keys?" she's saying, looking at me blankly.

"When you came over to ours that night. You let yourself in with the spare keys from the estate agents," I remind her.

"Oh *yes*, I forgot about that." She calls to Emily, "Speed up, or we'll never get you home," and then she turns back to me. "I gave them back to him."

"To Tom?"

"Yeah, I dropped them off with the documents that night. I gave them back to Tom. He has them." She sounds panicked, like she's trying to convince me.

"Oh, of course, I didn't mean . . . I wasn't *accusing* you of . . ."

"Sorry," she says. "It's just that no one ever believes me. I understand that you'd be worried about someone having the keys to your house, but I don't have them. And I don't want you to think I'm lying—ask Tom, he has them."

She's now opening the little gate that leads up the path to her house, and Emily's yelling about ice cream.

"Yes, Emily, calm down," she says, rolling her eyes at me.

Sam has pulled away from the little girl and is now clutching my hand. Visiting friends is all very new to him.

"Do you mind Sam having lemonade? It's homemade," she asks once we're inside. I've followed her into the kitchen while the children are grabbing some toys to take out onto the lawn.

"I don't mind at all," I say.

She fills a large glass jug with ice that clinks as she adds the lemonade straight from the fridge.

"Coffee, tea or something stronger?" she asks with a wink. I opt for coffee, and she puts the kettle on.

"I love the kitchen," I say, looking around at the warm pink walls, the old beams painted cream and pretty floral cushions and curtains. It's quaint, a bit like Chloe, who seems to wear lots of dresses and bright lipstick. She's pretty in that way too, with mid-length blond hair, a round face, clear skin.

"Yeah, my sister says it's a bit pink—but I love pink." She smiles and calls through to the kids to come outside with us. We all troop after her into the tiny, sunlit garden, where Emily immediately starts climbing the apple tree.

It's probably me, but I feel like there's now an awkwardness between us after I questioned her about the keys.

"Do you mind me asking about Emily's dad?" I ask cautiously. Sam said Emily's father is dead; this may or may not be true, but either way I need to tread carefully.

She doesn't answer.

"Tell me to mind my own business, it's just that I know you're getting over a breakup, so I just wondered if . . ."

She shakes her head. "Nothing to do with Emily." She looks like she's about to cry.

"I understand if you'd rather not—"

"Thanks, I'd rather not, don't want to get upset in front of the kids."

"No, of course not, sorry, I shouldn't have asked."

"Rachel, please don't apologize—a friend should be able to ask anything. I just get upset, that's all."

Poor Chloe. She's lost the father of her child and then goes on to be hurt by someone else. It's so sad—here she is in her hometown, surrounded by familiar friends and places, but she doesn't have anyone of her own. She's too young to be a widow. I can see now why she's so keen to welcome us into her world; she's probably lonely like me. I know I have Tom, but he works away, and that's not going to change anytime soon, especially with the swimming pool cost, so Chloe and I both need some kind of companionship. Our kids get along, and so do we; this feels like fate, like we were meant to meet. I'm smiling, the sun is shining, we're in a lovely little garden, and my boy is running around playing cowboys with his new friend.

"Life doesn't get any better than this," I say, and I sip my coffee, close my eyes, and lift my face to the sun.

When she doesn't reply, I open my eyes to see she's watching me. I feel slightly uneasy, but I smile, and she smiles back, immediately responding to what I just said.

"It's okay, I guess," she says.

"It's *perfect*—don't you love being in the sunshine with happy kids?"

"Yeah, but your garden's bigger, with a swimming pool and happy kids!"

My stomach lurches at the thought. I hope Chloe isn't like everyone else, resenting us for having that great big threatening thing in the garden.

"I don't even like it," I say.

"Really? But you're so lucky, it must be wonderful to swim every day and great for children."

I shrug.

"Oh God, that must have sounded terrible. I wasn't asking to be *invited*," she says earnestly as she touches my arm. "It's just that I've heard all about it from Tom. He was so excited when he discovered the old swimming pool in the foundations."

"Yeah, well, it's not everyone's idea of heaven."

"Tom said you'd love it. He couldn't wait to show you."

I roll my eyes. "It isn't quite like that."

"Oh?"

"I have this... Oh, it sounds stupid, but I don't even swim. I'm scared of water." I'm not ready to tell her everything. I'll save my life story for when we know each other better.

"Oh wow, no wonder you're pissed off. Does he even *know* you?"

"He's just so excited and in love with the whole idea, I think he just assumed I'd be carried away by it too."

"He doesn't understand you, does he?"

"No, not about this he doesn't," I say, feeling disloyal to Tom, but seeing for the first time in a while. "I know it sounds bonkers, but it feels like a constant malevolent presence in the garden, like it's waiting for me, waiting for Sam."

"You're giving me the creeps, Rachel, and it's such a shame you feel like that. It's nothing to be frightened of," she says rather glibly.

"That's what everyone says but it's not true," I hiss, and she recoils slightly. "Sorry," I say, feeling bad. "I didn't mean to snap, I know it's irrational, but I'm terrified, and nothing and no one can change that."

I feel the rush of blood to my head, like the rush of the sea coming toward me as I stand on the shore. It's swallowing everything up, stealing what I love. I see the cold, dark grave in my garden, deep and determined. My fear of water is shaped by what happened, and I'm back there now.

A beautiful day, a beautiful family at the beach. Mummy smiling at her little one, Daddy making sandcastles and the little boy helping. The spade's too big for his little hand, and the parents laugh affectionately at their precious boy with his determined chin and chubby knees.

I feel the sting of tears. I have to stop. I mustn't go there—I need to stay here in this garden, in the now, with Chloe and the children.

"It's not just a swimming pool," I say, "it's so much more than that."

FOURTEEN

"If it upsets you so much, why doesn't Tom get it covered over?" Chloe suggests logically. But this isn't about logic, it's about two people who have their own needs and desires and fears, and we both have to make compromises, especially me.

"He could make a play area for Sam instead? It's your home too, Rachel, and if you feel unnerved by it, you'll never be happy."

"I think it would kill him to cover it up," I reply. As much as it scares me, for Tom it's like a source of pride, energy; it's something *he* created—the last thing he wants to do is destroy it.

"We have these money issues," I tell her. "I have an inheritance from my dad and though Tom's grateful for it, he also resents it, feels like he should be the provider, the one who gives me what I want. It's old-fashioned, I know."

"Yeah, the 1940s called, they want your husband back," she says, smiling at her own joke.

"Yeah, but he's always been the rescuer, you know? When we first met, I had some mental health issues, and he helped me, saved me really. I'm okay now, but that's been our dynamic. Tom still looks after me, even though I don't need him to do that as much anymore."

"I guess if you're happy to let him, that's okay?" she replies rather disparagingly.

"It's fine, we're happy," I reply defensively. Her comment is challenging, makes me feel weak and causes me to momentarily question my relationship with Tom.

"Anyway, what I'm trying to say, rather clumsily," I admit, "is that the pool is Tom's way of showing his love. He built it with his bare hands for me, so it makes it even harder for me to reject it."

"Yeah, but if you're scared, then—"

"I know it doesn't make a lot of sense, and it's hard to explain. But Tom's mum left the family when he was just a kid—she walked out and said she'd be back soon. He's still waiting."

"Oh, that's so sad."

"It is, and as a child, he blamed himself; he felt he'd somehow disappointed her. I think that's what motivates him—he doesn't want to disappoint anyone, especially me, and despite my fear, he just saw an opportunity to please me by building a swimming pool."

"Is that his love language, do you think?"

"I hadn't thought of it that way, but yeah, I think it probably is." I'm now distracted by Sam following Emily up the tree.

"Be careful, Sam," I say. "Why don't you and Emily play with the toys you've brought outside?" I add, hoping Chloe takes my cue and asks Emily to come down from the tree.

But she seems to have drifted off and her eyes are soft. I think she'd love a Tom of her own. "They're fine," she says quietly, almost to herself. "He's a little boy, he *should* climb trees."

She's right, of course, and I feel slightly shamed by this. "I know, he should, but I worry about him."

"It's natural to worry about your kid, Rachel," she says gently.

"The world feels like a big, confusing place to Sam at the moment. Moving here was a big change, it's hard enough for me, but for a little kid like him it makes no sense. Everything's different, and I worry he's stressed. I check on him at night and he's restless, always dreaming. I hope he settles."

She sits for a few moments, watching him. "I'm no expert, but I don't think there's anything to worry about with Sam."

"I'm sure you're right..." I murmur, watching the children as Emily climbs the tree high and Sam sits on a safe, lower branch. I breathe a sigh of relief when he seems to get bored and starts to move down, but just as he does, Emily moves down too. Now she's calling to us and waving and the next thing she's on the ground sobbing.

"Are you okay, Em?" Chloe calls as we both instinctively leap out of our seats to comfort her. "What happened?" Chloe asks as she helps the still-crying child to her feet.

"Sam pushed me!"

"No, no. I don't think he did, Emily," I offer gently but assertively, while Sam starts to protest from his safe lower branch. "I didn't, *I didn't!*"

"He didn't," I say to Chloe, "I was watching."

She shakes her head. "Don't be silly, Emily, Sam wouldn't do something like that," she says to Emily, who does seem to be a handful.

Before things escalate, she wisely brings up the prospect of cake and ice cream, which seems to distract them.

I stay in the garden to watch the kids while Chloe goes off to the kitchen to get the promised goodies. The children are now sitting on the grass in a huddle, and I can't hear much, but I do hear Emily say, "Shall I show you?" Sam nods and follows her down the garden, and given the rather messy end to their tree-climbing, I feel I need to monitor this. Emily's a few months older, but I'm guessing at least a year wiser, and I fear that Sam may have rings run around him by the bright and feisty little girl. So, I stand up and follow them discreetly, intrigued to know what she's going to show him. And when they stop, I loiter by the small apple tree and watch as she finds a long twig and starts poking at what looks like fresh soil.

"Is that where he is?" Sam's saying excitedly.

I'm really not sure if I want to see what "treasure" she's about to unearth. I'm not good with dead birds or worms or whatever this might be.

"Can you see him?" Sam asks.

"No, you can't see his face, but look, it's here—look, Sam."

Sam bends down clumsily, his little hands resting on roughened knees. I hold my breath and await the slimy worm or slug, or even the ants' nest that Emily is about to poke awake.

"Here, Sam," she's saying, "this is where Daddy's buried."

God, I hope not! Why would she *say* that? I hope Sam doesn't understand, and I'm about to intervene when Chloe reappears.

"Chocolate, vanilla, or strawberry?" she announces as she marches across the garden with a tray full of ice cream, cake, and a large glass jug of something bright pink.

"I want all THREE!" Emily yells.

"And me, all THREE!" Sam echoes. They are so distracted by the ice cream, I hope Sam's forgotten what Emily said.

"Sam, I didn't hear the word *please*," I say.

"PLEASE!" he shouts, and Emily follows suit, which becomes a loud and, I have to say, rather annoying chant.

Chloe glances at me. "Big mistake—you can count on our Emily to even make the word *please* grate on your nerves. Drives my sister mad." She chuckles as she spoons ice cream into two bowls.

The children eat their ice cream and cake on a picnic rug a little farther down the garden, while Chloe pours the bright pink drink into two glasses.

"Cocktail?" she says.

"I don't usually drink in the day," I say, feeling like such a prima donna, "and Tom's away and I'm the only one looking after Sam—"

"Oh, it's low-alcohol, mostly fruit juice and lemonade," she says, handing me a large one.

"Thank you." I take it from her and notice she's even put a parasol in it. "This is lovely," I say, taking a sip, "is it watermelon?"

"Yes, my favorite. I put crushed ice in it."

"Like being on holiday." I swirl the parasol in the cold, fruity drink.

As we sip on our cocktails, we talk about our lives, her ex-boyfriends, how I met Tom. But she doesn't speak about Emily's dad—perhaps like me there are some things that are so painful she doesn't talk about them? Having spent time alone with her, I think she struggles in the same way I do. We've both had difficult relationships and experiences that make it hard not to sometimes feel a little paranoid around others.

"I don't trust people easily," she tells me. "I feel vulnerable, I worry that bad things are going to happen."

I understand exactly what she means, my own experiences have caused me to expect the worst in life. But Chloe's different, her openness and vulnerability make me feel I *can* trust her, despite her obvious flakiness. I feel relaxed chatting to her, like we've known each other forever, and before we know it, we've emptied the jug.

"I feel a little woozy," I say. "Are you sure that cocktail was low-alcohol?"

"Yes, *I'm* okay. Wonder if you have heatstroke—that can sometimes feel like you're drunk. I had that on holiday once, and I vomited for twenty-four hours nonstop."

"Great," I murmur. Just hearing this makes me want to heave. "I think I need to go home and lie down," I mumble. I stand up, and the world fizzes. I walk a little way down the garden to Sam and realize I'm really not well. "I feel dreadful," I say to Chloe.

"Why don't you have a lie down upstairs for a little while?"

I'm sorely tempted, and I'm sure Sam will be fine with Chloe and Emily, but I just want to get home, the way you always do when you don't feel well.

"I feel terrible, not sure I can walk. I'm so sorry but would you mind giving us a lift home?" I have this overwhelming need to lie down on my own bed.

"I'm sorry, I don't have a car," she says apologetically.

I plonk myself back on the garden chair and try and gather myself together.

"I'll get you some water," she says, looking concerned and disappearing into the house. She returns with a large glass of cold water, which I drink slowly, and by the time I've finished I feel slightly better.

"We'd better go," I say. "If that heatstroke hits me again, I won't be able to leave this chair, let alone your garden!"

Chloe insists on accompanying us home, and I'm grateful. It's good to know there's someone with me to take care of Sam if I have a relapse as we walk.

"Do you mind if I post a letter on the way?" she asks.

"Of course not." I'm sure I'm slurring my words; I still feel dreadful.

We begin the short walk to our house, but it feels like I'm climbing Everest. And when we get near the post office, it turns out Chloe needs to post a birthday card, which she hasn't even bought, then she has to buy the stamp, and she spends five minutes on her phone trying to find the address to send it to. Throughout this time, the kids play shop and "buy and sell" each other envelopes, causing chaos while I prop myself against a wall.

During all this, someone comes in and starts chatting with Chloe. I can't see the other person, but they're having a long talk. I've really had enough now, I just need to go. It's warm and stuffy, and the longer I stand here, the more nauseous I feel.

Finally the woman talking to Chloe, who I recognize as another mum from preschool, steps away, says bye to Chloe and starts looking through the greeting cards. She picks them up, reads them, and puts them back; all the time I'm aware she's watching me out of the corner of her eye, and eventually she pretends to notice me.

"Oh... hello. It's Sam's mum, right?" She smiles, still holding one of the cards in her hand, now using it as a fan. "Warm day, isn't it?"

I nod. I'm aware this may seem rude, but if I open my mouth to speak, there's a good chance I'll vomit.

She's wafting the card at her face and observing me like some Victorian noblewoman watching a peasant. "Are you *okay*?" she asks, concern and horror on her face.

She isn't smiling, and even in my wretchedness I feel her inquiry is more about expressing her disapproval than asking how I am.

"I'm fine, thanks," I say, dying inside.

She raises her eyebrows.

"I have heatstroke," I add, hearing the slur in my voice, and dying again.

She half smiles. "Oh, I *see*." She flutters the card faster and walks away in disbelief and disapproval.

"What was *she* saying to you?" Chloe says when we eventually leave the shop.

"Oh, the woman from preschool? Is she a friend of yours?"

"No," she replies adamantly. "Jennifer Radley is a snooty cow who thinks she's better than everyone else. I can't stand her."

"Mmm, well, she doesn't like me, that's for sure."

Her head whips around. "Why, what did she say to you?"

"Oh, nothing really, I reckon she thought I was drunk."

"Judgmental bitch," she says under her breath. "Watch your back with that one, she's dangerous."

FIFTEEN

I wake at 7 a.m. with a terrible headache to my phone ringing by the side of my bed.

"Rachel, it's Chloe," she says when I pick up, and even in my sleepy state I detect the anxiety in her voice.

"Hi," I say gruffly, a little annoyed at being woken so early.

"I have a confession to make."

"Oh?" To be honest, at this juncture I don't care, I just want to grab another half hour of sleep before I have to wake Sam.

"It's the cocktail I gave you yesterday. I'm so, *so* sorry, I got carried away. I meant to put a few splashes of vodka in with the fruit juice and lemonade, but I was . . . over-enthusiastic."

I'm pretty pissed off, and despite her being a new friend, I find myself berating her. "Chloe, I wish you'd told me that yesterday. I would have had just one glass if I'd thought there was a lot of vodka in it. Bloody hell, you let me get wasted, and I was in charge of my son!"

"I'm so, so sorry, Rachel, I just wanted you to have a good time."

"I was having a good time—I didn't need *any* alcohol."

"I'm sorry, really sorry. Forgive me?"

I say I forgive her, but this bothers me—why did she do something as reckless as add too much vodka? She doesn't know me well enough to be so laid-back about it; anything could have happened. I know it wasn't malicious, it was just stupid, and I blame myself now for believing her, and for letting her refill my glass. I won't allow that to happen again.

"I wish you'd tell that Jennifer Radley that it was your fault," I say. "The way she looked at me as I slid down the wall of the post office—she thinks I'm a wine mum," I say crossly, still stinging from Jennifer's scorn.

"Oh, she's a stupid cow, take no notice of her. She's never worked a day in her life, married some rich bastard, and now looks down on everyone with *his* money!" Her vitriol is real.

"Wow. You really don't like her, do you?"

"I bloody don't."

"You said she was *dangerous,* is that why?" I ask, aware of the irony of my question, having heard the same about Chloe from Tom. "Has she done something to hurt you?" I am determined to find out what she means.

"Yeah, we used to be best friends, until she stole my boyfriend."

"Oh, really?" This is interesting. I think about the perfectly groomed Jennifer Radley in her designer clothes, reeking of expensive perfume. Butter wouldn't melt. Clearly she *is* dangerous as far as boyfriends go.

"Yeah. She was determined to get him the minute she found out he and I were together—she sent him letters, told him stuff about me. It was awful, Rachel, I almost had a breakdown."

"I'm so sorry, that sounds horrible. When did all this happen?" I ask.

"It would be . . ." She pauses to count. "I'm thirty-three now, and I was fourteen so . . ."

Oh. "So you were at school?" My interest is suddenly *not* so piqued.

"Yeah, after that our friendship was over."

So Chloe has held on to that resentment all these years, when Jennifer probably doesn't even remember her teenage boyfriend. I guess there's dangerous and then there's *dangerous* . . .

With Tom away, I only have the chance to write when Sam's in preschool, but I feel too rough to work today. I also feel very isolated and alone. Rosa's got shifts with an agency this week too, so I can't even call her till later. It's been a long morning, and I feel the need to talk to someone, even Chloe. After the vodka incident I'm not as easy about her as I was. Can I trust her? I don't know, but I do believe that it was harmless, she genuinely just wanted me to have fun. It was clumsy and stupid, but I'm prepared to give her another chance—she's friendly and seems kind, so I'm going to be cautiously optimistic about our burgeoning friendship. So, after thinking this through, I've been looking forward to seeing Chloe when I collect Sam at preschool. But when I get there she's chatting to a group of mums. My heart sinks when I see that Jennifer's also part of the group. I feel embarrassed after yesterday's exchange in the post office. I hope Chloe explains to her about my condition, and that I didn't deliberately get drunk.

What must she think of me?

I consider going over and addressing it, making light of it, but she and Chloe are now deep in conversation, which makes me question Chloe again in my mind. Only this morning she was saying on the phone how much she doesn't like Jennifer and that they aren't friends. But it's not for me to judge—they go back a long way and Chloe can't just ignore Jennifer if she engages her in conversation, that would be rude. I have no other friends here yet, and don't want to give up on Chloe so soon just because she's being polite to someone she doesn't actually like. But it makes me wonder if she might be a bit two-faced, and if I can trust her? So, I decide not to join them. It wouldn't be easy as they always stand in a tight little circle leaving no room for anyone to enter. Besides, I have to get off quickly because we have the dreaded swimming lesson later.

Sam's tired from his morning at preschool, so once we're home, I let him nap on the sofa. I need him rested for his swimming lesson. It's now after two and Rosa should be finished with her shift, so I take my phone out onto the patio and give her a quick call.

"I don't want to even talk about it because I know I'll sound like a spoiled brat, but I'm dreading this swimming lesson," I say.

"You're not a spoiled brat."

"I am—I'm complaining about a bloody swimming pool when some mothers can't even feed their kids."

"I think it's perfectly reasonable for you to have an objection to a ton of water in your backyard. Bloody hell, Rachel, after what you went through. Have you told him how you feel?"

"He doesn't *get* it—he thinks it's all about the money. He says I've changed."

"He's such an arse. Did you tell him about going to that estate agent's house after preschool yesterday?"

"No, I still haven't. I like her, and the more he disapproves the more stubborn I feel, he can't tell me who to be friends with. Chloe's a bit flaky, okay she wouldn't be my *first* choice, but I don't have much choice. I don't know a soul down here, and with Tom away, I need another adult to talk to. It was good to sit in her garden and have a couple of drinks watching the kids play."

"Good, about time you chilled out and had some fun," she insists. "Keep meaning to say, thanks for the pictures you sent of Sam in the garden—I can't believe how grown up he is. It must be at least a year since I last saw him, he was still a baby then."

"You'll have to come down for a week or two and stay?" I offer.

"Mmm. Actually, I was thinking, how would you feel about me staying over one night next week?"

"Oh my God! I'd *love* that, and Tom will still be away so we can have a girlie evening."

"Yeah, I thought he might be. He doesn't really approve of girlie evenings, does he? Come to think of it, he doesn't approve of *me*."

I laugh it off, but she's right and has obviously picked up on his vibe.

"I'm probably going to come down to your part of the world soon anyway, I might have mentioned Great-Auntie Jean and Great-Uncle Ron?"

"Yes, they must be about a hundred by now?"

Rosa chuckles. "Not quite, she's ninety-four and he's ninety-two, her toy boy she says. They're still going strong, but he had a fall a couple of weeks ago, they live in Devon, so not too far from you. I said I'd go and stay with them for a bit, they need some help, and I need a change of scene, and I can come and see you too. I'll call them to arrange it then let you know when I'll be down—is that okay?"

"That's brilliant. You can stay over and we can get drunk and dance around the kitchen?" I suggest.

"Sounds great! Perhaps we'll have a silent disco so we don't wake Sam."

"Yes, and talking of which, I'd better go. I have a tortuous afternoon ahead of me watching him swim."

"Ahh, you've got this, Rach, you can do it. You're the strongest woman I know—you are made of iron. Let's face it, love, you've had to be."

We say our goodbyes and I head off to wake Sam up. It's good to talk to Rosa; she's my best cheerleader, and I hope I'm hers.

We've both been through some hard times, and in the few years I've known her she's had some horrible relationships. The last guy she broke up with stalked her for months, and she lived in terror. Still does, because she has no idea where he is, and when he might turn up again.

"Are you looking forward to swimming today?" I ask Sam as he eats his hummus and pita bread soldiers.

"Yes!" He's beaming.

"A man called Chris is going to teach you to swim like Daddy."

"I can swim already," he's saying, distracted by the war he's creating with his pita bread soldiers. I just smile—I know he can't swim, but he has been in the pool a couple of times with Tom just to get him used to it.

I help him put on his swimming shorts, aware for the first time of the waves rumbling in the far distance, which troubles me. It must be the way the breeze is blowing today, but I try not to think about the sea, or the warm westerly breeze gently rippling through the pool. On holiday I used to love the sound of the sea in the distance, the promise of sand between my toes and hurling myself into the waves. But now the sound of the sea is an ominous warning that makes my stomach churn.

"Mummy, that's too loose, Daddy makes it tighter." Sam's voice is screechy, and it jolts me back to now. I'm all thumbs as I try to tie the little lace that draws the shorts tighter around Sam's waist.

"Sorry, darling," I say, trying to hide the panic in my voice.

"Mummeee! It needs to be *tighter*." Anxiety lifts his voice an octave.

I try and pull it tighter and tighter but I need to stop. I need to calm myself. So I just put my head down in my lap, needing somewhere to hide.

"Mummy, what are you doing?"

"I just felt a little bit sick," I lie, "but I'm okay now." I lift my head, which feels like lead.

I look at my little boy's face: he's smiling but on the edge of something else. Fear?

He was excited a minute ago—have I erased his excitement and replaced it with my fear? Tom's right; I pass this on to my child. It's *my* horror, these are *my* memories. I take a deep breath, tell myself to get a bloody grip, and concentrate on looping the lace through my fingers.

Finally, I get it right. "There you go, we don't want your shorts falling down in the water, do we?"

He half smiles at this—like most kids, he loves slapstick, and the mere prospect of one's trousers around the ankles is the height of hilarity.

"Are you trained in first aid?" is my opening line to Christopher Hutchinson, the swimming instructor, as I open the front door to him.

"Yes, I am fully trained in saving lives. Your kid is safe with me. Oh and hello, I'm Chris," he says, reaching out to shake my hand. He has an easy smile, but that doesn't comfort me; I see it as a sign he might be too laid-back.

"Rachel," I say, smiling in return, "come and meet Sam."

He's wearing a blue track suit, and his mop of curly hair bounces as he follows me through the house, and I make introductions, attempting to seem relaxed. But I see the judgment in Chris Hutchinson's eyes: to him I'm just another over-anxious middle-aged mum. He thinks I waited too long to have my child and now I'm too old for the basic building blocks of parenting.

But he doesn't know that I'm different. It isn't only my maternal instinct and late motherhood that make me vulnerable to terror when my child is near water.

"Let's go then." I take a breath and with Christopher, walk on wobbly legs into the garden. I am fully dressed, my child is ready to swim, his armbands are fully inflated, and I'm holding his tiny hand for grim life as we walk toward the water. I have a first aid kit by the pool, and as much as I don't want to do this, as much as every nerve is raw and my mind is screeching *NO!* I remind myself that I'm doing this for Sam.

At the bottom of the garden, I open the arched doorway and, holding Sam back with one hand, gesture for Chris to walk through ahead of us, a safety measure of course.

"Wow!" I hear him exclaim as Sam and I follow him through.

"This is amazing. You are one lucky kid, mate." He ruffles Sam's hair, and Sam seems excited again.

"This is Christopher," I remind Sam.

"Call me Chris," he says.

I nod in acknowledgment. "Chris has come to teach you to swim, remember?"

"But I can swim *already*," Sam is saying, rolling his eyes like adults are so stupid he can't believe it.

I look at Chris and smile wearily. "He can't. He's paddled around in the shallow end a few times with his dad, but he can't swim," I explain.

"That's good," Chris says. "So you're used to water, mate?"

Sam nods. "Yes, Daddy's friend taught me to swim and dive and I can even swim under the water..."

Knowing we're back in imaginary friend territory I shake my head at Chris and he responds with a knowing look.

"Well, are you ready for some fun?" Chris says, walking toward the pool.

"Er, he needs to know how dangerous water is, as well as it being...fun," I say quietly to Chris. "As we now have this *beast* in our back garden, it scares the hell out of me that one day he might just climb the wall and..." I don't need to finish the sentence. Chris acknowledges my concerns with a wink, takes Sam's hand and begins walking toward the water, then turns to see me standing there, probably white as a sheet.

My instinct is to grab my child and run, but I stand and watch the man taking my child into six feet of water.

Daddy takes the little boy to the edge of the sea, his tiny hand in Daddy's big, safe one. The mummy is smiling and waving. She always smiled then; she was happy all the time. Now Daddy's going in farther, and he lifts the little boy onto his shoulders. He waves at Mummy, who waves back. Still smiling.

SIXTEEN

I hold my breath as Sam is lowered into the water in Chris's strong arms, and he holds him as he floats on the turquoise. It's a beautiful blue, almost the color of Sam's eyes, but I know beneath that placid turquoise lies something deadly. I can't get my breath, I can't watch, but I can't look away.

It's torture, but Chris is here: he's experienced, strong and sure. He also has first aid training—*nothing bad is going to happen.*

"I don't need these." Sam's referring to the armbands, which are preventing him from drowning.

"I think your mum would like you to keep them on, mate," Chris replies.

"Yes, I would," I stress, feeling for a sun lounger and sitting on the edge of it without taking my eyes off them.

"But I don't need them," Sam's muttering to Chris.

"Yeah okay, mate." I hear the sympathy in his voice; he feels sorry for Sam, having such an overbearing mother. I look away, ashamed. This isn't how it should be—it's about Sam, not me.

"Hey, *you've* done this before!" Chris exclaims as Sam starts to move his arms in a breaststroke. Tom has obviously shown him some of the moves, but I'm surprised to see him going so confidently and speedily too. I reckon Tom has brought him to the pool more times than he's let me know. I don't mind, sometimes it's better not to know, and it means he can already swim, which is a good thing. He's smoothly cutting through the bright turquoise, the sun shimmering on the water, his legs moving in and out, arms propelling him forward. Chris stays close, talking him through the movements as I sit back down on the end of the sun lounger.

"The boy can *swim!*" Chris calls, looking over at me. "He wasn't kidding, he's *good!*"

I'm shaking. My heart's beating so fast I'm almost breathless, but I'm holding on. I'm glad he can swim, but I just want him out of the water. I'm trying to envision us eating dinner later, playing ball on the patch of lawn, tucking him safely into bed when it's all over and he's truly safe.

The lesson continues for an hour, with Chris merely perfecting some of Sam's strokes. My kid is like a fish, swooping under, floating easily on the surface and even doing a backstroke. When Chris suggests he jump in, I nearly have a coronary. Watching my child teetering on the edge, about to jump into a vast expanse of merciless water while someone I don't really know shouts, "Yes!" is terrifying.

"I'd like to see him without armbands," Chris says once they're out of the pool. "I know you're nervous, and your husband mentioned that you're not comfortable with water, so I agreed to the armbands. But I don't usually teach with them—I think they can be dangerous as they give a child a false sense of security."

I take a breath, just glad it's over—for now. "Okay," I say reluctantly. "Perhaps next time, if you hold on to him?"

We all leave the walled garden, and I make sure to lock the door, checking it a couple of times before I walk with them both up the garden. I breathe a huge sigh of relief at being away from that deadly blue.

"He can obviously swim, but I don't want him to be overconfident and take risks," I say regarding the armbands.

"Mrs. Frazer, with respect, I think we need to *build* his confidence, not tear it down."

I feel attacked. "I'm not saying that..."

"Look," he says, moving closer—he smells of swimming pools and I want to be sick. "Your husband explained that you have issues around water, and he's keen those issues aren't..." He's trying to be tactful, but it's a bit late for that.

"Yes, I have *issues* around water. I know my husband means well, he wants to *cure* me, he always has," I say quietly, so Sam won't hear. "Thing is, Tom's a fixer, wants to make everything better, but I'm afraid this is something he can't heal."

Chris looks a little bemused by this. Tom clearly hasn't told him why I have issues around water, for which I'm grateful. But if I don't explain this, he won't understand why I'm behaving in this way around Sam's swimming, and I need him to if we're going to get anywhere. So I turn on the TV in the sitting room for Sam, give him a drink and a snack, and return to the kitchen, where Chris is now sitting on a stool at the island.

"I know I might appear anxious and fussy around Sam when he's near water. I hate that, and I wish it wasn't the case. But there's a reason for my anxiety."

He takes a sip of water and waits for me to continue.

"There was... an accident." I can't bring myself to talk about it to a stranger.

"Oh, I'm so sorry."

"It was a long time ago—twenty years now. I'll never get over what happened, I know that, but I do wish I could at least move on so I don't entangle Sam in my fears."

"I understand," he replies. "Do you swim?"

"Growing up in Manchester, I never had a reason to learn, but as a kid I always loved being by the water."

"But you haven't been near water since the... accident?"

I shake my head.

"Okay," he says slowly, like he's thinking about it.

"Before you even suggest it, I've been through therapy and it didn't help."

"I wonder if perhaps exposing yourself to water might be the answer."

"My husband suggested that, didn't he?"

"No... not exactly. Your husband wants Sam to swim but said you were nervous about him being in water."

"Yes, I am. He's four, and in an ideal world I'd have waited until he was a little older."

"The younger the child, the better the swimmer," he offers.

"It's just that I'm scared of water—I know what it can do, so I'm scared of my child in water." I pause, finding it hard to talk about. "It's not easy for me to live with a swimming pool in my backyard. I wish things were different, but that's how I am."

"That's understandable... but perhaps it's about perspective? A pool in the garden can be a positive, especially for Sam. But what about you? Have you thought about swimming, Mrs. Frazer?"

"No. And call me Rachel, please."

"Okay, so would it totally freak you out to get into your own pool and learn to swim?"

I almost faint at the thought. "Yes, it absolutely would. I haven't been near water since... since... well, forever."

"Well, if you ever change your mind," he says tactfully, "I'll teach you. I like a challenge." He finishes his water.

"Thanks, I appreciate that," I say, "but hell would have to freeze over first."

He smiles at this. "Okay, fair enough, no pressure. So I'll see you again next Wednesday?"

"Yes, of course. We've paid you in advance for the month, haven't we?"

"Yeah, I mean, he can swim, but I'll keep teaching him for as long as you want Sam to have supervision in the water."

"How about until he's twenty-five?" I half joke.

Chris chuckles at this. "I would probably have to hand him over to my younger colleagues before that—I'll be an old man myself."

"And who knows, I may even have overcome my fear of water by then," I joke.

I walk him to the door, and as he steps out I notice a brown parcel on the doorstep. "This must have come while we were down by the pool," I say.

"Hope it's something nice. See you next week." He bounces off down the gravel path, waving.

Once inside, I put the parcel on the kitchen counter and grab some scissors. It takes a while as it's well wrapped with thick parcel tape, and when I finally rip off the brown paper, there's more taped-up paper underneath. Hearing me rustling paper in the kitchen, Sam wanders in from the sitting room, where he's been engrossed in the TV.

"Is that a present, Mummy?"

"I'm not sure, darling, I hope so."

He climbs up on a stool to "help," and we both tear at the paper excitedly, only to find that there's another layer.

"This is like pass the parcel, isn't it, Sam," I say, throwing another sheet over my shoulder. What started as a fairly large parcel is getting smaller and smaller. "I hope this isn't a joke and there's nothing inside," I say, giggling.

"A joke, a joke, Mummy." He laughs, then his little face goes back to concentration mode as his eager hands rip some more at the paper.

Eventually, we come to something solid—it's in bubble wrap and we have to keep rolling it out, but as we come to the "gift" inside, I get a weird feeling. I think about feeling watched, being here alone, the neighborhood kids or someone else using our pool at night, and how some local people might not be too pleased about us living here.

"Darling, I've just realized what this is," I say to Sam as I stop unraveling the paper around the "gift."

He looks up at me. "What?"

"It's a present for your birthday. I forgot I ordered it. We shouldn't be opening it, it's a surprise! Oh no!" I make like we've been naughty and try to giggle about this.

He looks crestfallen—talk about taking candy from a baby. But something tells me this isn't something he should see. If I'm wrong, then I'll say I made a mistake, but if I'm right, then I can't let him see it. So, with the contents still tightly wrapped in what looks like their final layer, I cut out a large square of the discarded bubble wrap and educate my son in the joys of popping it. To my relief, he immediately becomes absorbed in popping the bubble wrap, giving me the chance to discreetly take what remains of the parcel to the bathroom.

"Won't be a minute," I say, and I quickly run in and lock the door.

Standing at the sink, I roll off the final layer of bubble wrap. I know immediately what it is and let out an involuntary whimper as the gift is revealed: my son's blue plastic sandals, taken from my memory box.

SEVENTEEN

I stand in the bathroom holding those little blue sandals against my chest. Sadness almost overwhelms the fear as tears roll down my cheeks, but I have to cry in silence. I don't want Sam to hear.

I'm not going mad—someone has been in our house, in our bedroom. Did they know about the memory box, where I keep it, and the significance of these old plastic sandals? Or was it just chance? Is it really teens secretly hanging around the pool, knowing that apart from the occasional swimming lesson, no one goes there day or night now that Tom's away? Or is it someone who knows me, really knows me, knows what happened that day at the beach?

I shudder. Whoever it is, and whatever their motive, I feel exposed, violated.

I head to our bedroom, on the ground floor and so easily accessible from the garden, and still clutching the sandals, I check behind the curtains and in the en suite bathroom. The bed is still as smooth as when I made it this morning; my makeup sits on the dressing table undisturbed.

I set the sandals down on the bed. To anyone else they're molded blue plastic for little ones, available at any shoe shop or supermarket that sells kids' clothes.

"Take them off, pleathe, Mummy," he demanded in his lispy voice as he lay on the sand, legs in the air. I did as I was told, and after unstrapping them from his chubby ankles, I tickled his toes. I still hear the echoes of his laughter... but now the landline is ringing and I have to return to the present, and run to the kitchen to answer it.

"Hello, darling, have you had a good day? Swimming lesson go well?" It's Tom.

"Yes... okay. You sound happy?"

"More relieved actually. I called your mobile, and when you didn't answer I was worried."

I tell Tom about the parcel on the doorstep, and what it contained.

"Oh God, Rachel..."

"Someone's been in the house. I don't know who or why or—"

"Look, just stay calm, this could be something or nothing. And first of all, you're going to hate me for asking, but are you sure?"

"Sure of what?" I say, looking at the confetti of ripped wrapping paper all around the kitchen floor.

"That you didn't just take the sandals out yourself. I know you often look in the box... Could it be that you just left them out and now—"

"Tom! I'm not *mad*. I know what happened. If I'd simply mislaid them, why is our son popping the bubble wrap they were wrapped in, along with floral wrapping paper?"

"Sorry, I really didn't mean..."

"I know, but I'm fine now, I don't do things like that anymore."

"I think you should call the police," he says. "It sounds a bit sinister to me. Was there anything else, a note, anything the police might be able to use to find out who sent it?"

"No, but I ripped all the paper off quickly, I didn't check for notes."

"Shall I come home?"

"No, Tom, it's fine," I say. "We are okay. No point in you

driving across the country until we know what's happened. And Tom? What about the keys?"

"Keys?"

"The house keys. Chloe said she gave them back to you."

"She didn't."

"I asked her yesterday. She said she gave them to you with the documents the night she came here."

"No, no, I don't have them."

My stomach lurches. "Do you think Chloe . . . ?"

"I wouldn't put *anything* past Chloe."

I feel sick, torn between disbelief and hurt in case he's right. "But why would she do something like that? She doesn't *know*—she wouldn't see his sandals as anything significant."

"Just chance? Just weird Chloe being . . . weird?" he offers hopelessly, then takes a deep breath. "I wish I could come up with an explanation for what's happened, love, but I don't understand it either. All I know is that Chloe Mason isn't what she seems."

Panic rises through me. "Oh Christ, Tom, I don't know what to do."

"Call the police now, tell them everything you've just told me, then call me back."

I put down the phone, call the police, and tell them all about the sandals. At first I'm sure the man at the other end thinks I'm joking, but when I point out I'm here alone with my son and terrified, he starts listening. I tell him about Sam saying he saw someone in the pool, and the abandoned orange towel on the patio.

"We've had things like this before down here," he admits in a rich Cornish accent. "It could be that someone resents you being in the county? You aren't Cornish, you have this big house, they might feel like you're taking homes from local people?"

"I agree, I've never felt comfortable about it myself, but it's not a second home," I stress.

"Or it could even be someone wanting to scare you so you'll be so desperate to move out, you'll sell for a low price?" he muses.

This sounds a bit Scooby-Doo to me, but what do I know? He makes yet another report, I give him all my details and he says he'll get back to me if they hear anything.

"Call us if you're worried about anything," he says and ends the call. He was nice enough, but I doubt very much they'll do anything; he didn't even offer to send anyone round.

I decide to put all the torn parcel wrapping and scraps of tape into a carrier bag to keep, just in case. If anything else should happen, this might be evidence. Holding the carrier bag in one hand, I sweep my arm across the kitchen counter to gather it all together, but as I do this, I see something pink. It's a Post-it note. Something's written on it. I can't see what it is. I don't want to. But still, as every nerve tingles in protest, I feel my arm reach out and pick it up. The words on the Post-it are written in red, and they chill me to the bone:

WATCH YOUR CHILD.

EIGHTEEN

I don't know who's responsible for the sandals or the warning note, but I've now logged both with the police, along with my suspicions. Tom was horrified and suggested I give Chloe a wide berth for a couple of days, and I agreed. I have no proof it was her, but I have to face the facts, and she looks suspicious, so I think it's wise to be cautious around her now. I don't want a scene, nor do I want to hurt her, I just need to keep my distance. So, I haven't stopped to chat at preschool drop-off or pickup, just waved politely and said I was in a hurry. But of course, we were fast friends, and my sudden detachment has seemed odd to her, and after a few days of this, she stops me one morning.

"Rachel, are you okay?" she asks.

I am just about to walk through the playground gates, but the distraught look on her face stops me in my tracks. She deserves my honesty at least.

"I'm sorry, Chloe, it's just..." I turn to see who's hanging around and might hear. I don't trust anyone at the moment.

"Come on, let's go for a coffee," she says.

"Okay," I agree, though I'm reluctant. I might be dining with the devil, but at the same time I need to clear the air and at least explain myself. I'm an honest person, and rushing past her every morning without explanation isn't how I should be dealing with this. I need to have a proper talk with her and let her know why I'm behaving this way, it's only fair.

As I have my car with me—meant for a quick getaway—she suggests we drive to a coffee place she knows farther along the coast.

"It's only a ten-minute drive," she says, so I agree and we get in the car.

"Chloe, we need to talk, but before we do, I just want to ask you: did you definitely give our house keys back to Tom, I mean literally hand them to him? Because he doesn't remember." I feel this is a little gentler than saying he's adamant that she *didn't* return them.

I'm looking ahead as I drive, but her head turns to me in alarm. "I told you I did, I *definitely* did. Don't you believe me?" She sounds hurt.

"Yeah. I believe you," I lie.

"What's Tom trying to say, that I *kept* them? Does he think I'm planning to rob the place when you're on holiday?" She's angry—so angry that I wonder if Tom's mistaken and simply forgot that she gave them back to him.

I'm sorry I mentioned it now; I didn't expect this reaction. She's really upset. "No, it's nothing like that, Chloe, honestly."

"What kind of person do you think I am, Rachel?"

"I'm sorry, I really didn't mean . . . I just wondered if you'd left them for him somewhere and they've been picked up by someone else. It's just that one or two things have happened lately and I wondered if someone has access to the house."

"What things?"

"Just let me park and let's find somewhere to talk."

She directs me into the town, and minutes later I pull up in a busy parking lot. It's a coastal town called Looe, with shops and restaurants and so many tourists we can hardly move.

"I know this place," Chloe's saying as we walk down the street toward the beach, past shops selling Cornish gin and buckets and spades—there's even a shop selling spells and magic.

She then takes me down and through some smaller streets, and I think about what Tom said, that she's not what she seems. I find her quite difficult to say no to, and ask myself why, at nine thirty on a weekday morning, I'm following her through a narrow lane down to a harbor.

"In here," she says, opening the door to a tiny and very old pub.

Inside it's quite dim after the bright sunshine outside, but it's nicer than it initially seemed. The tables are shiny wood like the floors, there's a well-stocked bar with every kind of gin on display, and the walls are covered in brightly painted seaside posters with declarations like "Life's a beach in Cornwall!" emblazoned across them.

Chloe finds us a little table by the window and orders two coffees.

"So, what's been happening, and why are you being weird with me at preschool?" She pushes her sunglasses onto her head, an intense, concerned expression on her face.

"I don't know what to tell you, really, I'm just keeping to myself because I don't know who to trust and—"

"You can trust *me*," she snaps, outraged.

"Yes," I reply weakly. "It's just that I think someone's hanging around the house, watching, swimming in the pool, trying to scare me." I watch her face, but she gives nothing away.

"*Scare* you? Why?" She looks puzzled.

"I really have no idea," I reply pointedly, and then go on to tell her about Sam seeing someone in the pool, the movements outside in the dark, the abandoned towel, and the sandals. All the time I'm waiting for her to give herself away. I watch her body language, check her expression for genuine surprise, but she's hard to read.

And after I've finished listing everything that's happened, she just shrugs, apparently taking it in her stride. "It's teenagers running around," she says dismissively. "Anyone who has a pool around here knows that teenagers use them at night, or when the owners are away."

"Yes, but in order to get into the pool, they'd have to come through the front door."

She shakes her head. "Remember, I sold your property, I've *seen* the scaled floor plan. That wall at the back of the walled garden leads directly into your neighbor's back garden. A teenage boy could climb it easily—your neighbor's garden, that's where they are getting in."

I hadn't thought of this, and it makes me feel slightly better. "So everything could be explained by that? Even the towel, I guess?"

Just then our coffees arrive; she thanks the waitress and leans back toward me.

"You're worrying for nothing. What does Tom think?"

"Well, when the sandals arrived, he told me to call the police. But they must think I'm mad. I already called them about the towel, and then I rang about the sandals then the note too."

"The sandals, yeah. That *is* a bit weird, I don't get that at all."

I don't respond. I'm not willing to get into the significance of the sandals with Chloe. I'm not sharing with her anymore. She gazes out of the window like she's looking for the answer. Then she turns back to me. "So why would someone wrap up an old pair of sandals and leave them on your doorstep?"

Does she know the answer to this? She's looking straight at me now, but I refuse to discuss it further, shake my head, and pick up the menu so I don't have to meet her eyes. If it *was* her, she's just enjoying a cheap thrill at my expense; if it wasn't, then why tell her so she can repeat my story to the mums at preschool?

She relaxes, sits back again. "Well, as long as nothing else horrible arrives in the mail, I'd get on with my life if I were you. Hey, they do a nice brunch here, shall we have something to eat?"

We decide on poached eggs on avocado toast, and Chloe goes

to the bar to order it. On her return she tells me about the artisanal bakery and the lovely gift shops nearby. "Ooh, there's a gorgeous candle shop here too, The Candle Company," she says as the waitress arrives with two Proseccos.

As one is put down in front of me, Chloe sees my face. "They're two for one—it won't do you any harm. I'll drink both if you'd rather have another coffee?"

I move the Prosecco toward her. I'm not falling for that again. But Chloe puts no pressure on, just orders me another coffee and carries on chatting.

"I love The Candle Company," I say. "Rosa is coming over to stay for the night and I want to make the spare room extra nice for her—perhaps we could pop in there before we go?"

"Absolutely," she says, downing the first Prosecco. "I love candles."

She rests her chin on her hands and leans forward. "I think we're alike, you and me," she says with a smile. "We have the same taste in everything. I love that shirt you're wearing."

"Oh, this?" I look down at the stripey blue shirt I bought just a few weeks ago online. "Yeah, it's so easy to wear—being a mum and working from home, I just buy simple stuff now."

"It really suits you—where did you get it?"

"Zara."

"Oh, I *love* Zara! See, I told you we are so alike. Will you send me the link?"

"Of course, as long as you promise not to wear it when I'm wearing mine. We'd look bonkers both turning up to preschool in matching shirts," I say, chuckling.

"Yeah, imagine Jennifer's face?"

"Oh, don't." I hide my face behind my hands in mock horror. "She already thinks I spend my afternoons getting drunk in your garden."

"I can see her sneering now. 'Oh, what are they doing now, playing twins?'" she says, giggling.

I laugh and wonder what it is that brings two people together. Chloe's almost ten years younger than me, we have little in common, but we have a chemistry. Our brunch arrives, and it looks delicious, but to my surprise, Chloe asks the waitress for two more Proseccos. I'm taking on board everything Tom says, and I agree in that I'm not sure I trust her. She's unpredictable, a bit flaky—but that's what makes her fun.

"God, I can't imagine you ever being friends with Jennifer Radley; she's so full of herself," I say.

"I try not to think about it. I was young and foolish," she says. "Rosa sounds like a very good friend," Chloe concedes, fingering the stem of her glass. "I don't have good friends like that. I envy you," she adds sadly. The Prosecco is making her softer, more vulnerable, as alcohol often does.

"Surely you have *some* good friends. What about the mums at preschool, are you close to any of them?"

She pulls a face. "The women at preschool are okay but we aren't friends. Not like you and Rosa are," she says almost enviously. "My sister's *like* a friend, but we aren't *close*—she's very different from me."

"In what way?"

She stops sipping her drink for a moment and looks up at the ceiling like she might catch the words she needs from the air.

"She's prettier, cleverer, more successful, has more money." She hesitates. "She was always the favorite."

"But you have loads of good qualities, Chloe: you're kind and fun and you're pretty too," I try to reassure her.

"Mmm, but her life's just been easier, you know? She just has this way with everyone, even Emily. She just walks into a room and everyone listens; men always fancy her."

"I guess Rosa's the closest person to a sister for me."

"Have you known her since school?"

"No, I only met her a few years ago—she nursed my father in the hospital before he died. Stuff like that fast-tracks a friendship more than years. It feels like I've always known her. I just knew from the first time I talked to her that she was my tribe, you know?"

"I reckon best friends are far better than sisters."

"I've known sisters who are best friends."

"I guess, but even best friends fall out sometimes, and you're kind of stuck with a sibling. I mean, if Rosa did or said something horrible, and really upset you, then you could just drop her." She knocks back some more of her Prosecco and, putting the glass down, says, "I mean, no one has to put up with shit from other people, Rachel—me and you, we are the ones that get pissed on."

I would never expect Chloe to use an expression like that. I wonder if it's the alcohol talking—she seems different, angry, even. I wonder who she's angry with?

NINETEEN

Chloe's now trying to attract the waitress. I hope she's going to ask for the bill and not another drink—I'm worried about the time. I'm not judging, but her easy, laid-back approach to the morning is putting me on edge slightly as we have to be back to collect the children by one o'clock.

"I think I was put off by the idea of best friends when I was at school. I always seemed to get the mean girl, Jennifer being the prime example."

"Nothing worse than having a friend who isn't a friend," I say, recalling those awful teenage years of toxic best friends. "Thank God we're adults. I look back now at some of the girls I used to know, and yes, exactly that—mean girls. Why did I put up with them?"

"Exactly!" She says this a little too enthusiastically, and as the waitress arrives and she orders another Prosecco—the two-for-one deal has ended, thank God—I wonder at the wisdom of this when we have children to collect later.

"You sure you don't want one?" she asks, nodding toward her own glass.

"No, I can't, I drove us here. Sorry to be a killjoy but we need to start moving soon to get back in time for the kids."

"Oh, yes, of course you do. My mum's picking Emily up today—why don't you call the school, and she'll pick Sam up for you too?"

"No thanks, I want to collect him. I didn't know your mum was around?" It was my turn to envy her.

"Yeah, me, my sis, Mum and Dad, we all live a stone's throw from each other."

"That must be nice."

"It's shit actually," she announces, too loudly. "They are always messing in my life, judging me when I don't quite come up to my sister's standards." She finishes the last of her drink. "Come on, then." She stands up suddenly, a little wobbly on her feet. "Shame you have to get back—perhaps next time we go out you could get a babysitter and we could go *out* out?" she says, attempting and failing to pick up her handbag from the floor.

I try to help her grab her bag, but we bang heads and she stumbles backward into an old man, who breaks her fall.

I apologize and help her up, laughing. "Chloe," I whisper, "do you really think I'd want to go *out* out with you? I couldn't keep up with your drinking, you're a beast!" We both leave the pub laughing, with what little dignity we have left, and I wonder again how I got here.

I'm living an isolated life in a house on a hill with no friends, just my little boy for company, but she brought me here today and we've talked and laughed and eaten lovely food. I know she also makes some bad choices—one might be men, and drinking too much might be another—but her company brings color back into my life. She's sometimes too loud, too silly, and I don't know if I can trust her—I don't even know her that well. But she's funny and kind, insisted on paying for brunch. Despite my doubts, I find myself back as her friend. It's like falling for a lover you know isn't right: he might bring trouble and heartache, and it won't last, but you can't help yourself—you have to go along for the ride. It's so conflicting. And as she grabs me by the arm and leads me skipping down the road, I'm laughing but hoping I don't live to regret this.

Chloe leads me across the road and to a small enclave of expensive shops, and eventually we arrive at The Candle Company.

"Oh, this is gorgeous," I say as we walk into the candle shop. We are both admiring the sheer luxury: clothes, perfumes, and candles, all in expensive, hushed tones of gray and cream and taupe.

"I want a house just like this," Chloe's saying as we walk toward a tablescape under a huge lantern attached with rope from the ceiling. Leaves and flowers adorn the table, and Chloe is almost lying face down in order to smell the fat, waxy candles that sit among the leaves, as if they also belong in the natural world.

"Everything is just exquisite," I murmur, fondling a white silk chemise that slips through my fingers like milk.

"I want to live here," Chloe says, holding out both arms, surrendering to the luxury, and catching another shopper with her hand.

"I'm so sorry..." She begins a long apology, and when it's over she returns to me, her hand over her mouth, just laughing.

"You are outrageous. I think the Proseccos have gone to your head," I say, feeling comfortable enough in her company to say this.

I pick up a rose-scented candle on the display and smell it. "That's lovely—it has a lingering, musky sweetness. It's very Rosa—I'll take that." I choose a boxed one.

Chloe picks up the rose candle, sniffs it, and pulls a disapproving face. "It's strong, bit musky for me."

"You're more of a freesia kinda girl. It's young and fresh," I say, offering her a diffuser to sniff.

She closes her eyes as I hold it to her face. "Yes, now *that's* more me," she says slowly, breathing it in. "I'm going to buy it. It'll remind me of today."

I still don't know about Chloe, or if I can trust her. She's a mystery, but I'm warmed by her innocence. She's having a good time and letting me know how special it is, and I find her openness refreshing.

"It's expensive," I warn, not sure if she's seen the price. It's decadent for me to spend that much money on a candle, especially as money is a bit tight, but I can't imagine how Chloe can afford it.

She's now clutching the diffuser to her chest like it's a precious urn.

We take our purchases to the till, where the assistant carefully wraps my candle in gray tissue paper.

"That will be thirty pounds, please," she says after putting the wrapped candle in a small but beautiful bag with *The Candle Company* written across in curly, swirling letters.

"Crikey, I knew they were expensive, but I didn't know they cost *that*!" Chloe says, loud enough for the woman to hear.

"Would you like to be on our mailing list?" she asks me politely while giving a disapproving glance at Chloe. I feel a little embarrassed. Chloe has no filter after a couple of drinks; I need to remember this and perhaps only see her for alcohol-free lunches in future.

"I'd love to be on the mailing list," I say, my way of compensating for my friend's remark, and I give the woman my name, email, and address.

"Oh, you're already on," she says.

"It must be someone else—Rachel Frazer is quite common. I don't recall putting myself on the list."

"Ahh"—she looks up from the computer—"no, it's not you. It's the same address and same surname, but it's *Tom* Frazer, not Rachel." She's smiling like she's solved a puzzle, but she's actually just handed me one.

"That's weird," I say.

"Well, it's all here," the woman says. "I can just change the

Tom to *Rachel* if you like?" There's something about the expression on her face that makes me feel uncomfortable. Then I realize, as we both stand and stare at each other, she thinks my husband must have bought something for someone else!

"Can you see what purchases he's made?" I suddenly hear myself ask.

"No, sorry," she says, shaking her head so vigorously I just know it's a lie.

"Oh... okay, I just thought he might have bought me something and I've forgotten."

"No, sorry, we don't keep that kind of information."

I look at Chloe, who seems to now be far more subdued. She says nothing, just looks wide-eyed from me to the assistant and back.

"I wonder when Tom's been buying from The Candle Company?" I say as we're driving home.

"It could be anything?" she offers. "I mean, he might have given his name and address for a competition?"

"Yeah, yeah, I suppose so," I reply. We drive for a long time without speaking, and I wonder why this is bothering me quite so much. Do I not trust my husband? It surprises me, and I get this weird feeling, the kind of feeling you get if you come home to find a broken window and you wonder if someone has climbed in.

"I guess he could have bought something for another woman," Chloe suddenly says into the silence.

I quickly turn to her. Our faces both have the same shocked expression, and then she says, "I mean, how well do you really know your husband, Rachel?"

TWENTY

"I miss you," Tom says when he calls that night.

"I wish you weren't so far away." I hear my voice in the darkness, croaky, on the verge of tears, and Tom tells me he's sorry he took the job.

"I popped into Looe today," I say to change the subject.

"Oh, nice. Did you go on your own?"

"Yeah, I like my own company."

"Ahh, I hate to think of you being lonely."

"I guess I am a bit—that's why I went, to get out, have a change of scene. I bought a candle from The Candle Company."

"Oh, nice..." I can hear his interest fading.

I've driven myself mad all evening wondering why he's on the mailing list for a candle company. It isn't a big deal, but I have to mention it to him or it will continue to drive me mad.

"But it was really weird—your name is on their mailing list."

"*My* name?" he asks.

"Yeah, and our address."

"How does that happen? Have I been hacked or something?" He seems genuinely surprised at this.

"I don't know."

Then I hear him chuckle.

"Why are you laughing?"

"I've told you before—I couldn't buy you anything without you knowing because you have to sign it off. Even when my payment comes in from the work I'm doing, I still can't surprise you because they add me to mailing lists, and you find out!"

"You bought me something?"

"Yes... I *might* have bought something for you..." he teases.

"Oh no, I'm sorry, Tom, I've spoiled your surprise." Relief floods through me.

"Let's pretend we never had this conversation."

"Okay, but don't feel the need to buy me gifts, darling, you know me, I'm not like that. Besides, you haven't been paid yet. Have they given you any indication...?" I hate to ask, but I'm worried about the bills.

"Yes, I spoke to them yesterday, they pay consultants quarterly, which means we have to wait a few more weeks. Ironic, isn't it? I work for a bank, and they won't give me my money," he chuckles. My heart sinks.

We chat for a little longer, and then we say goodbye, but I put the phone down immediately feeling embarrassed when I realize how I must have sounded about the candle. I behaved like a suspicious wife, which isn't like me, and it looks like I got it all wrong because the gift was for me anyway. I'm touched, but a little part of me wonders if he was telling me the truth. *I guess we'll know if and when he gives me the gift?*

Later, with Sam in bed, I sit in the lounge with the TV on. I feel tense in the evenings now. Restless, I decide to go keep an eye on the pool from Sam's room. A luminous blue rectangle in the dark. I watch for a long time, but to my relief, I don't see anyone.

TWENTY-ONE

"Mummy's friend is coming later today," I tell Sam as I get him ready for preschool this morning.

"Who's that?"

"Her name's Rosa—you probably won't remember her. She used to stay at our old place, but it was usually late, and you were asleep. She's been working away for a year, living in Ireland. You were only two when she last saw you."

"Ahh, can I stay awake to see your friend, Mummy?"

Laughing, I reply, "No, you can't, you'll be asleep in bed. We have a lot to catch up on, and it will be boring for you, sweetie." I ruffle his hair.

"Is Emily's mummy your friend too?"

"Yes, she is, but not like Rosa."

"Is Ro . . . Rose . . ."

"Rosa?"

He nods. "Is she your *bestest* friend . . . bester than even Emily's mummy?"

"Yes, she is. But as I've said before, darling, we can all have lots of friends," I press. "We don't just have to have one." I hope this is going in; I do worry that Sam only ever seems to play with Emily.

After I've taken him to preschool, I pop in the village flower shop for a fresh bouquet to go with the candle I put in the spare room for Rosa.

"You live in the big house, don't you?" Mrs. Pickering, the florist, says.

I cringe at the description—it makes me feel like I'm lording it over the village, which couldn't be further from the truth. We might have a big house, but we have very little money.

"Yes, we've been here a few weeks now."

"Well, it's lovely to meet you finally. Your husband has been in a few times."

"Oh? Not like him to buy flowers." I manage a smile.

"Oh yes, he has."

I vaguely recall some white roses in the house when I arrived; he must have bought them to make everything nice for my arrival.

"Ah yes, I remember now—I thought for a minute he'd been buying them for someone else!" I'm joking, but I must sound like a jealous, insecure wife, and I'm neither of those things. *Am I?*

She stops cutting stems and, putting down the flowers she's holding, she leans over the counter and puts her hand on mine. "I wouldn't worry—men do silly things, lovey."

Now I'm a jealous and insecure wife.

"Mrs. Pickering, if there's anything you think I should know...?"

She immediately shakes her head, and to my paranoid mind it looks like she's attempting to shake something out rather than reject the idea of my husband's infidelity.

"Oh lovey, I didn't mean anything, I was just saying that in *general* men..." Her voice fades, then she quickly changes gear. "Now, what can I do for you?"

Her reaction has shaken me a little, but I carry on and choose some white hydrangeas to put on Rosa's bedside table next to the candle. Then I go into the deli next door and buy pâté and cheese and nice bread.

I don't think about Mrs. Pickering's remarks again until much later, when Sam's in bed and Rosa's arrived.

We are sitting on stools in the kitchen and the island is covered in the detritus of what I optimistically called "a cheese and wine evening." But it's just me and my bestie, eating and drinking, and talking and talking and talking.

"I can't believe I haven't seen you in over a year!" she's saying, hugging me for about the hundredth time while balancing a wineglass in one hand.

"So, what's it like living here? Are you and Tom okay?" she asks.

"Yeah, yeah, we're fine." I tell her about the conversation I had with Mrs. Pickering the florist and how it's been playing on my mind.

"I don't know why you're worried, Tom isn't the kind of bloke who'd buy flowers for *you*, so he certainly wouldn't buy them for someone else," she chuckles.

"I know, I guess I'm feeling a bit vulnerable because he's away."

"Yeah, why is he working away?" she sits back, to hear my explanation. "I mean it's not like you need the money is it?"

I hesitate before answering. I don't want to be disloyal, but Rosa's my best friend. "He's spent quite a lot of money on getting stuff done here and—"

"Well, as much as it pains me to say it, he's done a good job. This place is lovely, tasteful too. Didn't know he had it in him. I bet you were heavily involved in the color palette and the soft furnishings though, am I right?"

"No, actually Tom did most of it."

"Really?"

"Yeah, I had *some* involvement, but as I wasn't here, I had to let him loose. I was looking after Sam while trying to work and sell the apartment, it was a full-time job, as you know. I didn't get a lot of time to think about the exact shades of walls in a house hundreds of miles away."

"I guess not." She stands down from her stool and reaches for the wine bottle, pouring more in both our glasses.

"So, what actually is he *doing* in Scotland?" She says this like she doesn't believe he's even there.

"Financial stuff, you know—working for a bank, corporate finance."

"You just keep throwing words at me, Rachel. You haven't got a clue, have you?" She chuckles at this while cutting herself some Cornish cheddar off the wooden platter on the island.

"You know me too well—I really don't. I know he is a troubleshooter; he goes into big banks when they're having problems and turns them around. But he doesn't discuss it with me in detail. It's all confidential." I sip on my glass of wine and change the subject; Tom wouldn't appreciate me telling Rosa about his job anyway. "But what about you? Any news on *him*?" I ask, referring to her ex-boyfriend, who's been behaving weirdly, calling her, turning up wherever she is.

"No, not for a couple of weeks." She looks around the kitchen again, and I see the tension in her eyes.

"You okay? This has been a horrible time for you, love." I take her hand.

"I'm good . . . I thought being in Ireland would help, but I still saw him on every corner, in my head anyway. Then as soon as I got back to Manchester it really kicked in. I was so triggered, you know?" She pauses, looks worried, and I'm worried for her, but typical Rosa, she manages to put on a brave face. "I'm glad to be away from Manchester, out of the area for a while. It's quite nice looking after my aunt and uncle, they're so appreciative I'll be spending more time down here. I can keep an eye on them, and pop and see you too, this part of the world is so lovely."

"Yes, it is," I say, not sure that I mean it.

"I don't know if I can live in Manchester again until they get him. I feel so paranoid in my apartment. I won't rest until he's behind bars."

"Could you move permanently down here?" I ask hopefully.

"I might, one day," she says with a smile. "Here's an idea: let's move Tom out and I'll move in? I'm more fun than him anyway, you know I am."

"Women friends are *always* more fun than husbands. But seriously, you can stay here as long as you like, just take some time to chill, to heal."

She shrugs. "Thanks, but for now I have to make my base with my aunt and uncle. I have to take my uncle for his hospital visit, and if he needs surgery, I'll have to hang around in Devon. But that's only about an hour away from here. I feel safer around these parts," she says with an attempt at a Cornish accent.

I smile at this. "Great! And you'll be so much nearer than the six-hour drive between here and Manchester. He doesn't know where you are, does he?"

"No." She shakes her head; her fingers play with the stem of her glass. "God, I hope not anyway, but even when my rational mind says, 'He isn't here, he *can't* know where I am,' I still wonder, you know?"

"When was the last time you heard from him?"

"When he stood in my garden in the middle of the night, waving at me."

My stomach lurches. "Sam said he'd seen someone in the night waving from our swimming pool," I blurt out, not thinking about the effect it will have on my friend.

Her face turns white.

"It was only a dream though, Rosa," I immediately backtrack.

"How do you know?"

"Well, we checked outside and it was obvious. Sam was asleep in bed, and you have to stand at his window to see the pool. It was *definitely* a dream," I say blindly.

But how do we know it was a dream?

"I bloody hope so." She takes a huge gulp of wine. I've clearly scared her, but I'm also a bit jumpy now. Who's to say her weird ex didn't follow her to Cornwall? What if he knows she has friends here and he was staking us out for when she turned up? I wouldn't dare even mention the damp towel, or the parcel containing my son's sandals.

She takes the knife and gazes at the cheese board, contemplating another piece. But before she cuts into it, she stops, looks around, and says, "Did I just hear something upstairs?"

"Sam's upstairs," I say, feeling the blood drain from my face.

"Oh?" She looks terrified.

I don't want to alarm her, but I stand up from my stool. "I'm sure it's nothing, but I'm just going to pop up and check on Sam."

"Do you want me to come with you?" She's holding a piece of toast with some pâté on it.

"No, you stay with your nibbles," I say, hiding the terror in my voice. "I'll be back in a minute."

I go upstairs, my heart beating ridiculously fast. I'm sure our conversation about Rosa's stalker ex has made us both paranoid, but I'd give anything to know where he is tonight.

The room is cool and dark, and Sam's dino nightlight is glowing softly in the dark. I can see him sleeping soundly, and while usually I would just gently close the door not to wake him, I feel the need to touch him, to hold him. So at the risk of waking him, I bend down and breathe in his milky, salty child smell, and for a few moments I forget everyone and everything. This is what matters, this little boy here—all the rest is noise, and I need to let go of everything else and hold on to this.

He stirs slightly, and I stand up, slowly moving backward toward the door as quietly as possible. But as I can't see where I'm going, I suddenly feel a sharp pain in the ball of my foot and yelp slightly.

"Mummy?" He stirs, and I remove the Lego from my foot, hoping he'll stay asleep, but no.

"Mummy?"

"Hello, darling, I was just checking if you were okay. Go back to sleep now."

"Is she still here, Mummy?"

"Who, darling, my friend? Yes, she arrived while you were asleep—you'll meet her tomorrow."

"She was in my room, Mummy."

I suppose Rosa could have popped in to see Sam earlier. "Ahh, Rosa, Mummy's friend, probably just wanted to see how big you've grown. You were a baby when she last saw you."

"No, not your friend. It was Emily's mummy, she kissed me good night."

TWENTY-TWO

"I know Sam thinking he'd seen Chloe in his room was a dream, but at the same time it's freaked me out," I say to Rosa when I return to the kitchen.

"I can tell—you're white as a sheet, love. Did he say who the woman was?"

"He said it was Emily's mummy, but he was confused, half awake."

"Well, that must be his imagination—this woman isn't likely to be hanging out in your kid's room is she?"

"No, but Sam's imaginings are all tied up with his friend Emily and her mum Chloe at the moment. Emily's his first proper friend, and we've seen quite a bit of them both recently."

I tell Rosa all about Chloe, how she let herself in on my first night here and then she was at the preschool and now we're sort of friends.

"You mean she just waltzed right in here?"

"I know, I know, sounds a bit weird, but she was dropping some documents off and thought we were out."

"How did Tom react to that? He can be very cool with guests, as I know only too well."

I flush slightly. Rosa sometimes popped around unannounced to our apartment in Manchester, and he felt she invaded our privacy, and it showed. "Tom was..." I look at her and smile. "Cool?"

She laughs at this. "Good old Tom."

"Yeah, but they knew each other before. They used to work for the same bank, and he used to visit her branch here in Cornwall."

Rosa has this permanent expression of doubt, which I have to confess echoes my own. "Sorry, but I'm still trying to get over the fact that she let herself in!"

"She was the estate agent, she had the keys," I say, feeling like she's focusing on something that doesn't really matter. "She says she gave them back to Tom, but he says she didn't."

"Whaaat? So there are keys of yours out there somewhere?" She's waving her arms like she's encompassing the universe.

"I've searched the house and can't find them, but she's adamant, and Tom's forgetful, she may have dropped them off and he's absent-mindedly put them somewhere."

She raises her eyebrows. "I guess."

"Tom says he doesn't trust her and keeps warning me off being friends with her, but I like her, so fuck that," I say, so she knows I'm not in agreement. I'm expecting a high five, some "you go, girl" response, but it's quite the opposite.

"Well, I'm sorry, but I'm with Tom—there's a sentence I never thought I'd say," she adds as an aside, to make sure I know exactly where she stands. "Rachel, I see a field of red flags—avoid, avoid, avoid!"

"No, you don't understand. Tom's just got her wrong, like he sometimes gets you wrong."

She rolls her eyes to acknowledge this.

"She's good company. I *like* her. She's a single mum—I think her partner died, but she doesn't like to talk about it."

"Probably because he's in the garden buried under her rose bushes," Rosa chuckles.

"Don't joke; her little girl, Emily, actually said that."

Her eyes are now wide. "You are *scaring* me!"

I laugh. "She's just looking for a friend she can trust. It must be a struggle to be on your own with a child," I add. "Sam plays with her little girl—they met at preschool, and I was relieved he'd found a friend. You remember I was worried about him mixing?"

"So, hang on, she turns up and lets herself into your house on the first night, then she's there at Sam's *preschool*?"

"Yes, but that's not weird, her kid just happens to be in the same class as Sam."

She looks doubtful. "I guess it's possible—have you mentioned it to Tom, that her kid's there?"

"Well, no, I haven't had the chance as he's away."

"I'm probably overdramatizing this, and it's probably because I have PTSD after all the stalking. But it just feels a bit predatory to me... Are you sure she's not looking for a new husband?"

"What do you mean?" I don't like where this is going.

"Well, she's obviously used to letting herself into your house. Maybe she did while you were away?" She's looking at me, wide-eyed.

I feel very uncomfortable. "You think Chloe and Tom...?"

Having introduced this bombshell, she simply shrugs. "What's she like?"

"She's about ten years younger than me, and very pretty."

And there it is; my insecurity is laid before us on the cheeseboard, between the brie and the blue.

"Does Tom *like* her?"

"No, like I said, he says he doesn't trust her."

"Yeah, but do you think he *fancies* her? Trust and lust are two quite different things," she adds mischievously.

I smile and shake my head. "You're terrible, Rosa. No, she's sweet, but she's not Tom's type. He says she's dangerous."

"*Dangerous?* Does he now?" I hear the sarcasm in her voice.

"Yeah, he says she's a gossip, that she has a weird relationship with the truth."

"There go those alarm bells again."

"Honestly, you're as bad as Tom. She's fine. A bit bonkers but not *dangerous*."

"You could invite her over to spend the evening? Work out if she really does have a *thing* for him?"

I feel like Rosa's making far more of this than it is just to get at Tom.

"That would be horrible, and I'm not worried about it. Tom's a good-looking guy, women find him attractive. It's not a problem. Anyway, if I invited her over, he dislikes her so much he'd make it obvious."

"Like he does with me?"

I feel my face going hot. "He's like that with everyone, Rosa, he's just not that sociable."

"You can say that again."

I change the subject; I want this to be a nice evening. "Let's not talk about grumpy old Tom," I joke. "Tell me all about your love life."

"God, you don't want to hear about that, trust me."

"I do. I'm an old married woman—let me live vicariously through you."

Just before she can begin, my phone rings—it's Tom.

"Hey," I say, "how are you?" I mouth his name to Rosa, who gets up and opens the fridge for more wine.

"It's lonely, and I miss you," he says, and I melt.

"I miss you too," I say, feeling a little awkward in front of Rosa, but not wanting to take his call out of the room and make her feel abandoned—after all, this is a girls' night.

"Rosa's here," I say.

"Oh. Really?"

"Yes, she's called in before heading back to Devon. Her uncle's ill."

"Oh, so she's staying over at ours?" he asks, vaguely surprised.

"Yeah, we're having a catch-up over a few glasses of wine."

"God, she didn't waste any time coming over!"

"Yes, we're having a great time, thanks," I say, glad I didn't put my phone on speaker.

"When is she going?"

"Sadly she's only here for one night." I pause for a second. "Yes, I know it's a shame but she has to get back to her uncle, he's not well."

"I doubt her being there will make him feel any better."

"Yes, okay, I'll give her your love."

"Are you trying to get me off the phone?" He's trying to sound light-hearted, but I can tell he's a bit put out.

"No, it's just that I haven't seen Rosa for ages, and we have lots to catch up on."

"So do we—I'm enjoying being back at work," he says, then goes on to talk about some of the people he's working with. I'm pleased he called, and if I'd been alone I'd have been delighted to discuss his new colleagues, but Rosa is now leafing through a magazine and I feel awkward that she's here to see me and I'm talking to Tom.

"Anyway, I'd better go."

"How's Sam?" he asks.

"He's . . . he's good."

"Any more nightmares, strange people in the garden?" He's joking, but now isn't the time. I wasn't going to say anything, didn't want to worry him, but as he seems not to be taking it seriously, I decide to mention it.

"Funnily enough, Rosa heard a noise just now, and when I went to check on him, he said Emily's mummy was in his room."

"Emily, his new best friend?"

"Yes."

"And why would he be imagining her in his room, do you think?"

"We've been spending time together."

"Oh good, so you've found a friend too?" He seems happy about this.

"Yes, but you won't like it, Tom." I roll my eyes at Rosa, who rolls hers back.

"Why won't I like it?"

"Emily is Chloe's daughter. We've become friends, and we've been round to her place and gone to the park with the kids," I say, relieved to be telling him. It was silly hiding it anyway.

"So, hang on, Emily is Chloe's daughter?"

"Yes, that's right."

"I don't understand."

"Sam's new friend is Chloe's *daughter*."

"But, darling, Chloe doesn't *have* any children."

TWENTY-THREE

"I reckon Tom must have got it wrong," I say to Rosa as I put down the phone.

"Tom never gets anything wrong... according to Tom!" she quips through a mouthful of grapes. Then she stops eating for a moment and says, wide-eyed, "So, if this kid isn't hers, then whose is it—did she steal someone else's child?"

"Christ, Rosa, your imagination is worse than mine," I say, but she has a point. I shake my head. "No, Tom's mistaken—he doesn't know her that well, so he wouldn't *know* if she had a kid?"

"Call her and ask her *now*," she demands.

"Yeah, that's what I'll do. I'll call her up and say, 'Despite seeing you every day at preschool with your child, going on playdates and sharing life stories, my husband says you have no children—discuss!'"

"Well, I think you need to find out pretty soon, if only to prove Tom wrong, which I will relish, of course," she says, standing up from her stool. "Okay, I have to be up at dawn and head back to Devon for an appointment with a handsome orthopedic surgeon—unfortunately it's my uncle's appointment, but I intend to steal the show."

"Does Dan... your..."

"Stalker?"

"Yeah, does he know you're in the southwest?" I ask casually. I feel like we're being watched, and though it may well be Chloe, I'm not convinced—she seems too *normal*.

Rosa looks up guiltily from her glass. "It worries me too, love," she says, realizing where my concerns lie. "He knows I have relatives in Devon, and when we were together I told him that my best friend was thinking of buying a place in Cornwall, in this village. I showed him the photo on the estate agent's website."

"Shit, Rosa."

"I know, but he wouldn't just come here," she says, sounding uncertain. "Though I never understood how he knew where I was when he was doing his thing. And no one's seen or heard about him for a couple of weeks, which makes me think—where the fuck is he?"

I'm now on high alert, every nerve is on edge, and I feel sick. "Is there any way you can find out where he is?"

She shakes her head. "Since he sent me that dead rat in the post and I got the police involved, he's disappeared off the face of the earth. I hope." She's trying to hide it, but I know she's scared.

"At least the police are on it," I say, hoping to God the Manchester police and their Cornish counterparts share a database.

"Yeah, I hoped the police would have arrested him by now, but they're always dealing with unhinged people who think they're in a relationship with someone they're not."

"Perhaps we should call the police here, let them know?"

"Already ahead of you," she says. "I called them last week

when I knew I'd be coming here. Gave a description, all his details, and the name and number of the guy dealing with it in Manchester."

I sigh with relief. "That's all good then."

"Yeah, I'm not putting my bestie and her precious little boy in danger."

"Thanks for doing that. I'm sure he won't turn up, but who knows? I'll never forget the night you called me after he turned up at your place with a knife."

"I thought he was going to stab me on the doorstep."

"And the police just came, took a statement, then left you alone in the house, terrified."

"Yeah, that was when I called you. You came and stayed the night with me—I was so bloody grateful."

"Tom was so good, said he'd look after Sam when I came to you," I say, always keen to get some credit in for Tom where Rosa's concerned.

"Did he? I just remember you being so supportive and listening to me while I whined all night," she replies, instantly rejecting Tom's involvement on any level.

"We didn't go to bed, just sat in your lounge on the floor. Every twig outside, every little sound, we both jumped." I pull my cardigan around my shoulders remembering that night.

"Oh God, Rachel, I literally could not go through that again. I'd kill myself first." She puts both hands over her face, draws them back through her hair.

"I'd kill *him* first," I reply, and I mean it.

"Well," she says, "I need to go to bed. Got to be up really early in the morning."

"Oh thanks, now you've scared me to death you're going to bed!" I joke.

We hug good night, and as she wanders off to bed with half a glass of wine, I hurry down to my bedroom. Once there, I go to quickly close the curtains, and as I do, I think I see someone run past the glass doors. I don't open the curtains again to look. I'm too scared, so I get into bed with the light on, clutching a heavy lamp. I don't get much sleep.

The next morning, Rosa has to leave early to miss the traffic, so she can make it back in time to take her uncle for his hospital appointment.

"I'll wake Sam—he asked about you. He doesn't remember who you are, but I know he'd love to meet you," I say as we walk across the landing to his room.

"I'm dying to see him, but promise me you won't wake him," she whispers. "It's too early and he'll just be tired all day."

She's right of course—it's five thirty and he might even be a bit grumpy—so I agree and quietly walk her into his room, where he's fast asleep.

"He's so precious," she whispers, gently kissing his forehead while he sleeps. "Thanks for letting me see him."

I suddenly notice he's clutching a fluffy lion. "Ahh, did you give that to him?" I ask quietly.

She reaches over and touches the soft toy; she shakes her head and we look at each other questioningly.

I'm *really* uneasy now. "I wonder where he got this from?" My mind is going in different directions, but I keep coming back to Chloe—I can hear his voice in my head: *Is Emily's mummy still here?* I feel a chill run through me.

Rosa puts her finger to her lips, then checks behind the curtains and the door. Only when we are sure the room's empty do we quietly make our way downstairs.

"Rosa, I'm beginning to wonder if Sam wasn't dreaming, and Chloe really *was* in his room?"

"Shit, Rachel," she replies anxiously, looking around like Chloe might suddenly appear. "Is she *really* so weird that she'd enter someone's house at night and go into their kid's room?"

"I honestly don't *think* so," I reply, unable to even comprehend this. I feel numb.

"Rachel, I don't want to scare you, but I think you need to be really careful."

Rosa doesn't scare easily, which bothers me, but now I'm questioning myself. Is it a toy I just don't remember? Is it a toy from preschool?

"Why don't you call the police?" she says. "Just tell them what Sam said and explain that this toy lion has come from nowhere."

I shake my head. "I'm sure the local police think I'm mad. I've called them a couple of times now, and when I hear myself say these things, I know I wouldn't believe me if I was them."

"Who cares? Better that you call them and report everything, then if there is any trouble . . ."

"I'll ask Sam about it first. He might have 'borrowed' it from preschool," I suggest. "It might fit into his lunch box—the kids sometimes do that not realizing it's stealing."

"Mmm, I hope you're right. I *hope* Sam took it rather than someone came into his room and left it here."

"Stop it, you're freaking me out."

"Sorry, but just promise me that if anything weird happens when I've gone, you'll call the police, won't you?"

"Of course I will."

"That little boy is so precious. And after what you went through, you *have* to keep him safe. I'm getting those same feelings I used to get about my ex."

"What feelings?"

"It's hard to explain, just instinct I guess, but this feels all wrong. Tom says she has no kids and Sam says she was in his room . . . ?"

I feel nauseous.

"And Rachel, whatever she's telling you, there's a strong possibility that, one way or another, she has *keys*!"

After Rosa leaves I feel really vulnerable. So, I double-check the front door is locked and put a chair against it, then go back to bed and read for a while, until it's time to wake Sam.

"Morning, darling." I open his curtains then go over to him in bed. "Time to get up," I say as his eyes open and he starts a slow smile.

"I don't think I've seen this lion before—is he yours?" I ask.

He nods; he doesn't seem too surprised to see him.

"Is he from preschool?"

"No, he's *mine*, Mummy."

I don't want to make a big thing about this. I need to check that Tom didn't buy it for him before he left and I've only just seen it. I could be overthinking all this: my concern stems from Tom saying that Chloe doesn't have any kids, so first of all I need to put my mind at rest and ask her about Emily.

I make toast for Sam and contemplate how to broach this with Chloe. I'm torn between rushing to preschool and asking her outright, or just asking casually when the opportunity arises. I'm still pondering this as I approach the school gates, feeling nervous. I see some of the other mums walking their kids in and wonder how one asks such a question of any mother without it sounding like you're accusing them of kidnapping.

Once inside, we hang Sam's coat up, and I take Sam into his classroom, where other children are now clambering up the climbing frame. All the time I'm looking around to see if there's any sign of them, and I'm aware that Sam's doing the same.

"Where's Emily?" he asks, looking up at me. His concerned little face breaks my heart.

"I'm sure she'll be here soon," I say. "Why don't you play with one of the other children until Emily is here?" I suggest.

"I can't."

"Of course you can—just go up to someone you like and ask if you can play with them."

He's shaking his head vehemently. "I can't!" He looks on the verge of tears.

"Why not?"

"Because they all hate me."

"Oh, sweetie, that's not true. I'm sure they all really like you."

I'm quite distressed but trying not to show Sam. "Would you like me to speak to Iris, ask her if she can help?"

He doesn't answer me so, still holding hands, we find Iris at the playhouse and I explain the problem.

"Oh goodness me, Sam, everyone here loves you. And the other children are super excited to play with you." She starts looking around the room for a likely candidate. But just as she seems to spot someone, Emily runs up to Sam, saying, "Let's go, Sammy!" She grabs his hand and whisks him off to the climbing frame, and Iris beams.

"Ahh, I'm glad she's here—those two are so cute. They never leave each other's side all day!"

"Oh, that's good I suppose, is it?"

"They are just close. You get that sometimes. It happens a lot with only children. I sometimes wonder if they're subconsciously searching for a sibling, you know?"

This feels like a kick in the stomach. I can barely answer her—I feel winded and just wave goodbye and make for the door.

Emily's here, so there's a chance Chloe might still be close by if she dropped her off. If I'm quick, I might be able to catch her, so I walk purposefully through the gates. I'm turning around, almost full-circle, trying to see if I can spot her among the other mothers, some leaving, some arriving, some standing around chatting and glancing over at me. I must look slightly crazed and desperate. I even ask a couple of the women hanging around the gate, "Have you seen Chloe, Emily's mum?" Jennifer Radley almost swerves to avoid me, and they all look at each other and shrug.

There's nothing else for it but to go to her house, so I head down to Fistral Drive, where she lives. After the short walk I ring the bell and wait. Then I ring again but no answer. I'm about to walk away when an old lady and her dog emerge from the house next door.

"Hello!" I say brightly.

"Oh hello, dear."

"I just called round to see Chloe—do you know if she's home?"

"Chloe?" She looks puzzled. "I know a lady lives there, only recently moved in. She has a daughter."

"Yes, that's right, that's Chloe."

"No, it isn't Chloe. The lady who lives there is called Natalie."

TWENTY-FOUR

My head is spinning. Who is Chloe? And why has she lied about having a daughter and living in that house? I wander aimlessly in the direction of home, my mind desperately searching for answers, but just as I'm turning the corner, I see a familiar figure. Chloe is on the other side of the road, leaving a coffee shop. Her blond hair flies behind her as she walks purposefully in the opposite direction of her house. Within seconds my feet are walking after her. I can't believe I'm doing this. I stay on my side of the road and walk a few yards behind her, which isn't as easy as it looks in the films. I must look very suspect.

"Are you okay?" I hear a familiar voice. Jennifer Radley—why is she always there when I'm being ridiculous?

"I'm fine, thanks." I try a reassuring smile.

"Did you find Chloe?" she asks.

"No, no, I didn't."

"She's up ahead on the other side of the road," she says, without adding "you idiot," but it's obvious that's what she's thinking.

"Yes, yes, there she is, thanks," I reply nonsensically before disappearing into the florists, which happens to be the nearest hiding place.

Mrs. Pickering greets me. "Hello, Rachel, what can I do for you today?"

I make small talk then buy a bunch of sunflowers because I feel I should. The process might also put some space between me and Chloe, not to mention Jennifer bloody Radley, who's now walking slowly past the florists and gazing in. And now I'm panicking because Chloe might get away, and I keep glancing through the window while pretending to care about what Mrs. Pickering is talking about.

"Are you okay, Rachel?" Why do people keep asking this?

"I'm great, thanks, just in a bit of a hurry," I say as she wraps the sunflowers agonizingly slowly. Eventually she hands them to me, I thank her, pay her, and run out of the shop.

I have no choice but to glide past Jennifer Radley, who clearly has nothing better to do than hang around trying to catch me out. Who can blame her? I must seem quite odd, especially as I'm now pretending to jog while carrying a great big bunch of sunflowers. But I have to keep going. I'm too close to my prey to lose her now, and just a few minutes later I'm rewarded. She stops and walks up the pathway to a big, old house, unlocks the door, and then she's inside, and I'm none the wiser. Something's driving me: I feel like nothing she's told me is true and so I decide to just go and knock on the door. It's none of my business, apart from the fact she's pretending Emily is her child, and she plays with Sam. If there's something weird going on, I have to know. So I walk up the path to the entrance, which has several steps leading to it, and look at the different numbers to the apartments inside, some have names on, but I can't see hers.

I shade my eyes to look at the windows, staring hard to see if there's any sign of her. It's not easy with the sun glaring down, but on the upper-left window, I suddenly become aware of something: a figure materializes from the darkness inside, and there she is. Chloe is looking down, watching me.

Our eyes meet but she doesn't flinch—no flicker of a smile,

or recognition even. I continue to stand there clutching the sunflowers, confused and uneasy. Then she moves away from the window, and after a couple of minutes, I hear the lock in the front door. It opens and she's standing there, expressionless, unfathomable. And despite the morning sunshine nudging into another beautiful day, I feel a cold chill run through me.

I'm now at the bottom of the steps looking up at Chloe. Those pretty blue eyes seem cold, the dimples created by her smile long gone.

"What are you doing here?" There's an air of inconvenience in her tone, like she's left a pan on the stove. I wonder fleetingly if, in answering the door to me, she's had to tear herself away from something urgent. Or someone?

She isn't talking, isn't filling the air with chatter and small talk, and I'm aware I owe her an explanation. But I don't know *how* to explain why I'm here without it seeming like I'm stalking her. "I missed you at preschool—I just wanted to say hi and you weren't home, so . . ."

"So you *followed* me?" she asks, one eyebrow raised, her delicate features showing only surprise.

I feel like an idiot. "Yes. I did, but only because . . ." I hesitate and realize I'm still clutching the flowers. "I wanted to give you these." I offer up the flowers. She's standing above me on the top front doorstep. I'm awkward and embarrassed, and to anyone passing it might look like I'm curtsying. She beckons and I follow her silently up carpeted stairs. A slight tang of damp and cabbage lingers in the air, and when she opens the door to her apartment, it couldn't be less like her little pink cottage.

The carpet's threadbare, a shabby sofa sits in the middle of the room, and a table in the corner is strewn with used crockery and paper takeaway cartons. No pretty muslin curtains, no flowery soft furnishings with pastel throws.

"What *is* this place, Chloe?"

"Home."

She walks to the table to stand in front of the detritus littering it. I think it's her way of trying to hide the mess. She looks ashamed, troubled.

"You own this too, along with the cottage?"

She shakes her head, leans on the table. "This is a rental. The cottage isn't mine, it's my sister's."

"Oh, I see. But why did you pretend?"

"I didn't. It's not *my* fault if you made assumptions."

"No, but you never once said it was your *sister's* house."

"Do I need to spell everything out? What does it matter to you? You're no different from Jennifer Radley, making judgments and assumptions."

"I'm actually *very* different from the likes of Jennifer Radley," I snap, offended. "Chloe, why are you being like this? I thought we were friends."

At this, she softens slightly—friendship is important to her; she wants a friend.

"We *are* friends. I'll never be your friend like Rosa," she adds, "but who knows, if she wasn't around, we could be one day, right?"

I'm really not sure about that, and what does she mean *if she wasn't around?*

"So okay, the cottage is your sister's, but you never made that clear. Why?"

She thinks for a moment. "Because I like the cottage, and sometimes like to imagine it's mine. I helped her furnish it, I chose the wallpaper, I did the same with your house, I suggested those green sofas," she sighs. "I guess I'm always living someone else's life, because mine's so shit, I can't afford fancy wallpaper and velvet sofas, I have to make do with damp walls and shabby seats," she mutters, resentfully.

I'm not really listening, I'm still processing the fact that her life is completely different than she led me to believe. I feel blindsided.

"And Emily, is *she* yours?"

"Emily's my niece."

"I thought..."

"Yeah, *you* thought," she says, like this is *my* problem. "I never *once* said she was mine, and did you ever hear her call me Mum?"

"I can't remember."

"Well, she doesn't, because I'm *not* her mum. I just look after her there while my sister goes off and has a big career and lives her exciting life. Why should *she* be pinned down by a child, Chloe will do it," she adds bitterly.

"But like the cottage, do you sometimes wish Emily was yours?"

"No!" She looks horrified. "I'm not a psycho. I told you my sister had a kid. I wasn't hiding anything from you."

I think of Tom's words: *She has a weird relationship with the truth.* Turns out he was spot-on—she's right, she never actually lied, but there's no denying she tried to pass off as her sister.

"I really wasn't trying to deceive you, Rachel. It's just that you were going on about how lovely it was and how you really admired my taste and the way I put things together. You liked me, liked my home, you were so nice to me. I wanted us to be friends, and it just went on until it was too late to tell you. I'm only ever a friend for a season or a reason. I don't know why, but people walk away from people like me."

"So you think not telling the truth will keep people close? It's probably *why* they walk away."

"You don't understand—how could you? You have this amazing house, gorgeous husband, good friends, wonderful life. Why would someone like you want to be friends with someone like me, who lives like this? Look at it." She gestures across the grubby little room.

"I don't choose my friends by their homes."

"I know. But you have this stunning, state-of-the-art place—it's worth over a million pounds. You don't have any idea how it feels to live here."

"Yes I do, I've lived most of my adult life in places like this, and I can only live in that house because my father died. I would go back to that little apartment now if I could swap and get my dad back. Houses mean nothing, but family is everything."

"Not my family. My sister is older—she got out before the problems started, had a career, traveled the world, and when she'd done all that, she married, had a baby, and bought that chocolate-box cottage. In the meantime, I had to give up the chance to go away to university to help my mum with my dad, who has Alzheimer's."

"You never told me that."

"No!" she yells. "Because I didn't *want* you to know. Who wants to know about me wiping my dad's backside, feeding him, putting nappies on him? No time for college or university; I had to get a job to help the family, and then after ten years I lost the job because some man told lies about me at the bank where I worked. Before I could find another one, Dad got worse and I had to stay here, do casual work at the estate agents and help Mum. It's been like that for years while our Natalie swanned around the world, FaceTiming us from fancy restaurants and texting photos of fucking sunsets! Then she got pregnant, but because she went to university and can earn more money than me, she and Mum decided it made more sense for me to look after Emily so she can have a career."

She puts her head down, and I feel so sorry for her, standing in her lonely room, bent with the weight of disappointment and unspent rage. "I do love Emily, I really do, but sometimes I just feel caught in the middle of everything."

"Chloe, that sounds so awful, but I understand you better

now. I think we should be more honest, don't you?" I say gently. "Friends don't judge friends. We are who we are, and we're here for each other."

"I understand if you don't want to be friends. It wasn't about you, I just hate my life," she says, wiping her eyes, "and sometimes it's just easier to be Natalie, and not Chloe."

I silently agree. I can only imagine what it's like to watch a sibling move on with their life and thrive, while you're left behind, sacrificing your own freedom.

I won't abandon her; she deserves some kindness and understanding. I also need to find out once and for all if I'm right, and she's harmless, just misunderstood.

"Hey, would you like to come over to ours one afternoon with Emily? The kids can play in the garden, and you and I can chat?"

"I'd love that, and Emily would too!"

"Okay, what about later today?" I suggest. Tom's due back tomorrow, and I know the last thing he'll want is to be greeted by Chloe.

"Wonderful! And thanks so much for not dumping me because I wasn't clear."

I think it was a bit more than lack of clarity, but I let it go.

"Be careful, Rachel, she's definitely not to be trusted. Just keep your eyes wide-open," Rosa says when I call her later. "Not telling you about her home or the kid is, in my book, just as bad as barefaced lying."

"Yes, I agree, but I'm watching her, and if for one single moment I think she's going to be trouble, I will end all contact. I know that will devastate her, she values our friendship, and that's why I don't believe she'll jeopardize it. At the same time, I don't want to ruin Sam and Emily's friendship—I think having her around is really helping his confidence. No, I need to keep her close for now, because the alternative is that I have to move

Sam to another preschool, and I can't do that to him, not when he's only just finding his feet."

"I understand. You're a good mum, Rachel, and I can see how you're putting up with her for Sam's sake," Rosa adds with a sigh. "I just hope you don't live to regret it. Just do me a favor, don't ever leave her alone with Sam."

TWENTY-FIVE

When we return with the kids, it's a beautiful afternoon, and they're so excited. I know I've done the right thing.

"I thought we'd have a picnic on the grass," I say, buttering bread to make sandwiches.

Chloe opens a plastic bag and takes out a box of cupcakes and a bottle of wine. "Thought we might need this." She winks at me. "It's so warm," she says, fanning her face.

She helps me pack the sandwiches into little plastic boxes and puts the plates and plastic drink cartons in the picnic hamper while the kids run around the sitting room.

"Shall we have a cheeky white wine now?" she asks.

"Perhaps with the food in a little while?" I say, making a mental note not to drink more than one glass. I've been here before with Chloe, and I need my wits about me. I didn't need Rosa to tell me not to leave Sam on his own with her, and I intend to stay very sober.

But while I continue to pack the picnic, she pours us two large glasses.

"Chloe, I'll get drunk," I warn. "I'm the responsible adult in charge of my child."

"Will you be the responsible adult in charge of my *niece* too?" she says, chuckling.

"Come on, kids, picnic!" I call, pretending to drink my wine but putting the almost full glass back on the countertop. Chloe can be so insistent—I just don't want the hassle, and it's easier if she thinks I'm joining her in a drink.

"You get the hamper and I'll get the more important stuff," Chloe says, picking up our two glasses of wine.

"I feel better now we cleared the air," she says a little later, when the kids have eaten and are now playing "castles," using the garden wall as a fortress.

"I'm glad too," I say.

"I was so shocked when you turned up at my place this morning. I felt terrible, like I'd deceived you."

I shrug. "I just wish you'd been clearer." I try to be tactful. I know she wanted me to think Emily was hers, and it might have been innocent, that she just wanted to be friends, but I don't think I'll ever completely trust her. Chloe has deceived me, whether she meant to or not, and she can be a bit crazy, but I'm fair and prepared to give her the benefit of the doubt to keep the peace, and for Sam's sake.

"So, where's your sister today?" I ask. She refers to her a lot, but only vaguely, nothing specific.

"Away on business."

"Yeah, but where?"

"No idea."

"Really? But what if something happens with Emily and you need to call her?"

"I have her mobile, and I think Mum knows where she is," she adds, then quickly changes the subject. "When's Tom back from Scotland?"

"Tomorrow. He's taking Sam to a cricket match, they're both excited."

"So you're on your own? Do you fancy getting together—we could go shopping?"

"I can't . . ."

"Why? Why can't you see me? It's a Saturday and you're on your own?"

"I have stuff to do," I say.

"Like what?"

One of the things that I don't like about Chloe is that she won't let go. If she wants something, she just keeps pushing, like wanting me to have a drink with her, and it's the same with meeting for coffee and playdates—she won't rest until I agree to a time and a place. She's pouring more wine now, despite me holding my hand up and telling her I don't want another drink—I've already emptied the first glass on the grass.

"So, tomorrow, what shall we do?" she asks.

"Chloe, I just need some *me* time tomorrow."

"No, let's have some *us* time instead." She's sitting up on the rug; her campaign has begun. "We could sunbathe by your pool, pretend we're in the Caribbean. I'll mix cocktails." Her excitement is building, and sometimes I find it hard to say no to her juggernaut heading toward me. But I will stand my ground, make her realize she can't steamroll me into something I don't want to do.

"No, I'm sorry, Chloe. I just want to potter around tomorrow, cook a meal for when they get back from cricket. You understand, don't you?"

"No, I don't understand," she says sulkily. She pulls her sunglasses from her head to her eyes and lies back down, momentarily shutting me out.

"So, Tommy's back tomorrow?" she murmurs. The way she sometimes refers to him like that suggests an intimacy I'm not comfortable with.

"Yeah, I can't wait to see him. I've missed him."

"Mmmm, I'd miss him too. Bet you can't wait to rip his clothes off."

"Calm down, Chloe," I joke, surprised at her candor, but I guess it's the drink talking.

"Am I wrong then?" She lifts her sunglasses onto her head again like she really wants to see my face.

"No, it's private, Chloe." I give a little embarrassed laugh. I've never been one to talk about my intimate relationships, even with my closest friends, and right now Chloe is little more than an acquaintance.

"But we're girlfriends, surely you've talked about sex with your girlfriends?"

"Yes, when I was about sixteen."

"Have you thought any more about him being on that mailing list for The Candle Company?" She's resting her head on her hand, plucking at the grass with the other. She's clearly pushing on a door, and I'm not letting her open it. My marriage and any doubts or concerns I may have are really none of her business.

"I mentioned it to him—he bought something for me and inadvertently put himself on the list."

She hesitates, and it seems she's about to say something else. I get the feeling Chloe likes to create trouble where there isn't any, and I'm about to make this point subtly, but I suddenly hear a door bang. It's coming from the house. "That sounds like the front door," I say, uneasily.

"Are you expecting anyone?"

"No, and I'm sure I locked it—who the hell?" I stand up and look above at the patio on the first floor, where someone is emerging from the house.

"Hey, I'm home! Are you in the garden?"

Tom! I go from relief to slight panic. What will he think, finding me and Chloe, a woman he doesn't trust, in the garden together drinking wine? The timing couldn't be worse because she's had a drink and saying things I'm not comfortable with. If Tom has a problem with this, I'm not sure I could defend her quite so vehemently as I have before.

"Yes, we're out here."

"I'm coming down."

"It's Tom!" I say, surprised, wishing to God she wasn't here and there weren't two glasses and a bottle of wine lying on the rug. It isn't that Tom disapproves of drinking, and I haven't even had any, but it's how it looks.

"Daddy!" Sam is calling and waving. "Emily's here."

"So I see," Tom says, attempting a smile, but it's more of a grimace.

He walks over to us. "I see Mummy's with *her* friend too. Hi, Chloe." I hear the accusation in his voice and feel like a teenager who's been caught drinking by her father.

"Hey, Tommy," she murmurs, lying back down, closing her eyes.

I cringe at this but try to override it with a bright smile. "I didn't expect you until tomorrow, darling," I say, going to hug him.

"Finished earlier than I thought." He hugs me back.

"Hey, Tommy, how was your long journey back?" she asks without opening her eyes.

"Terrible, I'm tired and exhausted and not much fun, I'm afraid."

I'm about to respond when she sits up. The straps of her sundress are pulled down and the top is dangerously low. I'm convinced her breasts are going to emerge any moment.

"Not too tired and exhausted to take your wife to heaven?" she replies, which even through her wine haze seems really inappropriate.

Tom doesn't answer her, lets it hang.

"I didn't mean anything—you're not offended, are you, Tommy?" she asks, her hand caressing her own neck as she makes full eye contact with my husband.

"Not at all, Chloe. But you must forgive me, I'm a tired, slightly irritable, middle-aged bloke, who's looking forward to falling asleep in front of the TV with his wife." If he's shocked by her behavior, he isn't showing it.

"I bet you weren't always like that." She's looking up at him, and he's looking down at her, and I see a look pass between them that turns my insides to ice.

TWENTY-SIX

"Well, I guess I'll leave you ladies to finish your drinks while I unpack and have a nap," Tom says, heading back up the garden toward the house. I'm still processing the look I saw pass between them. Do I have anything to be concerned about or am I overthinking things?

"I'll just go and get another bottle," Chloe says, and before I can stop her, she's skipping barefoot up the garden to the house, and to Tom, leaving me with no choice but to stay and watch the kids.

I know a sober Chloe would have been more thoughtful, more subtle even? But her flirting and now this move to get another bottle have made me feel a frisson of jealousy and resentment toward her. It's irrational, I know—I'm sure she hasn't gone back to the house because Tom's there, but I don't like how it's made me feel. I'm a forty-two-year-old woman in a happy marriage and I've nothing to feel insecure about. Have I? Since we moved here, I've changed. It's almost primal, I suppose—I'm in new territory, with new people, and I'm unsure of myself and others. But I need to get a grip because now I'm even doubting Tom! Why am I starting to feel like my foundations aren't as strong as I thought they were? I trust him implicitly. Don't I?

Suddenly I hear a peal of laughter coming from the house. I'm even more on edge now—what the hell is she finding so funny? Tom says all kinds of mean things about her to me, and I could see he wasn't pleased to see her, and yet there's this ease between them, like they've been friends for years. Something bothers me; I think I've always felt this, from the night she first turned up unannounced and let herself in.

I turn back to the kids, who are both chatting away. I'm too preoccupied about Chloe in my house with Tom to listen to their conversation. I check my watch—she's been in there about ten minutes now. How long does it take to grab a bottle from the fridge? I don't even *want* any bloody wine, and I'm not sure she should have any more either as she needs to get Emily home safely.

I can't even wander nonchalantly up to the house to put my mind at rest, because I need to stay here with the children. I've already asked Emily twice not to climb the wall and she's ignored me, and she's now entwined herself around the ivy and is shimmying up the wall.

"I can see it, I can see it!" she yells, referring to the pool, causing my stomach to drop.

Please don't ask to go in.

"Can we go for a swim, Rachel?" she asks.

I just shake my head and try to smile. I'm waiting for a tussle, but she seems to accept this—though she continues to climb up the wall and shout "Pool!" every two minutes.

Why is she still in the house? What's keeping her? Every minute is agony and I *need* to go inside if only for peace of mind. I can't take this uncertainty or the pain of unease another second. I could leave the children here—I'm sure they'd be fine.

It's only a short run to the house, a matter of moments. But I know all too well how quickly lives are changed in seconds, and I'm not leaving them alone.

"Ice cream time, kids," I suddenly hear myself call, and they follow me happily up the garden. I don't know what I'm expecting but I ask the kids to sit and wait outside on the patio where I can see them.

"No moving, and whoever stays still the longest gets a prize," I promise blindly, knowing they will keep me to this.

Then I hold my breath and go inside. The patio doors lead straight into the kitchen, which is empty, but the wine has been taken out of the fridge and is sweating on the counter. I don't call their names, just walk through the silence of the sitting room.

Where are they?

I walk through into the hallway and hear a noise upstairs. Then suddenly Chloe appears—she's bouncing down the stairs, her hair all mussy and her face pink.

"Where have you been?" I ask. "I've been waiting ages out there."

"I just went to the bathroom," she replies.

"Where's Tom?" I ask.

"Don't know." She holds up her hands like she has no clue as to his whereabouts. I'm not convinced.

"There's a downstairs bathroom," I say, knowing she must be aware of this as our former estate agent.

"I prefer the large mirror and lack of kids upstairs," she says with a smile.

I don't return her smile; I feel sick. "Talking of kids, can you keep an eye on them?" I ask.

"Yeah, sure." She stands at the bottom of the stairs, and I feel her eyes on me as I run past her two stairs at a time. I just know Tom's up there, but I'm suddenly scared of how I'll find him—will he be lying on our spare bed, the covers messed, the bed linen reeking of her perfume? I look in all three bedrooms, including Sam's, because you never know. Each time I call him then walk through the rooms, but there doesn't seem to be any sign of him. I'm actually relieved. He wasn't up here with Chloe after all, he must have popped out. I need to get a grip, my imagination is running away with me at the moment.

I head back down the stairs and Chloe is still standing at the bottom. *What is she waiting for?*

"Are the kids okay?" I ask, irritated that she's abandoned them.

"I checked, they're fine."

I don't believe her, so I push past her, through the hallway then out into the kitchen and outside. As soon as I get to the big glass doors, I see them and head out there, thankful that they're safe and my husband hasn't just been in bed with Chloe. I almost laugh at myself—what's wrong with me? I'm used to Tom working away, but it feels different here. I've become so insecure. I must be going mad to think anything was happening between Chloe and Tom.

But she's so pretty, and he's middle-aged and vulnerable. Mrs. Pickering's face is bearing down on me: *Men do silly things, lovey.*

Where is he?

"Rachel, can I talk to you?" Chloe's standing behind me.

"Of course," I say, "but we need to keep our eye on the kids," I remind her, maneuvering her out onto the patio.

"Oh, of course," she replies, like she's completely forgotten they are here.

I give them the promised ice cream and turn to her. "You wanted to talk?" I'm not in the mood for a Chloe drama now. In fact, the more I get to spend time with her, the more I'm realizing that she isn't as much fun as I thought she was.

"I don't want to talk in front of them because it's a difficult conversation I have to have with you."

"Okay, should I be worried?" I ask, a veil of unease falling over me as we move to the sofa at the far end of the patio.

Following me, she comes too close and whispers in my ear, "I just want you to know that what I'm about to tell you isn't meant to hurt you—it's meant to save you."

TWENTY-SEVEN

Dread swims in my stomach as I wait for her to continue, but she just stares ahead, absently.

"So, what is it?" I ask sharply.

She doesn't answer and I have the feeling she is quite enjoying the build-up.

"Chloe?"

She shakes her head. "I need you to promise you won't get upset, and that you won't hate me when I tell you this."

"I'm promising *nothing*, Chloe."

"I couldn't bear it if you hated me and ended our friendship over this." Her head's down and she's fiddling with her shell-pink nails.

I shrug. "Well don't tell me then?" I'm not playing her silly game.

"But it's in your interest to know."

"Okay, so *tell* me then." I'm so frustrated with her. "The kids will finish their ice cream in about two minutes, so we don't have a lot of time for this. Either tell me or don't."

She takes a deep breath, pauses for effect, I'm sure, then says,

"Okay, a little while ago, when you were still in Manchester and Tom was here alone..."

My stomach begins to swirl. I'm glad I'm sitting down because I feel unsteady, but I brace myself for what she's about to say.

"We...we were both on our own. We went for a drink, talked about our old friends at the bank." She looks at me.

"Okay."

"Rachel, there's no easy way to say this..."

Now I start to feel sick and have to remind myself that this woman tells lies.

"Thing is..." she continues. "Tom and I slept together."

"Oh?" I'm dumbfounded. Is she telling the truth? I very much doubt it. If she is, then I'm horrified; if she's lying, I'm just as horrified that she could lie about something like this. I don't know what to say or think.

"Yes and it...blossomed. We had a relationship, an affair, whatever you want to call it."

She looks up with big, sad eyes. I should feel hurt or anger, but my overwhelming feeling is one of disbelief.

"It's over now," she says, preempting my question. "I think for Tom it was temporary—as soon as you came here, I was dropped," she continues, in a dramatic tone. "I thought he loved me, but he just wanted someone to sleep with."

"And you made friends with me *knowing* this? What kind of person does that?" Why would she pursue a friendship with the wife of someone she's sleeping with, or even *imagining* she's sleeping with?

Tears spring to her eyes. "I didn't know you then—all I'd ever seen were photographs. He told me you were controlling, that you only gave him pocket money, that whatever he did, it never made you happy."

"That's simply not true. Tom would *never* call me controlling."

"Well, he did, and I feel so guilty now because when he

came up with the idea of turning that walled garden into a pool, I encouraged him. I found a contractor, helped design the layout, the colors, I even ordered the tiling. I didn't know you were scared of water, that you couldn't swim..."

"I don't want to listen to this anymore." I try to stand up, but she pulls me back.

"I *knew* you wouldn't believe me, but you *have* to! He told me when you saw the pool you ran away, you hated it, said he'd ruined the space, turned it into something horrible. He made out it was you being unreasonable, but back then I didn't realize you have a fear of water."

This hits me like a blow in the stomach. That's *exactly* what happened, and those are the words I used. How could she know that?

"So, if this is true, you were still seeing him then? Even when I came here, even after you'd met me that night, after I'd seen the pool?"

She nods guiltily.

"You wanted to be my friend while having a relationship with my husband?"

"I told you, as soon as you arrived, he dumped me, but it lingered on a few more weeks—I was in love with him, Rachel."

"Have you any idea how painful this is for me to hear? Even if you're lying, this is really twisted, Chloe."

"It is. But it's the truth."

"I think Tom's popped out, but as soon as he's back I'm going to ask him about all this," I say, calling her bluff.

"No, God, no."

The horrified expression on her face is a relief, her bluff has been called.

"Why wouldn't you want him involved? Is it because this is all a big lie?" I ask.

"No. I'm scared of him."

I laugh openly at this.

"He isn't what you think he is, Rachel," she says earnestly.

"Really? And what do *I* think he is?"

"You *think* he's a good husband, a decent man who's built this place for you, and who loves you regardless of your wealth."

"My *wealth*?" I don't see my inheritance in those terms, especially as it's now all been sunk into this house.

"He resents the fact you have all the money and your hands on the purse strings. He *hates* it, Rachel. He's obsessed and hates that your father only left it to you—he says your father didn't trust him, but now I know why. Your father was a very wise man."

I'm shaken again by the intimate knowledge she seems to have about us; it could only have come from Tom. But why would he say these things to her? This worries me the most, because under what circumstances other than pillow talk would he be discussing the minutiae of our finances, and his feelings around my father, with Chloe?

Is she telling the truth?

"You don't believe me."

"I don't know."

She now seems to gather herself together, like she has a battle on her hands, and she sits upright and looks around, presumably to make sure no one is within earshot.

"We got together almost as soon as he arrived—he was lonely, so was I. Together we created this. We'd sit together on those winter evenings talking about how the house would look, the style of wallpaper, paint colors. He didn't always choose what I'd suggested; he'd come back from being with you in Manchester with lots of new ideas, and he'd usually go with those. That's why I knew as soon as you arrived that he'd choose you."

I don't say anything at this point, but Tom never came back to Manchester while he was here. He was too concerned about leaving the house on its own, and he certainly wouldn't have trusted Chloe to keep her eye on it. She must be lying.

"We'd drink wine in the garden, long before your glass

balustrade or swimming pool." She's waxing lyrical now. "There was garden rubbish everywhere, deliveries of cement and bricks and all kinds of ugly stuff. But it was beautiful just to be here with him. He said he loved me. He said one day we'd live here together. I believed him."

Now I know this is all just lies. "This house is in my name, so there's no way he could live here with anyone but me."

"There are ways," she says, trying to sound mysterious.

I call her bluff. "I need to speak to Tom," I say, trying to pull away from her, but she now has my wrist in her grip and the children are only a few yards away.

"No!" I see a glint in her eyes, a kind of madness driven by unrequited love. And that's when it all clicks into place—Chloe isn't lying, because she believes what she's saying is true. She's a fantasist, a delusional stalker.

"Let go of me," I say quietly so as not to alarm the kids. But she's glaring at me, her teeth together like an animal about to bite. Looking into those glinting eyes, I hear Rosa's voice and wish to God I'd listened to my friend. I see a field of red flags.

"Chloe," I say gently. "I think it's all in your mind."

"No, no one ever believes me. Rachel, *please, PLEASE?*" She's clutching me, tears rolling down her cheeks. I've never seen anyone so desperate, so out of control.

Alerted by her raised voice, the kids both look up and stop what they're doing.

I look over and smile at the children. "Calm down. Now can you *please* let go of me, take Emily, and go home," I say quietly and forcefully. She seems to realize this could scare them and finally lets go of me.

"*Please* don't do this, Rachel, we're friends. If I lose you, I have nothing." Then her demeanor changes from begging to aggression, wild and unbridled, as she clutches once again at my arm.

I see the crazy in her eyes and I'm actually quite scared, especially with the children here.

"Why is it *me* you're angry with?" she hisses, baring her teeth. "It should be your fucking *husband!*"

She's shaking her head, tears streaming down her face—as scared as I am, I'm also worried about her.

"That's enough, you're going to upset the kids," I say. I glance over at them, now digging in the as yet unplanted vegetable boxes, apparently oblivious to the drama unfolding at the far side of the patio.

"I think you need help, Chloe, someone to talk to who can help you work through what's going on. But first, we need to get you home. Emily needs to be with her mum."

"She's working late. And my mum isn't home, she's at the hospital with Dad."

Now I'm *really* concerned. "I don't think you should be on your own with Emily when you're like this," I say. "Why don't I walk you home and Emily can stay here with Sam? Tom will look after them. Your mum or sister can pick her up later."

"I am perfectly capable of looking after my niece!" She's trying to contain her anger, but I feel it simmering just beneath the surface. I've never seen her like this.

"Do you have a number for someone I can call?"

"You're not having anyone's number. They'll think I'm the liar, not him!"

"Right now, that isn't an issue. I'm concerned about Emily," I say gently, trying to calm her down.

"No, you're not, you're concerned about your perfect husband and your perfect life, and you can't let anyone get inside it and find out the truth. But I got inside this house. Inside your life, your bedroom. I worked on the interiors. Oh yes, you were surprised at his 'decorator's eye'—he doesn't have one. I chose the sofas you sit on, the color of the walls you stare at. And I was the one who swam naked in your pool with your *husband*." Her voice is weird, staccato, doesn't sound like her. "We made love in the moonlight. He said his marriage was over, but you don't want to hear that, do you? You just want to call someone to *remove* me."

She twists her mouth, like she's trying to stop it from speaking. I feel like she's going to say something else, then thinks better of it.

"You don't *have* to believe me"—she's calmer now—"but I'm not the only one, Rachel. He's seeing someone else."

TWENTY-EIGHT

I stand over her, eager to get her out of my home.

"Chloe, you'd better go," I say.

"But there's more, Rachel."

"I don't want to hear it," I reply, shaking with anger. "Just *go*, please."

She seems surprised by my rage, which illustrates further how out of touch she is. She has no idea what she's saying and how it's making me feel. I realize now why she has no real friends. This is her MO: reel someone in, make them think she's their friend, and then try and make them as crazy and insecure as she is with elaborate lies.

"So, you're throwing me and Emily out?"

I nod, and staring at me in disbelief, she stands up. "Come on, Emily," she calls, listlessly. Ignoring Emily's protests, she walks past the kids and moves robotically across the patio. By the time she reaches the kitchen, I'm behind her, and Emily has followed. I am escorting them out, wanting to make sure she leaves, that I actually watch her go—I don't even trust her to do that now.

And just as we're all walking toward the front door, I hear keys in the lock and Tom walks in.

"Where have you been?" I hear myself blurt out, accusingly.

"I went to get some more wine, we've run out." He lifts the shopping bag he's holding. I know Tom, and he's making a point, that Chloe has drunk all the wine, but she doesn't pick this up.

"You shouldn't have bought more wine on my account," she says presumptuously.

"I didn't," he says. "Are you guys leaving?" He looks relieved. She nods but says nothing.

"Chloe has to get Emily back, don't you?" I can barely look at her, but I'm aware she's making no move to go, just standing there.

She's now looking at Tom with those big, victim eyes, and I wonder fleetingly if she'll tweak the narrative of this afternoon for the preschool mums, alienating me even further.

"Come on, Emily." Chloe grabs her niece, who's still objecting to this unexpected early departure.

"You said we could go in the swimming pool," she whines.

"No, I *didn't!*" Chloe's face flushes; she obviously did.

"You did, you *promised* we could go in!" Emily screeches at her.

I've never given any invites for the pool. Chloe knows it's *way* out of my comfort zone. So why would she promise Emily?

"Shut UP!" Chloe's saying through clenched teeth, but Emily shakes her off and runs back out into the garden. Chloe's now storming after her. "We can go in another day," she's saying in a low voice.

"You *promised* me *today*."

"I know but . . ." Chloe's looking over to see if we're listening, then lowers her voice so I don't hear any more of the argument until Emily screams, "You're a bitch!"

This takes my breath away. Tom and I look at each other with wide eyes—now I *know* where Sam's newly expanded vocabulary has come from.

Tom rolls his eyes and wanders through to the kitchen now, abandoning this horrible mess. I stand and wait for them to return and leave. I have no intention of going out to the garden—I'll let Chloe deal with this child and this problem. I just want them gone.

"Emily said you promised more ice cream," Chloe says as she sweeps back into the house. "But I told her you want us to leave, so we can't stay for more ice cream." She stands there, her face in mine. Does she really think she can use emotional blackmail on me?

"They've had enough ice cream," I say, not willing to light this bonfire. "Time for home now." I smile for Emily's and Sam's benefit, while Chloe stares at me in silence for too long. I'm dreading what she's going to say next; she clearly has no boundaries. But after a few seconds, she turns on her heels, dragging the kicking child, and slams the door behind her.

"What the hell was all that about?" Tom's saying, a bemused look on his face.

"She's just so bloody difficult. You were right, she's a nightmare, I don't know what her problem is. I don't even know why we're friends."

"I warned you. Didn't I *warn* you?" he repeats as I follow him back into the kitchen.

"What's for dinner?" he asks vaguely, like that's it, we've discussed it, and it's over. "Have you killed the fatted calf for my return?"

"No, because I thought you were home *tomorrow*," I point out absently, still in shock at what Chloe said earlier about the two of them.

He's now opening the fridge and gazing inside for inspiration. "Let's have a takeaway tonight," he suggests, closing the fridge door.

I can't even answer him; my blood is boiling and food is the last thing on my mind. I'm so wound up by what she said and the way she left, taking offense that I'd asked her to leave. She behaved like I was the one being unreasonable, when she'd just told me she'd slept with my husband, had a relationship with him before I got here. And even if that *isn't* true, it's bound to upset me. Can't she see that? I'm beginning to wonder if Chloe can see anything.

Tom's now opening the kitchen drawer, taking out some pizza and Chinese takeaway leaflets, and wafting them in his face like a fan. "Where in the world shall we go?" he's saying in a stupid voice. "Culinarily, I mean."

I can't smile at his clowning around. I need to ask him outright about what Chloe told me, so I suggest to Sam that we put his programs on the TV in the other room. He is of course delighted about this, and once he's settled, I return to Tom in the kitchen.

"She said the two of you have had an affair."

I'm surprised to hear myself say it out loud.

He stops fanning the takeaway menus and stares at me.

"Chloe?"

"Who else?"

"What? What the *hell*?" He seems genuinely confused.

"She said when I was in Manchester, she saw you all the time, that you slept together in this house... in the pool." My flesh feels like it's on fire. I hurt all over and need soothing, and only Tom can do this by telling me it's not true.

I *need* that affirmation.

He picks up on my pain and, carefully placing down the fan of leaflets, walks toward me. He puts his arms around me, kisses my forehead. But he doesn't say she's lying, he doesn't soothe me; he holds me for a long time, then he says, "I think you and I need to have a chat." His voice is low in my ear, and I'm not soothed. My flesh burns on as he takes me by the hand and leads me out onto the patio.

My mouth is dry as I sit down on the garden furniture. It's cooler now, and Tom thoughtfully brings out a throw from the sofa, placing it gently around my shoulders.

He brings his chair close to mine and sits down, then takes a deep breath; he seems to be searching for words—for what? To console, to explain, to confess?

"I'm not surprised to hear she's said these things." He takes my hand and looks into my face. The seriousness of his expression makes my world tilt a little.

"When I told you Chloe was dangerous, I wasn't being flippant or dramatic," he starts. "I could have told you a lot more, but I didn't want to scare you. Perhaps I *should* have, then you'd have listened?" He says this almost to himself, a reprimand. "I told you she's trouble, and in Chloe's case this takes many forms, but this isn't the first time she's lied in an attempt to break up someone's marriage."

"Really?"

"I remember when she worked at the bank someone telling me she had this habit of fixating on unattainable men. Bosses, senior executives, often married." He pauses, shakes his head. "She would *create* opportunities to be alone with them, and always did her research, like finding out their favorite place for lunch and turn up, or suddenly have a spare ticket for a band she knew they liked. At first it was never *that* obvious. She was a nice, friendly, pretty girl, and even if she was a little overt with the flirting... well, not many middle-aged men had a problem with that."

"So it wasn't a problem?" I say, confused.

"It wasn't a problem—until she became really fixated on this particular guy. She'd got him in her sights, but for once he wasn't interested, and she wasn't used to that. She became fixated, called him at all times of the day or night, knowing his wife was there with him."

"That's scary."

"She'd made it her mission to know all about him, about their home, their kids—she'd watched him so intently for so long; she was a woman possessed. She even started following his wife, trying to befriend her."

"Just like she has with me?" My mouth goes dry.

He looks at me, raises his eyebrows. "Yes. Exactly."

"Christ, Tom, you said she was trouble. But I had no idea she was this bad. Why didn't you tell me about the guy at work?"

He shrugs. "Because I didn't want to scare you. I knew you weren't as keen to move here as I was, and I worried if you knew all that, you might change your mind about staying here. Let's face it, if I told you there was this psycho running around, you might have just packed up and gone back to Manchester. Besides, I didn't know you'd become friends while I was away. You kept that from me."

I feel terribly guilty at this—he's right, I went against his advice and brought her into our lives.

"I feel a fool," I say, "but I liked her. I had no friends here and thought she was fun."

"Oh yes, she plays her part well. She seems to know *just* what a person needs, and offers it to them on a plate. In your case it was friendship," he murmurs.

Listening to him, I wonder if Tom was ever sucked into her vortex. And given what he knew about Chloe, why did he agree to let her work on the house purchase?

"When she was assigned to our house sale, why didn't you ask for a different estate agent?" I ask.

"I did, but they said they were short-staffed, and when they asked me why, I didn't want to cause trouble for her. I mean, we've all made mistakes, and everyone deserves a second chance. I thought perhaps she'd changed, or that the story I'd heard was exaggerated. At the time of buying the house, she was so helpful, seemed professional, and I made it clear we were happily married."

"Do you think her obsession is now centered on you?" I ask.

He gently caresses my hand. "I don't know. If I'm honest, it never occurred to me that she might be interested . . . never imagined she'd even *think* about an old codger like me in that way."

"She seems capable of falling for anyone who gives her five minutes of their time," I say, stamping on any possibility he might be flattered by her attention. Tom isn't stupid, but he is a man and the middle-aged male ego can be a fragile animal.

"I'm now seeing everything from a different perspective with Chloe," I continue. "Like the other day she asked me where I got my blue striped shirt from, the one from Zara—I sent her the link. I was flattered that she liked it, but now I'm wondering if she's trying to copy me? Do you think she wants to *be* me . . . married to *you*?"

"Who knows? But I wouldn't be surprised if she's fixating on you too. You've shown her kindness and friendship, and people like Chloe often feed off that."

"Yes, that makes sense. She seems to think our friendship is far deeper and meaningful than it is. But I've only known her a matter of weeks."

"To her a few weeks is a lifetime. You need to back away now, Rachel," he says gently.

"I have, it's over," I say firmly. We both look down at the table, avoiding each other's eyes, because Tom and I both know that with someone like Chloe, it's *never* over.

After dinner, when Sam's safely tucked up in bed, we watch TV, but it seems neither of us can stop thinking about her, and how things are starting to make sense.

"What you've told me explains some weird phone calls I've been getting," Tom suddenly says.

"Like what?"

"Salesmen phoning up saying I've asked for information on double glazing, home repairs, stuff like that. I assumed it was because I'd been booking builders for the house, and they'd passed on my information."

"Isn't that illegal?"

"Probably, but it could be computer cookies too. It was annoying, but harmless, but if it's her..." Then he lifts his head back. "Damn, that explains the pizzas too."

"What?"

"While I was away, I had a pizza delivery to the hotel. Twenty-four pizzas."

"Shit, what did you do?"

"I sent them back, said they'd made a mistake. But from what I remember, this is the kind of thing she did with the guy at the bank all those years ago. There was always some drama in reception over stuff he'd apparently ordered—it was her!"

"Oh God, I hope this isn't a sign of more to come."

His eyes widen. "I wouldn't be surprised."

"Oh of course she has mine too," I say. "God only knows what other information she harvested from our conversations."

"Well, I suggest you change your number or be prepared for some weird phone calls and texts."

"She knows where we live too." I want to cry. "I *can't*, it's my work mobile too, I'm barely getting work as it is. Oh God, we really don't need this." I sigh, longing to be back in gray, rainy Manchester with Rosa.

"Perhaps if I let her down gently, she won't do anything weird?" I say hopefully.

"Don't assume for one minute that she'll walk away—be prepared for some push-back. We have to be extra vigilant, Rachel, and *promise* me you'll never leave Sam on his own."

"I *wouldn't*, I've never left him on his own," I reply, affronted that he even needs to say that. But then again, he warned me about Chloe and I went ahead. I have a history of doing stupid things. I think about the time Chloe offered to collect him from preschool to take back to her house and I shudder.

"I think you may have mentioned about you working away again next week. I don't want to be alone and a sitting target, might see if Rosa fancies a few days down here."

"If that makes you feel better." He squeezes my hand. "And Chloe definitely didn't give me back those keys, so she still has them. But don't worry, I'll call first thing and get the locks changed as soon as possible."

I'm just nodding, my head filled with fear, regretting my own naivety.

"And, Rachel, when I'm away, if you're at all concerned or something happens that worries you, however small or insignificant, you *must* phone the police."

I'm scared. The childlike innocence, the flaky, unpredictable behavior that I'd found so endearing, is nothing of the sort; it's a mask for something far darker. I was so desperate for a friend, and hell-bent on proving I could make my own choices, I ignored my husband's warnings. I feel stupid and reckless. I've allowed someone into our lives who won't let go, and it might already be too late.

TWENTY-NINE

"Chloe's texted me twice already this morning to ask if I've changed my mind about spending the day with her," I tell Tom as I hand him Sam's rucksack to take to the cricket match.

"It's like nothing happened, like she didn't say all that about you and her, and didn't slam out of the house."

He rolls his eyes. "This is the problem—from what I remember, she doesn't give up. Just like the guy at work, she pushes and pushes. It's relentless."

"Until something happens?"

"Yeah..." He raises his eyebrows. We both know what I mean. She obviously set out to hurt us; that's why she turned up that first night, and she now wants what she came for.

"Have you called about changing the locks?" I ask.

"I've called an emergency locksmith, left messages, just waiting for them to get back to me. I'd like to keep the police informed too, tell them she has the keys."

"Good idea, perhaps you could explain the situation and see if they can advise us?" I suggest. "I think it would help if they heard it from you, Tom, because I've called them loads of times and they just don't seem to do anything. I reckon the whole bloody police force around here think I'm a madwoman."

I don't say any more as Sam has put down his crayons and is watching us.

"There are some drinks in there and some flapjacks," I say brightly, gesturing at the bag Tom's now holding.

"Thanks, we'll get a burger or chips or something at the match for lunch."

"Burger, burger!" Sam's jumping up and down now.

"I thought the cuisine would be slightly more refined at the cricket—I expected cucumber sandwiches," I remark in a posh voice that makes Sam giggle.

"Not quite," Tom replies, "but after the burgers there's usually homemade cake." This prompts a "cake, cake, cake" chant from Sam, who's excited to be going out on a "boys only day" with Daddy.

I watch them leave, waving from the window. It's good to have Tom home—I missed him, and so did Sam.

I finish an article I'm writing for a lifestyle magazine, and after a couple of hours I send it off. It's always good to complete a written piece and I reward myself with a cup of coffee on the patio and enjoy the sunshine. But turning on my phone, my stomach lurches to see Chloe's sent four more messages *and* she's tried to call. A wave of nausea washes over me.

I reluctantly open up the messages, dreading what they say. They're as bad as I expected, each one more demanding and urgent and creepy than the last.

Rachel, where are you? I called you. Hope you're ok? Xxx

I have something to tell you about Tom. Call me back xxx

Rachel, is Tom there? Has he hurt you? Is Sam okay? Xxx

Rachel, I'm SO worried about you. Please call me or at least text me back. PLEASE! Xxx

What the hell is she up to now?

I consider forwarding them to Tom, but realize that's selfish. He's at a cricket match with our son—why spoil his day? These are just silly, overdramatic texts—she's playing some stupid game and the lack of response from me is escalating the drama from her. She's trying to play with me but is instead driving *herself* mad. Will she stop if I just text her back to say I'm fine? I don't know, so I call Rosa.

"What the actual fuck?" is Rosa's opening gambit when I tell her that Chloe and I have fallen out and she's now crazy-texting me like a woman possessed.

"Oh my God, Rachel! You made friends with the village weirdo. The only answer is to go back home to Manchester now. You can stay in my apartment, leave Tom there, and you and Sam move in with me. It was never your dream anyway."

She's joking, but knowing her true feelings about Tom, I think it's only half a joke. Yes, it's true, living here is Tom's dream more than it is mine, but he hasn't forced me—I came of my own free will. But Rosa's my friend, and very protective of me.

"She's now accusing my husband of having an affair with her," I announce.

Rosa's silence says it all. "What. The. Hell?" she finally says.

"Obviously I don't believe it."

"To be fair, babe, I don't either. Your husband is a lot of things, and never say never, but I don't have him down as unfaithful."

"Me neither."

"But *she* is scary as hell."

"I know, but she seemed okay at the time."

"Okay? *Okay?*"

"Yeah, she seemed, I don't know ... lonely, kind," I say, feeling gullible and stupid, desperately searching for why I liked her. I think of Tom's word, *beguiling*, but Rosa would laugh. "She could be fun and had a sense of humor too," I offer.

"Ted Bundy had a sense of humor." She isn't buying that either.

"Yeah, well I learned a harsh lesson. Chloe isn't kind or funny and she isn't okay. Yesterday she seemed really unhinged. I'm trying not to freak myself out ..."

"Sorry, but I think you *need* to start freaking yourself out. She has keys, Rachel. Bolt the doors and call the police. Now!"

"Tom's going to call them, and we're also getting the locks changed. Tom called the locksmith."

"*Finally* Major Tom gets his arse moving," she says.

I ignore her dig at my husband—there's no point in defending him to Rosa; she'll never change her mind about him.

"So the locksmith is on his way?" she asks.

"No, Tom just texted me actually—he heard back from him just now and he can't do the locks until next week because he doesn't have our locks in stock. They need to be ordered because the doors are old, and universal locks won't work, they have to be made specially to fit."

"Trust Tom to have posh locks." She sounds disgusted.

"It's an old house, Rosa, it isn't a *class* thing!" I love her but I sometimes tire of her putting Tom down.

"Well, if I were you, I'd barricade myself and my kid in that house until Larry the Locksmith turns up."

"That will be days, and there's no point us all staying indoors scared," I say, despite the fact that it's just what I want to do. "I think she's just desperate to make friends with me again, that's all," I say, aware I'm trying to convince myself as much as Rosa. "I mean, it's not like she's going to climb into our bed while we're out and be waiting naked under the sheets."

"That's *exactly* what she'll do. *After* she's boiled your pet rabbit."

"Rosa, stop, you're giving me the creeps now." I feel a chill go through me, imagining her in our bed now, wrapped in our sheets. And dead rabbits all over the garden.

"I bet she's already been in your bedroom, rubbing up against your linen," Rosa says.

"Don't. She mentioned that she'd seen a photo of me in a red dress, and that's on our bedroom wall, so she's obviously had a good look around."

"Or she told you that because she wants you to think she's been in your bed?"

"Perhaps? But I reckon she saw it before I even moved here—she was our estate agent, so had access." I hear myself making excuses for her, but I'm just trying to stay calm. At the moment I have no choice but to stay here and barricade ourselves in. In order to stay sane, I need to believe we are safe here for now, even if in my heart I'm not truly convinced.

"Oh Christ, imagine her writhing around on your bed thinking of Tom—it makes me shudder," Rosa's saying. This isn't helping.

"Stop it, Rosa, you're creeping me out."

"What I find most disturbing is that she's probably been having fantasies about your husband while being your friend."

"Yeah, *pretending* to be my friend. Going shopping, having Sam and me over to tea, and all the time she's . . ."

"Ugh I know! It's too much, I can't even."

"I dread seeing her again, it's going to be so awkward. Thank God it's Saturday today and I don't have to see her at preschool."

"Can't Tom take Sam to preschool?"

"Yes, while he's home, but he goes away again next week. I was thinking . . . do you fancy coming over?"

"Of course I can. I'm still at my aunt and uncle's but they should be fine on their own in the evenings."

"I'd love that, thanks Rosa." My heart lifts a little. "I just keep thinking about those crazy texts she sent me. I haven't responded, but I wonder if I *should*?"

"Why?"

"Because it might just stop her if I say, 'I'm fine, no one's hurt me, please stop texting'?"

"No, no, no, do *not* respond. If she thinks she has an open line of communication with you, she'll keep on and on—remember, I know all about stalkers. Block her."

"I would, but I worry that might escalate things. I think I need to respond to her in some way, or she might use it as an excuse to come over. You know what she's like: 'I was worried about you, Rachel, because you didn't respond,'" I say in Chloe's voice.

"Well, my guess is it's stalking Saturday in Chloe's world. She's spoiled for choice, and is either stalking you or Tom today."

"Thanks for the reassurance, Rosa." I suddenly have this image of Tom and Sam watching cricket, oblivious to her standing in the distance, watching them. I feel sick.

THIRTY

After talking to Rosa, I finish my coffee and check my phone. *Ten more messages, all saying the same thing:* "Call me" or "Are you okay?"

And something takes hold of me, my anger overtakes my fear. I go into the back of my wardrobe and pull something out that I haven't worn for years—a swimsuit. I put it on and, opening the doors of the bedroom, walk slowly down the garden. Chloe scares me, but not as much as the swimming pool, and if I can cure that, then surely I can deal with her. But grief and fear are unpredictable—they grab you around the throat when you least expect it—and as I open the door to the pool, the sun glints on the bright blue water, and I'm triggered.

I lean against the garden wall, take my time, breathe, and stand very still. All I can hear are seagulls and the gentle lap of water. *Nothing bad is going to happen.*

Eventually I sit by the pool. I have to breathe; if I don't, a major panic attack is just a moment away. A bird suddenly swooping, a bee buzzing, and a devastating flake of memory landing on the flat, shiny water toy with me until I can't take any more.

Mummy's walking through the sea, staying at the shallow

end, calling and calling. Salt water splashes and sunshine hurts her eyes, but she can't close them until she's found them. She goes deeper, ankles, knees, then thighs, shocked by the weight of water as she wades through, fighting the force, pushing on against the tide, unable to stop until she finds them.

You never get over it; you just keep going *through* it. Again and again.

It's time on my own when the ghosts emerge; they exist in the space in my head and expand, rising from the ashes. The pool is one of those places where I come face-to-face with them, and it's terrifying, but in facing my fears I know I will overcome them. Chloe is nothing compared to what happened to me before.

I nod while looking straight ahead, swallowing nervously. I'll always be nervous, but Chris, Sam's swimming teacher, said his advice to nervous swimmers is that it's not about eradicating nerves, it's about managing them.

He told me to put the bad memories in that wicker storage box by the pool with Sam's armbands, which he doesn't need anymore. The memories are the same: they'll never go, but psychologically, it helps to stow them away.

I stand on the edge of the pool; the floor tiles are sunshine-warm on the soles of my feet. The water's flat and calm and improbably blue from the chlorine. And I'm petrified.

I hold my breath; it feels like my heart is stopping. I sit down on the edge and allow my feet to touch the cool water, and as they do, my breath is taken away.

Sitting here, I realize this is the first time I've been alone by the pool. Aware there's no one else here to save me if I go under, I feel a frisson of fear. *Nothing bad is going to happen.*

This is my time to be strong, to move forward, take the challenge, be present for everyone, and I stand up and walk to the steps. Putting everything into the box in my mind, I slowly place each moment, each horrible second, into the box and close the lid, and only then do I take a first step alone into the pool.

Ankle-deep, I'm aware of the sound of rustling leaves, down and down. Now waist-deep, I hear birdsong and seagulls squawking in the distance. I focus on me. The water. Here and now. Not then.

I'm alone in a huge expanse of blue, an enormous sky above me. Sun beating down. I stand still, feeling the water around me. I am euphoric and terrified at the same time. I feel powerful but fearful, conquering, scared of death, but so alive for the first time in forever.

Suddenly, a cloud covers the sun, the pool turns gray, and a breeze ripples across the water. I'm aware of crunching footsteps on the stones through the garden. *Thud, thud*, the footsteps chime with the beating of my heart. Someone is now moving the door handle on the other side of the wall.

"Tom?" I call. "Is that you?"

The door in the wall opens slowly. I'm extremely vulnerable now, exposed, right in the middle of the pool. Nobody knows I'm here, and there's no one to save me if whoever is on the other side of that door means me harm. I'm shaking as the door opens; adrenaline and fear thrum through me as I wait. And then I see the blond hair, the blue flowery dress, the heels. She's crying, mascara running down her face like black tire marks, her lipstick a bright red smudge across her face.

"Rachel, why haven't you been answering my calls?"

THIRTY-ONE

I'm shivering in the sunshine. Standing in the middle of the pool, I instinctively back away from where Chloe's standing, but in doing so, I seem to be moving into deeper water. My feet are just touching the floor, and one step, one slight push in the wrong direction, I will go under. *I will drown. I can't swim.*

I'm numb with fear as she walks toward me; her dark shadow moves with her to the pool.

She's standing right on the edge now, looking down at me. "I thought we were friends. That's why I told you the *truth*. Why don't you believe me?"

I don't speak; I mustn't upset her. I don't know what she might do. Don't know what she's capable of. She's just standing over me, swaying slightly. I concentrate on the daisy pattern of her pale blue dress, my mind on survival and scrambling for an escape. The light material flutters in the breeze that's now rippling through the water, an undercurrent of anger replacing the still warmth before she arrived.

"Why didn't you answer my texts?" Her head tilts to one side questioningly.

I shake my head. "I just need some time alone." I continue

to move away from her, even though it means I'm heading into deeper waters. I'm scared of her, I want her to go, but more than anything I'm scared of the water, and I *have* to get out of the pool. I try to move, but it's holding me down. My legs feel like lead; the weight is unbearable. Panic rises rapidly in my chest, filling me up like water.

I don't know what to do.

I'll try and get out, might stand and talk, might make a run for it—I can't judge it yet. I keep moving slowly, I even try to swim a little, but I *can't* swim, and suddenly it's dark and silent and it's hard to breathe. I've slipped under. Panic and fear are tightening my limbs; my arms and legs feel tied. The pool is swallowing me whole.

I could die here, and Chloe would watch.

My head is filled with the past.

The waves are reckless, the current brutal, showing no pity. The little boy screams for his mummy, but the sea has him in her arms now. Daddy screams for help, but the sea doesn't listen. Mummy stands locked in terror watching them. Terrified, she's weak and helpless as others push past her, almost knocking her into the sea to save her family. Piercing screams and frantic splashing. Followed by the terrible silence.

I breathe and gasp and splutter. Reaching for the side of the pool, I cling to it, recovering myself, not knowing where she is and whether I'm safe yet from her or the pool itself.

Finally, I look up slowly—I can't see her. Has she gone? Or will she suddenly appear in the water and leap out at me like in *Jaws*? I can almost hear the slow, thumping music as she swims unseen, the pool colluding with her wishes, hiding her.

But there's nothing. Nothing but silence.

Then I see it, the shadow on the water; she's standing over me.

"Rachel, I have to talk to you," she says. "Why are you avoiding me?" The expression on her face is one of confusion and frustration. She's standing guard over me.

If I try to climb out, will she push me back in?

She doesn't speak, just continues to stare down at me like I'm a rare specimen she's just discovered in a rock pool.

"Will you let me get out?"

She shrugs. "Only if you'll listen to what I have to tell you."

"I will, I promise."

She seems to consider this for a moment, and, nodding, she steps back slowly.

"I need to tell you everything," she says.

My heart sinks; I don't want any more of her crazy stories. But I take this as her agreement for me to leave the pool, and still clinging to the side, I start to move toward the steps. I'm pushing through the water, and when I finally feel like I'm getting close, I reach out for the metal bar on the steps.

Relief floods through me, until she suddenly yells, "No, Rachel!" making me start.

I'm clutching the metal stair bar, about to heave myself up, but she bends down, her face in mine.

"Not. Yet," she says softly.

"Please?" I let go of the metal bar, my anchor—I'm now floating, surrendering against my will to the water.

"No. We can talk while you're there—I don't want you running off."

My heart sinks, down and down and down into the pool.

"Chloe, I can't—you know I'm not comfortable in water." I'm trying not to panic.

"I know, I was surprised to see you walk down the garden and come in here."

She was watching me. She's been here ages.

I'm angry but also scared. I try to move along the ledge back toward the metal bar and the steps, but she walks with me, like she's getting ready to block me if I try to get out.

"I *need* to get out!" I insist.

"I don't trust you. I think you'll run before I can say what I came here to tell you. It's for your own good, Rachel."

"I can't concentrate on what you have to say while I'm in here. I'm scared and I might have a panic attack."

After considering this, she glances around, and to my relief, she nods her head and steps back.

I move quickly before she changes her mind and heave myself out of the water.

Once on solid ground I walk briskly away from the poolside and grab a towel.

Within seconds she's next to me.

"You have to believe what I'm about to tell you. I'm not crazy." She grabs me by the upper arm, and I'm surprised at her strength.

"Chloe, why are you doing this?" Alarmed, I try to pull away but she just squeezes more tightly. "You're hurting me—friends don't hurt each other!" I exclaim, showing pain rather than anger, which seems to have an immediate softening effect.

"I'm sorry, I don't want to hurt you, but *someone* does," she's saying earnestly, still clutching at the soft, fleshy part of my arm, her nails digging in now. I feel weak, unable to pull away, the fear of water has drained me.

"Get *off* me!" I'm squirming in pain, desperately trying to pull away, when suddenly there's a knocking then shouting coming from behind the door in the wall.

"LET ME IN, NOW!"

I spin around. "Rosa? HELP ME, Chloe's here!"

"Shit," I hear Rosa mutter loudly.

I turn back to Chloe, who's still attached to me by her nails like a limpet. "You've locked the door?"

"I didn't . . . I *didn't* lock the door." She pushes me and I land hard on the floor tiles, groaning as searing pain shoots up my ankle and calf. For a few moments I'm dazed—all I can see from the floor are Chloe's feet running away, running fast toward the back wall, then Rosa's sandaled feet thumping past me.

Rosa must have jumped the six-foot wall. But Chloe's fast, and she's now trying to scramble up and over the wall at the other side of the pool. It leads to other gardens, and if Rosa doesn't grab her, she could go anywhere, but Rosa's hot on her heels.

"You okay, Rachel?" she calls behind her.

"Yeah," I manage as she continues on toward Chloe, who's now clutching at the ivy, crying hysterically. She's desperately trying to use the twisting fronds like rope. She might be strong, but she's tiny. Rosa must be a foot taller and thirty pounds heavier, and used to playing women's rugby. From my prone position, I silently urge her on as she tackles Chloe like she's on the pitch.

"What the *fuck* are you doing here?" Rosa runs at her, head down like a bull, and as Chloe screams, Rosa pushes hard into Chloe's back with her head. This brings Chloe down from the wall with a bump. Suddenly everything stops: Chloe is lying on the ground, Rosa standing over her, gasping for breath. For a moment I think she might be dead, and my heart starts to bang in my rib cage, but she suddenly rises, like the killer in a slasher film. She seems to have this superhuman quality and can't be destroyed.

I try to move to help Rosa tackle her, but the searing pain is stopping me from putting one arm down to leverage myself, and I fall back.

"You don't get to ruin my friend's life!" Rosa's yelling, now holding on to Chloe, who's swinging at her, roaring like an animal in pain.

"Is that what you wanted, a *fight*?" Rosa's in her face. "Thought you could hurt my friend, did you? Well, you picked the wrong one, you nasty little bully," Rosa's spitting through gritted teeth. "You think it's okay to ruin her life? Have you any idea of what you put her through?"

Chloe's now kicking out at her and catches her shin hard. Rosa yelps but keeps her hand on Chloe's neck. Chloe is flailing around, her arms lashing out at Rosa, who's holding her firmly while she's scratching at her, spitting and swearing. Chloe's a dirty fighter; she's small and delicate but uses her nails, and she is now using her teeth, taking a bite at Rosa's arm.

"You little *bitch!*" Rosa yells, and instinctively lets go as blood begins to pour from her arm. "Call the police!" Rosa yells over her shoulder at me, but I'm already moving along the floor toward a sun lounger, where I manage to lift myself to my feet. I can barely stand; the pain is surging down the whole of my left side, from my shoulder down to my ankle. And I still can't reach my phone, which is by the side of the pool where I left it when I started my swim.

I stagger in slow motion toward the pool and finally manage to grab my phone. But just as I reach it, there's an enormous splash. They both land hard in the pool, and all I see is water and arms and legs and fear. I hear the screams of pain and panic. Shrieking heads desperately come up for air, but still they fight. Rosa, who's bigger and stronger, is trying to push Chloe under, but the basic, primal fear of death urges the slighter Chloe to continue to fight, to breathe. I can't watch, I have to turn away, and suddenly I'm back there.

It's some time later when I am able to pull myself from the past. All is quiet now; no screaming or fighting or fear, just the familiar and horrifying silence of the aftermath.

THIRTY-TWO

Rosa is lying on the tiles. I can't see her moving, but I focus on the pool, the turquoise shimmer, something floating on the water. Blue flowery fabric. Chloe's dress. I manage to drag myself around the pool—I've obviously sprained my foot, and the pain sears through my sole and up my leg.

"Rosa, are you okay?" I call as I get closer to where she's lying in a pool of water on the hard, tiled floor. "Rosa?" I call louder, unable to look again at the pool—in my mind's eye I see Chloe's lifeless body in the water.

To my relief, Rosa stirs as I reach out to her, and opening her eyes, she stretches like she's just awoken from a long sleep.

"Hey, that bitch *bit* me!"

"I'm just glad you managed to pull yourself out of the water," I say, feeling guilty that I wasn't able to help her.

I turn to look at the pool. Rosa's eyes follow mine, and when they alight on the crumpled fabric, the blood drains from her face.

"Shit, is she . . . ?"

"I don't know. I'm not even sure what happened, but she put up a fight."

We help each other up, and as my foot won't take my weight,

I have to lean against a lounger while Rosa walks the few steps to the pool, calling Chloe's name. She turns back to look at me and shakes her head. "No sign of her," she says, clearly relieved.

"Thank God!" Relief washes over me, and I half sit on the lounger before I fall down with pain and shock. "Did she leave her dress in there to make us think she'd drowned?" I ask as Rosa walks back to where I am.

"I remember tearing it as she was biting and scratching me. It probably came off and landed in the pool." She looks back at what remains of the daisy-sprigged blue dress. "She must be running down the road somewhere now in just her underwear," she says, laughing.

I'm not as resilient as Rosa, and not yet ready to laugh. "Thank God you were here."

"Yeah, when I talked to you on the phone, I just had this *feeling*. I can't explain it, but after what you've told me about her... She's obviously unhinged and knew you were alone..." She looks at me. "Oh, love, I'm sorry you had to go through that."

"It's just awful, you think you know someone..."

"Yeah. That's how I felt about Dan, and it's what put me on alert today. It just makes me so angry that one person can do that to someone else. Even if they aren't there watching from the shadows, they might as well be, because it fills your mind."

"I shudder to think what might have happened if you hadn't turned up. She could have pushed me in, and I would probably have drowned." I glance over at the pool, the potential murder weapon.

"Well, I reckon we've scared her off now—hopefully that'll be the end of it."

She helps me back through the garden, my support; I can barely walk and the pain is horrendous.

When we get back to the kitchen, Rosa sits me down and takes a look at my ankle with her nurse's eye.

"It's painful, but just a sprain," she announces, going to the drawer where we keep all the first aid stuff. "You need to keep off it for a few days, no weight-bearing."

"Not only are you my knight in shining armor slaying dragons, you are medically trained. The universe sent you to me."

She rolls her eyes. "Okay, would you ask the universe to send someone to me, tall dark and handsome with muscles, please?"

She's just strapping up my foot when the door goes and I hear Tom's voice talking to Sam.

"Hi guys. We're in here. You're early?" I call into the hallway from the kitchen.

"Sam got bored, and it's hot out there," Tom replies as they take off their shoes. "I thought it wise to cut our losses before he kicked off," he's saying as he walks through the door. His face drops slightly when he sees Rosa, who discreetly disappears to the bathroom, but he recovers well and is immediately concerned about my ankle.

"I can't say too much," I say, glancing in Sam's direction so he knows this isn't a conversation we can have in front of him.

"Oh?" He looks worried now. "Come on, buddy, let's put the TV on," he says, ushering him quickly from the room before he can see my ankle being bandaged. "See Mummy later, she's busy at the moment."

Sam never needs to be persuaded to watch TV, and Tom soon returns to the kitchen alone.

"Chloe was here," I start. "Rosa got rid of her, she was brilliant." Rosa's walking back into the kitchen and I smile at her, but she shakes her head dismissively.

Tom doesn't seem to want to hear how brilliant my friend is—perhaps he feels guilty about not being here? Perhaps he wants to be the one who "saves" me?

"So, did she hurt you?"

"She pushed me and I landed hard on the ground. That's how I got the injury."

"Shit," he murmurs, looking down at my leg.

"It's just a sprain," Rosa says without looking at him.

"Have you called the police?" he asks.

"No, they won't do anything..."

"I told you, Rachel, you have to keep the police informed." He takes his phone out and calls them, and gives them details. "Yes, my wife has already called you about this matter," he says, irritated, but eventually is dismissed and puts his phone back in his pocket.

"I told you, they do nothing."

"No, but we need to build the case against her," he murmurs, "and we have to report everything. I can't work away again if you're in this state," he says. "You can't walk properly. And with Chloe at large, and the police not exactly helpful, I don't fancy your chances if she decides to pay another unexpected visit."

"You aren't going until next week, I'll be fine in a few days," I insist.

Rosa is shaking her head doubtfully. "You'll be able to walk, but it could be a week or two before you're properly back on your feet, and able to run." She hesitates, I know she doesn't want to scare me. "I mean you might have to run, Rachel—you have to think of Sam. I mean, if she were to—"

"Okay," Tom is saying, "I'd better call work and let them know."

"Hang on." Rosa is raising her hand like she has the answer. "You can still work away, Tom—I could come over and stay in the evenings, if you like?"

"No, that won't be necessary," he starts in the official voice he uses when he thinks people are being stupid.

"No, *really*, I can. I have to be with my aunt and uncle during the day, but I can give them dinner about seven—they can watch TV and get themselves to bed. I can then drive over here in the evenings, and as long as I leave here about seven in the morning, I'll be back to get them up..."

"That would be great," I say.

"Yes, that would be helpful," Tom reluctantly concedes. "But what about during the day?"

"I don't want to scare you guys, but I've lived with a stalker. If Chloe is going to come back, it will be when it's dark," she says in a low voice so Sam can't hear us.

"Well clearly she doesn't have a copy of The Stalker's Handbook, she turned up in daylight today," Tom contradicts her.

Rosa ignores his sarcasm, she just looks at me and, cutting Tom out, says, "Rachel, the offer is there. I can be with you every night he's away, just let me know, okay?" Having now finished strapping my ankle, she stands up. "I'll get going—I told my uncle I'd be back soon and that was"—she glances at her watch—"about an hour ago."

"Yes, you must get off. Thanks for everything, love," I say, patting her arm.

She bends down and hugs me. "I'm here for you, just remember that," she says, standing up straight, ignoring Tom, who mutters, "Thanks," and stands there, just waiting for her to go.

"I wish you weren't so bloody obvious," I say after she's gone. "Why do you always have to be off with Rosa? She's never done you any harm."

He shrugs. "How do you *want* me to behave? Would you have liked me to bow and scrape?"

"Don't be stupid, you know what I mean. We've talked about it so many times before, it's just so . . . petty!" I snap.

"She's the petty one," he replies, proving my point.

"I just wish you'd be a bit nicer, if only for me."

"I saw her to the door."

"Yeah, thanks for that, but it was obvious you weren't motivated by politeness—you couldn't wait to see the back of her. You'd have liked to kick her out of the door, I'm sure."

"Was it that obvious?" he jokes.

"You're such a child, Tom," I say, trying not to be angry, remembering that he's only just come home and I need to be kind. "Just try and be nice next time, for me?"

"Can't promise—she's such a know-it-all."

"Well, she knows a lot, she's a trained nurse, and her fighting is pretty good if this afternoon is anything to go by."

"Chloe isn't exactly Tyson Fury."

He obviously feels somehow threatened by Rosa so has to put her down.

"Well, I was impressed, and I'm going to take her up on her offer to stay while you're away."

"Up to you, but I could always cancel work."

"We need the money. Sam and I will be *fine*," I say, sounding confident. But inside I'm ragged and crumpled, and my mind is filled with death and drowning, and the flowery blue fabric floating on the surface of the dreaded pool.

All Mummy can hear is people screaming, and they're pulling her back through the water. She's trying to reach them but she can't—they're too far away, hands reaching up through the water, desperate to be saved. She hears her little boy yelling for his mummy. She still hears him. She always will.

THIRTY-THREE

It's been a few days since Chloe's visit, and she's made no contact. I'm torn between feeling relieved and concerned that her lack of contact is just a prelude to something bigger, more dramatic. Tom delayed starting work by a couple of days, so he could be around in case of any problems. On Monday and Tuesday he took Sam to preschool but said there was no sign of Chloe. Emily was delivered and collected by an older woman—I presume that was Chloe's mum. So is Chloe avoiding preschool and me? Has she finally let go, or is she simply waiting?

Tom had to start work today—this time he's in Newcastle, and though it's a seven-hour drive at best, he says he'll come home if I need him. But Rosa will be around, so hopefully we'll be fine.

He left early this morning, and Rosa's coming over later tonight once she's settled her aunt and uncle and I've put Sam to bed.

I'm hoping Chloe might have gone away for a while. She once mentioned a friend in Jersey—perhaps she's spending time with her? I hope so, but in the back of my mind I find it hard to believe she's just walked away; she's too intense, too obsessive. And I was stupid; I thought we were friends and shared too much.

As Rosa pointed out on our call yesterday, "You told her *everything*. She knows your routine, and she knows when Tom's going away. She might have been waiting for him to go so she can make her way back into your life. But not on my watch!"

Rosa is the wing girl I need right now, and she calls me soon after Tom has left this morning. "Are you okay? Anything to report?"

"No, officer," I joke, "he's only been gone seven minutes."

"A lot can happen in seven minutes," she says. She's joking, but she's right, and I lock the big glass doors in the kitchen, which I would usually keep open to let the fresh air in.

I appreciate my friend's protectiveness. Tom says it's too much, but it comes from a good place. She used to be in the army—it's where she trained as a nurse—and I sometimes think she misses the thrill of military life, and what I find intimidating and scary, she sees as a challenge. I just hope she doesn't need to use any of her army training over the next couple of weeks while Tom's away.

He's worried too. Before he left this morning, he was offering to stay home and call in sick.

"We'll be fine," I tried to reassure him.

"Okay, but don't be too shy to ask for help. In fact, one of the other mums has offered to drop Sam off and collect him for us," he said. "I got chatting to her when I picked Sam up the other day. If we notify the school, they'll allow her to pick him up in our absence."

"That's kind of her, but my foot's much better now. As long as I take it easy, I'll be able to walk him slowly there and back."

"Well, I just thought I'd let you know that there's someone who'll help if you have ankle problems . . . or any other kind." We both knew what he meant.

"Which mum is she?" I couldn't imagine any of the mums at preschool being concerned about me—they barely know me.

"I can't remember her name, she wrote it on a piece of paper, hang on." He rummaged around in his jeans pocket. "Here, it's Jennifer, and here's her number—she said to call her if you need anything."

I looked at the piece of paper he'd handed me and saw the scrawled name and number. "Jennifer?" I saw the slightly sneering woman who always seems to witness me in some state of distress—or drunkenness.

"Yeah, she said she doesn't live far from us, she'd be happy to help."

"She used to be a friend of Chloe's—they went to school together," I said, looking at the piece of paper.

"Oh, really? Are they still friends?" He looked concerned.

"The opposite, from what I gathered from Chloe."

"Oh—well, that's funny, she didn't seem surprised when I said you'd had some issues."

"You haven't told her about Chloe, have you?"

He looked a little guilty. "It was mostly about your ankle, but I did say Chloe had got very close and seemed a little . . . odd."

"Oh, I'd rather you didn't discuss it—I don't want everyone at preschool knowing our business."

"I agree, but to be honest, Rachel, I think at this stage the more people who know, the more they will look out for you when I'm not here. She's a nice woman and seemed concerned about you."

"Did she? That's nice," I said, trying not to sound sarcastic. I wanted to throw the paper in the trash.

Hell will freeze over before I ever call on that mean girl for help.

Earlier this morning I dropped Sam off at preschool for the first time since the incident at the pool. It was such a relief not to see Chloe, but now as I walk to preschool to collect Sam, I'm feeling rather nervous. I stand safely by the railings, waiting for the bell to signal when we can walk inside and retrieve our children. More than anything today I just want to collect my little boy and get him safely home. I gaze around the playground at the parent groups, some big, some small, some alone like me, and it's then I see her. A jolt goes through me as my eyes go straight to hers; she's staring at me so intently, I immediately look away. For the next few minutes before the bell rings, I don't look in her direction, but from the corner of my eye I can feel her stare burning into me. When the bell rings, I wait a moment until she's gone inside before I go in the same direction, praying that she doesn't try to engage me.

"Mummy, look what Emily gave me," Sam is shrieking the minute I walk into the preschool classroom. He's running toward me with a rather unwieldy box of Legos. I try to smile, but it feels more like a grimace. Is she watching? I wouldn't dare turn around to look.

"That's very kind of her," I say, "but that's a *big* present, and it isn't your birthday or Christmas, so I think we need to politely give it back."

His lower lip falls, his chin begins to tremble and my heart sinks. "But Mummy, she *gave* it to me, it's a present. It's *mine!*" His voice holds a threatening whine, a tantrum alarm which has the effect of alerting the other parents. It's a warning to others that this kid is about to blow. I'm not looking, but I'm sure they're all discreetly glancing over, secretly glad it isn't their child. They say pick your battles, and taking a toy from a child in a public space is rarely the right time to choose that battle. But this isn't just an expensive box of Legos, it's so much more.

"No, Sam, I'm sorry," I start, "we have to give it back to Emily."

"NO, MINE!" he yells, defiantly clutching the box to his chest, his arm span barely wide enough to hold it.

I stand for a moment feeling totally lost. *How do I deal with this?* To everyone around me, this appears to be a generous gesture that should be appreciated, not confiscated. But I know the Lego isn't a gift from Emily to Sam; it's an olive branch from Chloe to me. And by allowing Sam to accept it, I may be forced to let her back in.

So, I focus, gather my courage, and kneel down to Sam's height. "Would you be a big boy and give this to Iris so she can return it to Emily, please?" I attempt to tug gently at the box, and for a moment he almost releases it. But then he realizes what's happening and shouts, "NO, MUMMY, pleeeeeease. Please don't take my Lego, Mummy!"

This is breaking my heart, and now everyone is observing the spectacle. Parents stop midchat, hold their kids' hands, and stand watching, while the schoolteachers stare open-mouthed at a mother trying to tear a much-wanted gift from her child's hands. Everyone loves to watch a slice of bad parenting to make themselves feel better, especially other parents. I long to sit them all down and explain, but of course I can't, so instead I begin to wrestle my child for his Lego. I'm gently trying to take the box while offering bribes under my breath, only too aware that Jennifer and her friends are staring and gathering their kids to them protectively. I just hope to God that Chloe has already left.

I have one last attempt and go for the assertive approach. "Darling, give Mummy the box," I say firmly, through gritted teeth. I read somewhere that there's a perfect tone that kids respond to, and I'm aiming for it. But my son is shaking his head, and still clutching the box. Clearly that wasn't the tone, and what's worse, he's now crying. A loud, wailing cry.

I lean closer and whisper in his ear, "If you give the box to Mummy, we'll go straight home and order exactly the same Lego for the postman to bring tomorrow." I'm aware that in my desperation I'm going against everything the parenting books say. I'm rewarding his bad behavior, but then who's really the one behaving badly?

He's rejected my final offer, seen the hypocrisy no doubt, and is now full-on wailing. I look beseechingly around me for some help or inspiration. But as there's none forthcoming, I tell myself I'm the parent, I need to get a grip of this situation. So, with all my strength, I snatch the box from him, place it on a nearby table and pick him up in my arms to leave. He continues to screech, kicking and screaming, and shouting, "Get off me," while making his body go rigid. I have no choice but to walk through the throng of gaping parents and head for home.

The short walk is tortuous as he sobs loudly, accusing me of "stealing" his Lego, but when he suddenly darts across the road toward an oncoming car, I am the one screaming. I run after him, instinctively putting myself between him and the car, which is now screeching to a halt.

"Sam! Sam!" I'm yelling through terrified tears as the driver glares at me. Jennifer! She sits there, her eyes boring into me while shaking her expensively highlighted head in total judgment. I want to die. I can't look at her. I just burst into tears and pick Sam up. Holding him close, I run home, praying that Chloe isn't following me.

THIRTY-FOUR

"What a total bitch," Rosa says later over a glass of wine when I tell her about my afternoon—Chloe staring, and Jennifer's judgmental gaze from her expensive car.

She arrived just after eight, when Sam was bathed and in bed, and though it's hours since the whole horrible pickup incident, I'm still feeling the shame and embarrassment. Rosa has listened intently to my retelling, and being that friend who's on your side even when you're in the wrong, she has curled her lip at Chloe and taken an instant dislike to Jennifer without even meeting her.

"I don't think she's a bitch, I just feel like she stands on the sidelines a bit, you know, watching."

"I know her type."

"Apparently at preschool, she asked Tom where I was, and when he told her about my ankle and that he was going away, she offered to collect Sam if I needed any help."

"Nice one, Tom. Why didn't he just put a post on Facebook and tell everyone that he was going away and you'd be alone and vulnerable with a sprained ankle?" She rolls her eyes.

"Well, *everyone* isn't the problem—Chloe is, and she already knows when he's away because I told her, being the idiot I am."

"You weren't to know," she offers, "but yeah, I bet she has a whiteboard on the wall of her apartment to track your comings and goings."

"It wouldn't surprise me—nothing would with Chloe. Apparently Jennifer stole her boyfriend when they were teenagers, and Chloe's never forgiven her."

"I doubt Chloe ever forgives anyone. And as they're 'former associates,' don't go telling this Jennifer anything either—it could go straight back to crazy Chloe."

"Okay, I won't, Detective," I snicker.

"If she's anything to go by, I don't trust *anyone* in this village. Mind you, I don't trust anyone, come to think of it."

"Wow." I smile at this.

"It's true, I don't. I trusted Dan, thought he was the best thing that ever happened to me, but I was lied to and love-bombed and . . . it was only when he took a knife to my throat I realized how stupid I'd been to trust him."

"I'm sorry, Rosa, I'm making this all about me and my problems, but you're still going through yours."

She visibly shivers. "Don't remind me, I'm still in recovery. Ironic, isn't it? I survived being in the army then get PTSD after a few dates with a guy from an online app."

We sit in silence for a moment, both processing this. Selfishly I hope my own experience is now over, and I don't have to go through what Rosa did.

"I just wish they could find him, but until they do, your situation is a distraction," she says with a sigh. "Instead of walking down a quiet street thinking it's Dan's footsteps behind me, I now think it's Chloe's."

"Your stalker or mine?" I make a lame joke and neither of us laughs, but we roll our eyes at each other then go back to staring into space, our lives ruined by people who claim to love us.

"What the hell does Chloe want?"

I shrug. "I wonder that myself. Does she want Tom, or does she want me?"

"Perhaps she wants your *life*, including Tom, the house... and Sam?" She offers this up like a suggestion, but I know it's her gentle way of warning me while trying not to scare me.

I nod slowly, thinking about the familiar way Chloe walked into our home, like she lived there. "If she *does* want Tom, and / or Sam, then in her twisted mind, she might want to replace *me*, so she can have them?"

We look at each other, and I see something like fear in her eyes. It chills me.

"Whatever Chloe wants, she isn't going to get it," she says, pouring us both another glass of wine.

"Do you ever ask yourself why you're here, Rachel?" she says. "You had a tough time losing your dad, uprooted yourself here for Tom, and now he's got you here he's working away and some random woman is stalking you."

"I don't see it like that," I reply, irritated that she's right. I hear what she's saying.

"Did you ever get the locks changed, by the way?" She takes a sip of wine.

I shake my head. "Not yet, the guy's ordered the locks, but they are coming from France and Tom says there's some Brexit issue that's causing the delay."

Rosa looks concerned. "I hope he gets them soon—you really don't want her to turn up and try those keys."

"Thing is, even if she did give them back to Tom, she could have had copies made," I say.

"You're a sitting target," she murmurs.

"No, I'm not. I've locked the front door, and the bifold glass doors lock from inside. I also have kitchen knives and a heavy marble rolling pin, and I'm not afraid to use them." I'm not joking.

"Yeah, well, put something in front of the front door, and

those glass doors might lock from the inside but they could easily be opened by someone who knows what they're doing, and I reckon *she* does."

Rosa stands up from her stool at the kitchen island, goes over to the glass doors and bends down to check them. "They can be opened *so* easily," she says, standing up, shaking her head. "She could be in and out and you wouldn't even know."

This sends a chill right through me.

"I wasn't going to say anything, but today, when I got back from taking Sam to preschool, I went in our bedroom and just had this feeling that someone had been in there," I say. "It was like last time, when I got the sandals—the pillows looked disturbed, and when I opened my wardrobe, I could have sworn one or two things had been moved around."

"Why didn't you say?"

"I didn't really think about it until you said that just now about the glass doors. I can't be absolutely sure—perhaps I'm just reacting to Tom being away and my imagination's running away with me."

"Possibly?" She nods in agreement. "And you're sure nothing was missing?"

"No, not really, but then . . ."

"What?"

"Oh, it might be nothing, but I couldn't find this blue stripey shirt I wear a lot. I know it must be around *somewhere*. I'm sure it'll turn up," I say to reassure myself before adding, "I wouldn't think twice if it was anything else, but Chloe loved that shirt." I look at Rosa, realizing what I just said.

"Really?" She sits back up on her stool, listening intently.

"Or it isn't Chloe, it's me who's going crazy?" I add a mirthless laugh to this in a vain attempt to trivialize it. But I can see by Rosa's face that she's not buying my fake flippancy.

"I *really* think we should call the police, Rachel."

"I called them myself on Monday after Tom had called them

Saturday, I reiterated what had happened and told them she must have a set of keys. I mean how else would she get into the garden and down to the pool? They said they'd send someone round to talk to her, but who knows if and when that's going to happen?"

"And if they do, she'll just say she doesn't have keys, that you let her in, and it's your word against hers?"

"Yeah. It's the same with my shirt. I can't say she stole it because I don't *know* she did, I have no proof. But it's missing, and I've looked *everywhere*."

She suddenly jumps. "Did you hear that?"

"What?"

"Something outside?"

"No, I didn't, but your hearing's always so sharp."

"That's the trouble, I hear everything, and it's usually nothing. It's probably just me getting jumpy for no reason," she says. But I know she's lying.

"I'm a grown-up, Rosa—if you did hear something outside, then be honest. What did it sound like? It's *my* house, and I have a child to protect."

"Okay, okay. I *think* I heard a woman's voice yelling," she says.

"Yelling what?"

"I don't know."

"Right, I'm going to check," I say, stepping down from my stool to go and see.

"No." She puts her hand on my shoulder. "If it *is* her, she might have made that noise so you'll do just that—go outside and leave Sam alone in the house. She doesn't know I'm here, remember?"

I feel the blood drain from me. "Remember last time you stayed over, Sam said she'd been in his room, said she'd kissed him good night. We thought it was a dream, but what if it wasn't?"

THIRTY-FIVE

"Well, as Chloe has no idea I'm here"—Rosa half smiles—"I'm going to go outside and scare the hell out of her, while you go upstairs to check on Sam."

Terrified and shaking, I do as she says and run out of the kitchen and up the stairs two at a time, despite the agony from my ankle sprain, hoping to God my baby is still asleep in his bed.

I run into his room, and the silence hits me like a wall. I immediately turn on the nightlight by his bed. There's a shape under the duvet, but it's too still and I can't see his face; holding my breath, I quickly lift off the cover to see if he's there.

"Mummy!" His voice is high; he sounds alarmed. Sitting up, he rubs his eyes, surprised to be awoken so abruptly. I immediately scoop him up, hugging him, telling him I love him. "Mummy!" he's chastising me grumpily, and who can blame him? It may only be just after eleven, but to a four-year-old it's the middle of the night.

He's frowning, but I just hug him closer, rocking him until he squirms and demands to go back to bed. I do as he asks, and he immediately goes back to sleep. I don't want to leave him alone just yet, so I check in his wardrobe and behind his curtains, feeling bad that I woke him, but as he's now sleeping peacefully, I go back to the kitchen.

"Is he okay?" Rosa asks.

"Yes, he's fine, just a bit pissed off to be woken by his hysterical mother." I roll my eyes. "Did you see a sign of anyone in the garden?"

She nods. "Don't freak out, but I think I saw her."

"No!" I groan.

"I could hear footsteps coming from the pool garden, but by the time I got there, she was disappearing over the wall." She seems a little shaken.

"It was *her* then?"

"I think so, love."

"How crazy to think she was here." I shiver outwardly. "What kind of madness makes someone wander around another person's garden late at night?"

"Don't know, but she's obsessed, she's not in her right mind." She's leaning on the kitchen island, looking out of the darkened glass doors into the distance.

"Who knows what she's capable of," I say, sighing.

"I'm worried about you and Sam," she murmurs, still staring through the glass.

"If it's all too much for you, I completely understand if you want to go home, Rosa. Sam and I can get a cheap bed-and-breakfast, I'll call the police and this time really make a stink so they keep an eye on the house."

"No, you can't let her win, Rachel, you are not leaving your home because of some lunatic who's just trying to scare you."

"But you've already been through enough. You've had your own troubles. This must be triggering for you."

"Yeah, it is, but I'm not abandoning you and that little boy. No way, sister." She turns and winks at me, then goes back to staring out the window. "Can you smell burning?"

My heart jumps. I breathe in. "Yes, I can."

"Oh God, Rachel, I think that smoke's coming from your garden. Shit, I can see flames too." She pushes the glass doors back and rushes outside.

I instinctively follow her and run outside, pulling the glass doors closed and heading after her. As I run through the trees, I see orange flames, and within seconds my mouth is filled with acrid smoke, which stings my throat. When we get through the trees I almost collapse. Smoke is billowing from the corner of the garden, and Rosa's single-handedly attempting to put out huge flames in one of the flower beds.

"Call the fire brigade!" she yells from behind the flames as she whacks them with heavy tree branches to try and stamp it out. I call and pace around, waiting for them to answer, aware that in her panic she's fanning the flames rather than putting them out.

"Rosa, get water from the pool!" I yell, but she doesn't hear me and then someone answers the phone and I have to move away from the smoke that's stinging my eyes and making me cough. By the time I've given my address and details and headed back to where she is, the fire is even higher and stronger.

"Rosa, come away, you can't do any more!" I scream, but she's still breaking off tree branches and whacking the fire.

In her desperation she might be making it worse. "Rosa, let's wait up at the top, they have to be let in to come through the garden."

"But the house, the house could burn down!" she cries. Through the smoke I see only the outline of her against the flames.

"There's nothing you can do, just come away from the flames!" I urge, but she continues to stay there, putting herself in danger to save our home. In the middle of this I'm reminded of something Tom once said: *Rosa would kill for you*. Watching her now, I think she'd die for me too.

I rush toward her, hoping in some small way to help until the fire service arrive, but then I realize something. If Chloe started this fire, she had a reason, and that might have been to get me outside and leave Sam alone in the house. What an idiot I am.

"Rosa, I'm going back to the house!" I scream. "I'm going to get Sam!"

She doesn't seem to hear me, so I just run like the wind up the garden and only stop running once I'm inside. Then I dash to Sam's bedroom, but his bed is empty.

"Sam, SAM!" I yell, tearing into his room, seeing the covers off his bed, the pillow on the floor.

Not again, not twice in one lifetime?

Then I see him, standing by the window. I almost faint with relief and have to hold on to the bed.

"Is it bonfire night, Mummy?" he asks, unable to tear his eyes away from the fire roaring outside.

I compose myself. "No, darling, it's just a fire," I say, joining him at the window. The flames are far enough away to mean we are still safe to be in the house. For now.

"Daddy's friend was there, in the garden. She's naughty, she had *matches*, Mummy. You should never pick up matches." He's shaking his head.

"Did you *see* her, Daddy's friend?"

He nods.

"Who was it, darling? Was it Emily's auntie, who we thought was her mummy?"

He looks confused and is now distracted by what's going on in the garden.

Eventually the fire truck arrives, and I run downstairs to let them in.

"I've got this," Rosa says, opening the door. "Stay with Sam."

So I go back to Sam's room and pull a chair to the window, sitting Sam on my knee. He's mesmerized, asking so many questions, watching the crackling sparks lift into the clear sky.

Within an hour the fire is out, and Sam's asleep in my arms.

I think about calling Tom, but it's now after 2 a.m., he's a seven-hour drive away, and there's nothing he can do. I'd rather call him tomorrow and tell him after the event, knowing we are safe, than call him now.

I put Sam to bed and head to the kitchen on shaky legs. I'm scared. I had no idea what she was capable of, but now I do, and I'm so scared.

Rosa is in the kitchen talking to a police officer, and as I walk in she introduces me to him.

"Your friend seems to think this is arson, Mrs. Frazer. But I just want to confirm with you that this isn't the embers from a barbecue, or if you've had any fireworks or candles out there this evening?"

I shake my head adamantly. "No, nothing like that. I agree with Rosa, it's deliberate, and we suspect it might be someone who..." I pause—how to say this without sounding like I'm crazy? "There's this woman who seems dangerous." I hear the word rebounding around the room.

If only I'd listened to Tom.

"She has keys to our house, I know her from preschool, she says my husband had an affair with her, but he didn't. And then she turned up and she stood by the pool and I think she would have tried to drown me. I can't swim, you see?" This has shaken me, and I want to tell him everything without sounding mad, but even to me it sounds like nonsense. "I've already called the police about it all," I add.

He doesn't react to this, simply takes down all the facts and details, and stops writing when Rosa says, "Tell him what you told me before, about how she wants your life. You think she's been stalking you, and you're worried about Sam, aren't you?"

"Yes, I feel for her, she obviously has mental health issues. But I think she wants me out of the way. I'm worried for our safety. I think she wants to be me," I add, grateful for Rosa's clear head and gentle prompting.

"So, if she wants to be you, what makes you think she'd light a fire in your back garden?" He so doesn't believe a word of it, clearly thinks I'm hysterical.

"I'm not sure, probably revenge because I've ended our friendship, and she wants my husband?"

He looks at me doubtfully. "You ended your friendship?"

"Look, Officer, Rachel's told me *all* about her, and the situation is untenable. My friend's being stalked, that's why I'm here—her husband's away and Rachel doesn't feel safe in her own home."

He's still looking at me like I'm a madwoman.

"She was our estate agent," I say, "before we were friends, but she did some weird things. She spiked my drinks, took my son's sandals from a box in my bedroom then sent them to me, said she had an affair with my husband. Then she turned up at the pool and stopped me from getting out—"

"Rachel says she's not just trying to take her husband and her child, but her house . . . her *life*," Rosa adds in support.

I'm nodding at this. "And I think my son said he saw her in the back garden with some matches."

"Oh shit, really?" Rosa's flushed with anger again. I can tell she wants to just go out there and find her.

"So where is your son now?" the officer asks.

"In bed."

"He's four," Rosa says.

"Okay, well, I have all the information I need so far," he says, obviously disappointed at the age of the witness. "Would you mind coming down to the pool with me, Mrs. Frazer?"

"I'll stay here in case Sam wakes up," Rosa offers.

The pool is the last place I want to go to tonight. In fact, if it was anyone other than a police officer inviting me, I would have refused. He's now shining his flashlight and guiding me through to the pool garden, where it's cold, quiet, and pitch-black.

We stand in the silence, punctuated by the constant, rhythmic hum of the pump, like a heartbeat throbbing, echoing my own.

"I'm nervous around water," I say after a few moments. "Is there something you'd like me to see?"

"Sorry, my flashlight is acting up," he says before it suddenly comes back on. He moves it around, finally throwing a beam of light onto the far wall. It takes a moment for me to focus on the brightness now shining on the gleaming wall tiles in the midst of all the darkness. Then I see it... on the white, lovingly plastered six-foot wall surrounding the pool, written in bloodred, dripping paint: *Drown bitch!*

THIRTY-SIX

I recoil at the scrawled message and turn away, stumbling in the dark as I try to get away from the horror.

How could she?

She was my friend, and it shocks me that someone I spent time with, shared my secrets with, could *hate* me so much that she'd try to burn down my house, with me and my child inside.

"We found a box of matches too," the officer says, "so it certainly looks like someone came into your garden tonight with the intent to set fire to it."

"It must be Chloe Mason, it couldn't be anyone else," I say adamantly.

"Okay, well, obviously we will talk to her. There's also a vodka bottle. Could it be yours, and someone took it from the house to use the contents as a fire accelerator?" He shows me the bottle in an evidence bag.

"Yes, it *could* be ours—my husband would know for sure. I don't drink vodka so I can't swear on it. Do you think she came in the house and took it?"

"It's impossible to say at this stage, Mrs. Frazer. But we'll have it tested for fingerprints to see if that turns anything up."

Eventually the officer leaves, along with the two remaining firefighters. I close the front door, lock it, and join Rosa in the kitchen, where she walks toward me and gives me a welcome hug.

"If you hadn't been here, I would have been in bed asleep, and I may not have smelled the smoke. The house could have gone up with me and Sam..." I can't finish the sentence.

"Shhh, it's going to be okay, I promise."

I pull away and open the cupboard, where I last saw the vodka. "It's not there."

Rosa takes a deep breath. We both know what this means: Chloe *has* been in the kitchen.

"When did you last see it?"

"Earlier today, I cleaned that cupboard."

We both look at each other, and I see my own fear reflected in her eyes.

I call Tom first thing the next morning. He is horrified. "I'm setting off now," he says, "I'm not leaving you alone ever again."

"We're fine, the police are all over it. Rosa was the one who smelled the smoke."

"Sounds like I have some groveling to do to Rosa?"

"Just a thank-you will be enough."

"So are the police looking into it?" he asks.

"Yeah, the officer said he'd call me today. I reckon the minute they speak to Chloe, they'll know it was her, and she'll be charged with arson."

"Okay, I have a couple of things to do here, and then I'm heading home—no arguments, I'm your husband, I'm Sam's dad, I have to come home and look after you."

Despite all the bad news, I put down the phone slightly lifted after talking to him. I love Tom with all my heart, and I'd begun to have doubts about him, but he's dropping everything now to head home, and I already feel so much better. And there might just be a thawing between my husband and my best friend, which makes my life more pleasant. I check the clock and, feeling a little easier, decide to go back to sleep for a bit before getting up. I'm so tired after last night, I curl up and drop off straightaway, only to be woken less than an hour later by loud banging on the front door.

Rushing to the door, wrapping my dressing gown around me, I open it slowly and peer out to see a smiling, middle-aged woman. I don't know her, but at least she isn't Chloe.

"Hello, Mrs. Frazer. My name's Maureen Richards, I work with social services." She shows me a plastic card with her name on it. "I'd like to have a chat with you, if I may?"

"Have the police been in touch? They've worked quickly," I say, opening the door and ushering her into the kitchen, where there are a lot of dirty cups stacked on the side from the drinks we made for the police and firefighters last night. Along with mine and Rosa's wine bottles and dirty glasses from earlier in the evening, it must look like we had a party.

"You'll have to excuse me—as you can imagine it was a very late one last night," I say, assuming the police have filled her in on last night's fire.

"It looks that way," she says, giving me a judgmental Jennifer Radley look.

"So has she been arrested?" I ask as I gesture for her to sit on a stool.

"I'm sorry, who?" She can't seem to take her eyes off the wine bottles.

"Chloe Mason, the one who set fire to my garden last night."

"Erm no, I wasn't aware that someone had set fire to your garden," she replies. "I'm sorry to hear that." Her eyes do one more sweep past the wine bottles. "But I'm here regarding another matter. It's regarding the welfare of your son, Mrs. Frazer. Someone has reported a concern for your child's safety and well-being. I'm here in the first instance to conduct a welfare check."

I don't understand. "I've been *reported*? Are you sure you've got the right person?"

She nods, raising her left eyebrow slightly as she does.

"What for? Who reported me? Sam is well looked after, he's healthy and happy and loved, and I really don't get it?" I'm just throwing words at her. God I wish Rosa was here to back me up—she'd send this woman packing—but she left an hour ago to see her aunt and uncle.

"I'm sorry, the name of the person who reported this is confidential."

"Oh, I know who it is," I say as the penny suddenly drops. "It's Chloe Mason, isn't it?"

"Like I said, I can't—"

"So someone, *anyone*, can just call you up and say, 'Rachel Frazer's not looking after her son properly,' and you come over and *investigate* me?"

"At this stage, this isn't an investigation. My visit today is routine, Mrs. Frazer, please don't be upset. When someone contacts children's services because they are concerned about a child's safety and well-being, it's our duty to take their concern seriously."

"Concern? Have you any idea how malicious this woman is? She's been in my home, taken things, set fire..." I'm about to regale her with Chloe's back catalog of stalking when she stops me.

"Mrs. Frazer, this is a different matter, and the purpose of my visit here today is to see your son." She stops talking for a moment and refers to her notes. "Sam. Is he at home?"

"Yes, he is, but he's still in bed."

"And he was here last night?" She glances pointedly over at the empty wineglasses.

"Yes, he was bathed and in bed before eight. My husband is away, so a friend came over to stay with us as I've been having some problems with the woman I mentioned, who set fire to my garden. The woman is the same one who reported me to you. She has mental health issues—she wants my husband and my son, and it would help her a great deal if she could have me charged with child neglect!"

"Nobody is charging you with anything at the moment, I just need to see your son and make sure he's okay."

"She's ruining my *life*," I murmur, walking toward the door to go and wake Sam.

It couldn't be worse timing—he's grumpy due to lack of sleep, and not in the mood to meet with anyone, least of all a stranger waiting to interrogate him. So to avoid any tantrums, I pick him up and carry him in his pajamas to a waiting Maureen Richards, with the promise of pancakes after she's gone, if he plays nice.

"Hello," she says in a rather patronizing tone to Sam, who immediately shrinks into my neck, his head turned away from her.

"Do you still have to be carried by your mum? You're a big boy, you can walk, can't you?" she says, throwing so much shade at both my parenting and Sam, we both feel attacked.

"He's fine to walk, but I've just woken him, and he isn't used to strangers," I reply without smiling.

"Would you like to come and sit with me and tell me about your favorite toys?" Maureen asks, ignoring my defensive response.

I'm desperate to step in and introduce the truly fabulous Dinosaur Island, which is, according to the website, educational, interactive and "helps develop social skills and your child's imagination." More importantly, I'm hoping Dinosaur Island will illustrate to Maureen just how enlightened, engaged, caring, and educationally aware Sam's mother is.

"We could play with your favorite toy?" Maureen's suggesting seductively.

"That would be fun, wouldn't it, to play with Maureen?" I urge, and Sam looks at me, appalled. I appreciate that prehistoric fun with a social worker isn't everyone's cup of tea, but I plead with him with my eyes.

"No."

"What about playing Dinosaur Island with Maureen?" I suggest, desperate now.

"No! I'm not *playing* with *bloody* Maureen!"

I am *dying*, and Maureen visibly stiffens, though I'm sure in her line of work she's heard much worse.

"Please don't say that word, darling, it's very rude," I say, silently cursing Emily, the child who taught him these words. "Why don't you show Maureen your Lego?" I suggest.

"Mummy stole my Lego off me. My friend gave it to me. I cried when Mummy wouldn't let me play with it. She said I was a naughty boy and couldn't have it. So she bought me some more."

This has come out in a tsunami of words and emotion. Sam has obviously stored up all this hurt and resentment but I thought he was over it. I feel so guilty I want to cry.

"It wasn't *quite* like that..." I try, then realize that even if I wanted to, I couldn't explain the full story to Maureen with Sam present, so I abandon it.

Maureen suggests she speak to Sam alone. "With your permission, Mummy," she adds, but it feels more like a directive than a request. I've nothing to hide, and so I agree to fifteen minutes and busy myself in the other room. It is the longest fifteen minutes of my life, in which I imagine all kinds of truly terrible scenarios. I can't lose Sam; I would never survive that.

When I return after the allotted time, Maureen's still talking to Sam, but it's about TV programs he watches. I'm sure the more potentially damaging conversations have already taken place.

"All okay?" I ask brightly, trying to cover my fear as the large wineglasses admonish me from the kitchen surface.

"Yes, thank you both for your time. I will need to take this back to the team before any decisions are made."

"Decisions?"

"Yes..." She looks at Sam. "Would it be possible to have

a quick chat while Sam watches a TV program in the sitting room?" she asks.

I agree and minutes later, when he's settled in the other room, Maureen asks, "Do you find it hard looking after Sam while your husband's away? Can you cope alone?"

"Yes, of course I can. But Chloe Mason has made things difficult—she tried to burn down my house last night, so forgive me if I'm a little on edge."

"You weren't alone with Sam last night when the fire happened, were you?" Her gaze wanders to the two empty wine bottles resting on the side.

"No, my friend was here."

"Did you both have a drink?"

I can hardly deny it with the evidence brazenly displaying itself across my kitchen.

"Yes, my friend Rosa drank a lot more than I did." I glance at the two empty bottles, knowing I had only two glasses, so Rosa must have finished the rest. "She has no kids," I add. Like it makes a difference. "I had a glass or two but was perfectly capable of looking after Sam."

She gives a slight nod, as if she doesn't really believe it.

"Is *drinking* the issue here? I mean, is that what Chloe said, that I'm not able to look after my little boy because I drink?" I'm horrified.

Maureen's face is a veil of discretion.

"If that's the case, then it's just another lie she's telling," I say, angrily. "The joke is, that afternoon when we went to her house—that turned out *not* to be her house—*she* was the one who got me drunk!" I say, remembering Jennifer Radley's face in the post office as I slid down the wall, and seeing that same expression on Maureen Richards's face now.

She shifts in her seat. "Drinking when caring for young children is a choice, Mrs. Frazer—one has to take responsibility for one's actions." With that, she stands up, lecture over.

"You have this all wrong, I don't drink, I'm *not* a *drinker*."

"That's not for me to judge. I will now take my findings back to the welfare team to discuss."

"But what will you say? Surely you aren't going to condemn me on a phone call from some madwoman?"

"I can assure you, no one is condemning anyone at this stage," she says, smiling, but her smile doesn't meet her eyes.

THIRTY-SEVEN

"What did the lady say to you?" I ask Sam later as we walk to pre-school together. It's a couple of hours later than usual, but I'll tell Iris that Sam had a dental appointment. I want everything to be normal for Sam after the unexpected visit.

"What lady?" He looks up at me.

"Maureen, the lady who came to see us this morning. Did she ask you any questions about Mummy?"

He shrugs. "Can't remember?" He so can. He might be four but I can read Sam like a book.

"Did she ask if you're happy with Mummy?"

"I told her you kept waking me up last night, and once you took me out of bed when I was asleep."

I can feel myself shaking inside. "But I was only checking on you, darling."

"You woke me *up*!"

"Sorry, I just wanted a hug." I'm lost. I can see how this scene could be misinterpreted to look like I was drunk who staggered in and woke him.

"Did Maureen ask you if Mummy likes wine?"

"No."

That's something, I guess.

"Can you remember anything else she asked you?"

"No!" His default mode recently has been grumpy; he must be reacting to something in me. It's my fault.

"Darling, you aren't smiling, you seem sad. Is there anything upsetting you?"

He doesn't respond.

"How can I make you happy? Shall we go out for tea?"

He shakes his head.

"What would you like, then?"

"Can Emily come to play at our house?"

My heart sinks. "I'm sorry, darling, but she won't be able to for a while, we're busy."

"Emily says if I don't let her play in our swimming pool, she'll kill me." I try not to react—I'm hoping this is just being used as a turn of phrase, and not a direct threat. But with an aunt like Chloe, who knows?

"Oh, sweetie, take no notice. Emily can be a bit mean sometimes, but Chris will be over one afternoon this week to teach you, and Daddy's home next week, so you'll have plenty of pool time."

I'm tempted to tell him that I'll join him in the pool soon too, but he might keep asking, and I don't want to put myself under pressure. I'm still recovering from my pool encounter with Chloe.

Once I'm back home I call Rosa. I can't face telling Tom about the social services visit yet; he's already had my early-morning call about the fire. I'll wait until he gets home and talk to him properly, it isn't something to discuss over the phone.

"Maureen gave me no indication when they'd be in touch with their conclusion," I say after telling her all about the visit. "But if it's negative, and there's the slightest chance that my parenting is in question, I'm getting a lawyer. I'm also going to get the police involved more fully in Chloe's activities. *She's* the one who needs investigating!"

"I agree," she says, "you can't be too laid-back about these things. Trust your gut and call the police. They won't judge."

"Yeah, I will. This social services report she made has really shaken me up. It's made me realize she'll stop at nothing. I know she's twisted, but this is psycho level."

"If you think calling social services is psycho level, that's nothing. I dread to think what's on her to-do list next!"

"Oh don't, you're creeping me out," I say, looking around me. I'm standing in the kitchen, alone in a big house. "Perhaps it's time I introduced myself to the neighbors?" Having lived in a cramped apartment for years with people above and below us, I miss that close proximity, that sense of community we had in Manchester.

"Yeah, I met one of your neighbors the other day," Rosa says. "He's about eighty-five with a walking stick—not sure he'll be able to fight Chloe off, she's a dirty fighter too."

"Luckily, I don't need an eighty-five-year-old with a walking stick, I've got you—she's scared to death of you."

"Yeah, and if I'm honest, I'm scared to death of her," she says, quite seriously. "I've been talking to a lawyer friend of mine who says you need to report *everything* she does. Everything! Even if it doesn't seem like a big thing, but if she turns up where you are, if you think she might be following you, or calling you.

"We've all watched those true crime documentaries where the victim ends up dead because they haven't told the police everything. The police are low on staff and resources, and things get missed—so you *need* to make them aware, make them listen. Start a diary, a dossier, of everything she's done so far and add to it as she does more stuff—because she will. Send it to me on email as you update it, so someone else has a copy just in case . . ." The silence hums between us; we both know what she's saying.

"In case something happens?" I ask, and for the first time I realize this might not just be game-playing.

"Look, I'm not going to sugar-coat it to make you feel better: you and Tom have to face up to the fact that this woman is a serious threat to you and your family. Log everything, record everything, film her if you have to. I wish I'd done that with Dan, but I doubted myself. I kept asking, 'Is he *actually* doing something wrong here?' But the fact that I couldn't sleep or eat, that he always seemed to be where I was, should have *told* me he was doing something wrong. I didn't listen to my own instinct. Don't make the same mistake, Rachel, and don't rely on the police—carry one of those kitchen knives."

Later, I head back to the preschool to collect Sam. I'm desperately hoping Emily is collected by her grandma again because after everything that's happened in the past twenty-four hours, I can't face Chloe.

When I arrive in the playground some of the parents are mingling, and I see Jennifer Radley, who smiles and gives me a cutesy wave. It makes a nice change from her usual look of disdain. I smile back, praying she doesn't come over. I'm sure on some level she's as nice as Tom says she is, but I'm not in the mood for small talk. She's with her usual gaggle of friends, and it's an impenetrable little group I now know I'll never be part of, and today that's okay, because I just want to be alone. My friendship, if that's what it was, with Chloe has scared me off new friendships for life, and I understand why Rosa doesn't have boyfriends now after what happened with Dan. So I stand alone, passively observing the others. Some parents rush straight from work; they seem anxious, scurrying, busy. Others, like Jennifer, have more time, and they dress for preschool, treat it like a social occasion surrounded by their tribe.

It's the blue striped shirt I see first. It jolts me out of my passivity as the adrenaline begins coursing through my body, lighting it up with fresh rage. If ever I doubted myself, now I know I'm not going mad. *Chloe is wearing my shirt!* I can't help but stare. The police must have been to see her by now. She's standing with Jennifer and the other women but looking around. Is she looking for me? She soon catches my eye, and I half expect her to look away in shame—after all, she tried to set fire to my garden last night while scrawling a vicious message over the pool wall. And now she's wearing my shirt, which she must have taken from my laundry basket. Again, my doubts are erased about Tom forgetting, she is the one who lied. She *does* still have the keys!

I try to calm myself down. I mustn't lose it here, in the preschool. I silently tell myself that she might have used the link I sent her and bought the shirt for herself. But in my heart, I know that's not true. I *know* she's been in my house, gone through my things and stolen it from me. And now I can *feel* her walking toward me, smiling brazenly in my blue striped shirt. She's coming closer and closer and I don't know how to feel, what to do.

I am breathless at how shameless she is: instead of showing any kind of guilt or doubt, she's standing here, parading my own shirt in front of me. She's put a belt around the shirt, tucking in her tiny waist, folding her hands together neatly in front of her, obviously pleased with the look. Rosa's right—this is psycho-level behavior, and that psycho smile widens until she stops in front of me and twirls around, hand on hips. Clearly referring to the shirt, she asks, "So, what do you think?"

THIRTY-EIGHT

"I'll never look as good as you in this shirt, but I love it!" Chloe's beaming.

I'm so shocked at her boldness I can't answer.

"I've been texting you," she says, "but you never text me back." She pulls her bottom lip down like a hurt, sulky child. I recoil slightly at this.

"I blocked you," I say, unsmiling.

"Oh Rachel, is this all because of what happened at your pool? Your friend got it all wrong—she thought I was going to hurt you, but I wasn't. But then she was *so* angry—"

"You started threatening me, like you've taught Emily to threaten Sam."

She looks at me with a doubtful expression. "I wanted to talk to you. I wanted to tell you what's really going on, but he's got to you, and you won't believe me. I lie awake at night worrying about you."

"Is that why you're wearing *my* shirt?" I ask, loud enough for Jennifer's little tribe to hear; they need to know what a liar she is.

She looks visibly shocked. "You *gave* it to me."

"Wow!" I don't believe this. "Is *that* your story?" My voice is raised now; I'm surprised to hear my own rage, bright and white. "You *stole* it, you know you did!"

A murmur moves like a Mexican wave through the throng of parents.

"Rachel, I don't know what you mean? You *sent* me this shirt, it was a gift!"

"Why would I send you my shirt?"

"Because... you want to be friends again?" she says doubtfully, looking around at Jennifer's group like I'm the crazy lady.

I briefly close my eyes dismissively and move to walk away. There's no point in arguing with her; she has no grip on reality and believes her own lies now.

"Why are you lying, Rachel?" she asks, sounding hurt, a half smile playing on her lips. "You know you sent me this shirt. I received it this morning in the post with that lovely note," she adds in a voice meant to carry. This is a performance, and she's loving it.

"You are deluded, Chloe."

"Okay." She looks up with a pantomime thinking face on. "More cynically then, perhaps the shirt is your way of compensating after your friend beat me to a pulp in your garden? Are you worried I might go to the police and report her for assault? I still could, I've taken photos of my bruises just in case."

"Well, that's certainly your style, isn't it? You're happy to tell all kinds of lies to social services about my parenting," I announce to the playground.

"I don't know what you're talking about," she says. "*You're* the deluded one."

I'm now so angry I turn to the audience, all clearly taking this in while pretending they aren't. I'm frustrated—it's futile talking to her. I need allies, witnesses, I need them all to see who she really is for their own good.

"Don't buy into the denials and wide-eyed surprise," I start, and I point my finger at her. "Last night she tried to set fire to my house while my little boy slept. She needs help!"

There's a murmur from the assembled parents, who seem so embarrassed they can't meet my eyes. Jennifer looks at her watch like she wishes they'd hurry up and let the kids leave so she can get away from this.

"I know how this looks," I continue, addressing Jennifer's group, and anyone else who cares to listen. "I can see by your faces that some of you might think it's *me* who's mad, but *listen* to what I'm saying. If I'd listened to my husband, I wouldn't be in this mess now. He warned me against her, said she was dangerous."

Chloe's clearly horrified and red with embarrassment; she tries to brave it out, sighing like she's bored and can hardly bring herself to respond.

"And now I've realized what she's up to, she'll be on the hunt for her next victim—it could be any one of you!" I say, angry that she's driven me to this public display of rage.

"But, Rachel, I wouldn't do anything to hurt you, I'm trying to save you, if only you'd listen to me." She has tears in her eyes, but I know it's all part of her victim act and all for the other parents.

"Save me? You almost killed my child last night, you lie about my husband, you come into my house and take my stuff. You're not trying to *save* me, you want to *be* me!"

"I'm not... I don't want to be you... Why would you even say that?"

"Chloe, you're wearing my bloody shirt!" I reach out toward her, gesturing at the shirt to make my point, but as I do she springs back, probably to make it look like I was about to hit her.

"Don't hurt me." She's now cowering, and some of Jennifer's tribe have stepped forward, presumably on standby to protect her.

What the hell has she told them about me?

Everyone is staring, and I see surprise and judgment on all their faces. They think I'm a bully, they think I'm mad, that I'm the one who's been targeting the younger, prettier woman because I'm somehow threatened by her.

"She's *lying*! *She's* the one who's mad! You have no idea what she's capable of," I yell. As I throw out the final line in my defense, I turn to see Tom standing by the gate, his mouth half-open in horror.

"Tom...I..."

He doesn't move, clearly appalled at my outburst. I feel sick. *How long has he been standing there?*

Before I have the chance to go to him, to explain everything—he still doesn't know about her call to social services—the door to the classroom opens, and Iris appears. It's clear by her demeanor that she's heard the commotion. She's been keeping the children back until she knew whether it was safe to let them out, and I feel so ashamed.

"Come on, Rachel," Tom's saying.

"What are you doing here?" I ask.

"I told you I was on my way, I can't leave you alone like this," he says, and another murmur goes through the parents' throng.

I lean into him as he puts his arm around me. "She's told more lies, Tom..."

"It's okay, it's okay," he's saying, maneuvering me gently like I'm a dangerous animal who's escaped from the zoo.

Tom's reaction, and the unguarded looks from the other parents as they gather their children close, is making me realize how I may have made things a lot worse.

"I can see how upsetting it must have been for you to walk in on me yelling like that, but once I tell you what she's done, you'll understand," I say as we walk home with Sam.

"Keep your voice down, we don't want him to hear," Tom replies, clearly shaken.

"She's reported me to social services, Tom," I growl.

He doesn't answer me, just continues walking, addressing Sam and pretty much ignoring me, and I don't blame him.

Once we're home, Sam becomes engrossed in the new Lego set that I ordered to replace the one Emily gave him, which gives us the chance to talk. "Look, I've been driven mad by her these past couple of days," I start and tell him everything, ending in how Maureen Richards interviewed me then Sam.

"God knows what he said to her," I groan. "But she seemed even more abrasive with me after she spoke to Sam."

"You didn't let her speak to him *alone*?"

"Why *wouldn't* I?"

"Because it was probably distressing for Sam—he should have had someone with him. What did Sam say, did she tell you?"

"No, but I know Sam told her I woke him in the middle of the night and took him out of bed."

"Oh, he's been dreaming again?"

"No, not exactly—I mean, to him that's how it must have seemed."

"So you woke him up in the middle of the night?"

"Yeah, but only because I thought Chloe set the fire to distract us and kidnap him . . ." My voice fades. I realize how crazy this must sound to him.

"*Kidnap* him? What the hell, Rachel?"

"Well, you were the one who kept warning me against her," I say defensively.

"I said she was dangerous, a stirrer, that she tells convenient lies. I never once said she would abduct our child!" His voice is raised; I don't think I've ever seen him this angry.

"Oh, hang on." I see a flicker of realization in his eyes. "Rosa was here. You two had been drinking?"

"No, I mean yes, but we only had a couple of glasses of wine," I say, knowing how this must look to him, especially as I've just been reported for drinking while caring for a young child.

"Look, I know how this all sounds, but I'm okay, I'm not losing it, *she's* driven me to it," I say, pleading for some understanding from Tom.

"I understand, but today at preschool, when I arrived and saw all those other parents gawping, I thought something big was happening. I was so shocked to hear your voice, the way you were ranting, Rachel, and it reminded me of how you were when we met."

"That was different, I was grieving, you know I was."

"Yes, but you were also irrational, like you are now. I don't doubt that Chloe's lied, and she may have even reported you without any evidence, but the way you were yelling, you were out of control, Rachel."

"Honestly, Tom, I feel like she's taking my life apart piece by piece, and her denials and fake calm just sent me over the edge. But you're right, I feel like I'm unraveling all over again. I behaved like a deranged idiot, and if Maureen Richards from social services *should* decide to investigate further, there are now at least twenty witnesses who'd confirm everything Chloe reported."

"I understand what you've been through, but getting anyone else to believe it is the problem," he says, calmer now.

"I just want Maureen to believe it, because she's the one who could take Sam from us."

"Sam's happy and healthy, and we're both good parents," he says reassuringly.

"Yes, but he tells stories, and he swears, and I'm worried about him, I'm worried what he said to Maureen."

"So what happens now, with the report she made?" he asks.

"We have to wait."

"Shit," he murmurs.

"Don't worry, we can fight this," I say. "I refuse to let Chloe win."

Tom's face is etched with worry. "I think she just did."

THIRTY-NINE

"Even Iris was looking at me with fear in her eyes when I was yelling at Chloe," I say to Tom, shivering in horror at the memory.

"Look, there's no point in going over it again and again," he says as he makes a pot of soothing coffee. "What's done is done. You lost it, and we're now dealing with damage limitation. I'm home now, there'll be no more girls' nights with Rosa, no accusations of drinking in charge of a four-year-old, and *no* arson attacks. Oh, and the locksmith's coming tomorrow, so hopefully no more stolen shirts."

I sink into his arms, all the tension and fear flowing from me. I'm not even irritated by his dig about my "girls' nights" with Rosa, because he's back and it's going to be okay.

"What would I do without you, Tom?" I rest my head on his chest.

"You'd be fine, probably better off without me. I feel partly responsible for all this. I was the one who wanted us to move down here. I tried to do everything to make you happy, make you want to stay. But unfortunately the first person you met was Chloe, and I feel responsible for that. I'm sorry, darling."

"Don't apologize, or blame yourself in any way. I stupidly fell into this friendship with her. And as you've reminded me more than once, you did warn me."

"Hey," he says, his voice lifting, "let's try and distract ourselves and have a romantic dinner tonight. I'll cook?"

"That would be so nice," I murmur, "but I haven't told Rosa you're back, she was planning to come over tonight."

His face drops. "She doesn't need to come over now, and we really don't want a romantic evening for three."

"I know but I feel a bit mean just saying, 'Don't come because Tom's here.'"

"You and I need some time together, and *you* definitely need some TLC, just call her and tell her that. If she's your friend, she'll understand," he says. "Look, you're exhausted—why don't you go and have a nap and a bath, take your time getting ready."

"Okay, that sounds good." I kiss him on the lips.

"After all, it is our anniversary."

"Oh no! I didn't even realize the date! Tom, I forgot all about it, I feel terrible. How could I forget? It's usually me reminding you."

"You've had a lot to deal with, and before I came to meet you at the preschool, I went shopping. I told you I'm doing dinner tonight."

"Now you're making me feel worse, you do a seven-hour drive, and you also remembered our anniversary."

"Please don't feel bad, you're supposed to feel good on your wedding anniversary."

"You must think I'm awful . . ." I really don't feel like celebrating tonight, but I'm touched that Tom remembered, and that he wants to celebrate.

"You've had so much to deal with since you came here, just relax. I've got this."

"Lovely, thank you, I'll jump in the bath now," I say, blowing him a kiss.

I stop in the doorway and turn around. "Are you sure about

this? You've had a really long drive—you must be tired. It's not all about me."

"I am tired, but I think I should spend some time with Sam."

"Good idea. He'll love that." I start to walk away then turn back. "Oh, and if you get the chance, will you have a word with him about swearing?"

"Again?"

I roll my eyes.

"I'll have a word," he chuckles. "Oh, and put that red dress on, I fancy you in that."

I blow him a kiss and head to our bedroom, where I call Rosa to tell her that Tom's home, and where my stripey shirt turned up.

"Oh my *God!*" She sounds almost as angry as I am. "You *knew* she had it, didn't you? How weird was that seeing her wearing your stuff?"

"Awful, I was totally creeped out, but also can't get over her audacity."

"Bitch," she murmurs.

I go on to tell her that Tom's home a couple of days early because of the fire last night, and to my relief she's fine about that as it turns out her uncle isn't very well.

"If I'm honest, I was reluctant to leave him, but I didn't want you to be on your own either, so for once Tom's come through," she half jokes.

"I'm sorry. Well, Tom's here now for a couple of weeks, so Sam and I won't need our security detail—you can look after your aunt and uncle."

She chuckles. "Fair enough. As soon as Tom knows when he's going back, let me know if you need me to take over, but with any luck, crazy Chloe'll be in prison by then."

"I just hope she gets the help she needs," I say. "Imagine how lovely it would be not to have to lock the doors and check behind curtains every time I come home?"

"Not to mention checking the back garden every night for bonfires," she adds with a chuckle.

I put down the phone. I'm so tired I decide to rest for a few minutes on the bed, but two hours later, I wake up. I'm surprised, but it's still early and I needed the rest, so feeling much better, I take a long bath.

Later, as I'm dressing, I hear Tom and Sam laughing in the hall. Tom chases him up the stairs and, after a quick bath, puts him to bed. I can't resist popping in to tuck him in too. I'm wearing my red evening dress, with matching red lipstick and freshly blown hair, and despite everything, I feel more relaxed than I have for weeks.

"Wow!" Tom says when I walk into Sam's bedroom.

"Wow!" Sam echoes, which makes us laugh.

I kiss Sam good night and head to the kitchen, leaving Tom to read him his bedtime story.

But once there, I'm a little surprised that the kitchen is as untouched as when I left it earlier. I thought Tom said he was going to cook something, but the oven isn't on, and there's nothing in the fridge, so I guess he's planning to order takeaway. I sit at the kitchen island and pour myself a small glass of wine, cursing Chloe for making me feel guilty about this small avenue of pleasure. But the cold white wine soon takes the edge off, and I find myself relaxing as I wait for my husband to come spend the evening with me. I don't care if it's a korma and a couple of poppadoms; it will just be lovely to spend time alone together. I'm contemplating the evening ahead when the doorbell rings, a jarring pierce of my bubble, and as I'm still on high alert, I jump and spill wine down my dress. I guess I'm not as chilled as I thought I was.

My immediate thought as I walk into the hallway is what if this is Maureen from social services trying to catch me out? Answering the door in a long red dress reeking from the wine I spilled is the last thing I should be doing. But whoever it is, they are insistent and keep ringing the doorbell aggressively. I pick up a vase from the hall table just in case I need to defend myself if it's Chloe on the doorstep.

I stand cautiously by the door and try to make out who it might be through the mottled glass, but I can't tell. It looks like a smallish woman, but she isn't blond, so unless Chloe's wearing a wig for disguise, it's not her.

I open the door slowly, peeping through the crack. I step back a little, surprised to see a glamorous young woman with shiny lips smiling back at me.

"Mrs. Frazer, hello?"

"Hello..." I say vaguely, unsure of who she is. She looks strangely familiar, but I can't place her.

"It's Iris, from preschool." She smiles, and I suddenly see her through the makeup.

"Hello, Iris, I'm so sorry I didn't recognize you. Gosh, you look so glamorous, not that you don't usually, I mean..." I open the door the rest of the way, feeling a little awkward. Only a few hours ago, Iris was looking at me with fear in her eyes after I'd raged at Chloe in the playground.

"Oh, you only see me in my uniform without makeup." She chuckles at this, and I smile with relief. She's clearly forgiven me for my outburst.

"Actually, Tom was supposed to answer the door to me."

"Oh, was he?" I ask, confused.

"Yes, I'm part of your anniversary surprise—he's so thoughtful, your husband," she adds as an aside.

"Surprise?" It must be obvious by my expression that I haven't a clue what she's talking about.

"Yes. I'm going to babysit for you."

This isn't making sense. "Oh, that's nice, but we aren't going out."

"Well, you aren't *exactly*, but I can't spoil the surprise."

"Okay," I say slowly. "Well, please come in and make yourself at home. Sam will be delighted, but Tom's just putting him to bed, so I'm not sure you'll see him."

"That's a shame."

"Not necessarily, I'm sure you have enough of the children in the day!" I joke.

She smiles and we both stand in the kitchen looking at each other, neither of us knowing what to say. She's Iris the preschool teacher, and her being here in our kitchen has changed the dynamic. I think she feels as awkward as I do.

"I'll get Tom so he can explain," I say, making my escape. "I don't want you getting into trouble for spoiling the surprise. There's some hot coffee in the machine, please help yourself, I won't be a minute."

I run up the stairs and grab Tom as he's quietly closing Sam's door.

"You okay?" he asks, looking alarmed. I realize that despite pretending everything's fine and Chloe can't hurt us, we're both on tenterhooks waiting for her next move.

"I'm good," I say. "Iris is here, but you said we aren't going out, and under the circumstances I really don't want to leave Sam."

"I don't either, and I racked my brain trying to think of how we could feel like we're out, *without* leaving him. Then I thought about eating outside, and realized that the way things are at the moment, we would both be happier and more relaxed if there was someone in the house to keep an eye on him."

"Yes, that makes sense."

"I nearly called Rosa, but then I suddenly had the brilliant idea of Iris," he says, smiling like he's just done something wonderful, which he has. But I'm unsure of leaving Sam with *anyone* at the moment, even Iris.

He picks up on my reluctance. "You would have preferred Rosa?" he asks, crestfallen.

"No, Sam hasn't met Rosa since he was tiny, he wouldn't know her. Iris is perfect."

"Yeah, of course—Rosa would be a stranger to Sam because when she's been here, she's arrived like the vampire that she is, under cover of darkness." He smiles to soften the remark.

"I don't know what I'd have done without her while you were away," I say pointedly. "As far as I'm concerned, Rosa saved my life."

He shrugs slightly. "Yeah, but I feel guilty I wasn't there to do it."

I appreciate his honesty, and kiss him on the cheek.

"It's so good of you to go to all this trouble, and Iris is a great choice, but we could just pay her anyway, send her home, get a takeaway and sit on the sofa all night, just the two of us?"

"Yeah, but she's here now, and it's our anniversary. I wanted tonight to be special, not a takeaway on the sofa. I ordered an amazing hamper that's waiting for us outside: champagne on ice, smoked salmon, strawberries, all your favorite things. We've been apart so much this year I just want you to know how much I love you. Did I get it wrong?"

"No, not at all, it's lovely. I'm being... I'm being very *me*, aren't I?" *Nothing bad is going to happen.* "I'm worrying too much and letting my anxiety spoil the moment."

He smiles and takes my hand, and we walk into the kitchen together, where Iris is waiting.

"Hey, Tom." Iris beams as we walk into the kitchen.

"Hey, Iris, I don't want to tempt fate, but I reckon you're going to have a peaceful evening. Sam's exhausted."

"Ahh I don't mind if he wakes up, that's why I'm here," she says, looking me up and down. "I meant to say earlier, you look lovely, Mrs. Frazer." She smiles.

"Thank you, Iris. Please, call me Rachel."

"Sam's room is at the top of the stairs," I say. "We haven't had a babysitter before, but if he should wake, Sam would be thrilled to see you."

"The feeling is mutual," she says. "Now don't worry about

Sam, he'll be fine. I'll keep checking on him. Is he excited about sports day tomorrow?" she asks.

"Oh yes, he is." I've completely forgotten, but I don't want to admit this. After Iris watched me fall apart in the playground at preschool, I now don't want to prove to Tom or my son's teacher what a fuckup I am by forgetting about sports day.

"And good job you mentioned it, because his sports clothes are in the wash. Excuse me one moment." I dash into the utility room just off the kitchen. I'd put the laundry basket in there this morning and *meant* to put on a wash before I took Sam to preschool, but with Maureen Richards turning up to accuse me of being an alcoholic, and concerned I might have my child taken from me, I'd completely forgotten.

I open the washer door and quickly tip the contents of the basket into it, then throw in the detergent to set it off. But I'm just about to leave the utility room when something in the washing machine catches my eye. I stare inside as it goes round but can't see it anymore, so I turn the machine off and wait for the door to release.

"Come on, Rachel, what are you doing in there?" Tom calls good-naturedly from the kitchen.

"Just hang on," I say, desperately waiting. Blood is pumping through me. My heart is thumping so hard I can hear it in my head.

God, I hope I'm wrong. Please, God, make me wrong.

Eventually, after what feels like hours, but is actually about three minutes, I hear the click of the lock releasing. Bending down, I open the glass door, and reaching in, I pull out the bright blue striped shirt. The shirt that Chloe loves. The one that I publicly accused her of stealing from my home.

FORTY

Tom and I walk hand in hand through our fire-blackened garden to our champagne picnic. We don't talk about the ruined plants or the piles of gray ash; they are a reminder of her, and neither of us want her to spoil this, like she's spoiled everything else since I came here. This evening, I want to look at the sky turning dusky pink, and the crescent moon that hovers among the almost lilac clouds. Tom's hand is warm, my child is safe with Iris, and everything is almost perfect. But I have this urge to stop walking and throw up in one of the flower beds. All I can think about is *her*. In my mind's eye I see the stripey blue shirt, which I *know* wasn't in that laundry basket yesterday when I looked for it. I moved beds, emptied drawers and cupboards, checked every single nook and cranny in every room in the house. The shirt was absolutely *nowhere* to be seen. So why did it turn up tonight, in the washing machine? It wasn't there before when I searched, and I know *I* didn't put it in the washer. Tom only came home today, so he hasn't put anything in there, and Sam sure as hell didn't.

Had Chloe come into our home and put it in the washing machine while we were all here? Again, after everything, I can't help but feel this minuscule fragment of doubt emerging in my head once more. Did I, in all the messy drama, just not see it? Was it there all the time? Is that why Chloe looked so shocked and hurt and incredulous when I accused her of stealing it? I can think of nothing else as we walk farther into the garden. I barely notice the sweet jasmine filling the air, and hardly register when Tom opens the door into the pool area. It's only when we're meters away from the pool that the familiar dread hits me full on like a wave.

I can't breathe, I'm gulping at the air for oxygen, my heart is pounding. I feel out of touch with reality, like I'm becoming detached from something solid. I'm floating with nothing to anchor me.

"Rachel, Rachel." Tom's voice is in my ear. He's holding me up as I stagger across the Italian tiled flooring. The scrawled threat glows in the blue light of the pool: *Drown bitch!*

"I don't want to be here," I say.

He's brought me to a blanket on the ground, an open hamper, I remember now. Our anniversary.

"Darling, sit down, just rest here, no one's going to try and make you go near the water. Look, I've set it back a little—we don't have to swim, I just wanted to bring you here. I want you to love this as much as I do."

My eyes are drawn to the message on the wall, a silent, stinging smack across the face.

He follows my eyes. "You didn't tell me about that. I saw it when I brought the picnic down, but by then it was too late to do anything about it. Don't look at it—I'll get it covered over, or erased."

I sit down beside him and don't look at the words, but the eerie turquoise light from the pool is present everywhere.

"She's always here, isn't she? One way or another she manages to ruin everything," I say.

I sit for a few minutes. Everything's blurry and after a little while I can focus on something other than the weird blue light and bloodred letters.

I notice that Tom has dotted the pool area with tealights in jars, like little stars reflected on the shiny tiles. The light from the pool seems to increase the darker the sky is, a glowing turquoise entity in the dusky darkness.

The champagne is chilling in a bucket of ice and two empty champagne flutes are on standby, but the disappointment on Tom's face makes me want to cry. I'm a bad wife as well as a bad mother. This isn't the romantic evening my thoughtful husband had planned. He's done this for *me*, from the lights in jars to the champagne to finding someone we trust to look after our precious little boy. He deserves a better wife.

"Shall we open the champagne?" I murmur, still overwhelmed but fighting it.

The smile on his face is worth it. He lifts the bottle from its icy bath, and with a flourish, he pops open the cork. It makes me jump, and as he fills my glass with bubbles, we laugh, in a fleeting moment of happiness. But then my eye catches the message, and it dampens the sparkle of champagne, drowning the moment until it can't breathe anymore.

Tom's arms are around me, my safe harbor as darkness descends and the stars emerge, and that little pop of pleasure that started with champagne is resuscitated. I begin to breathe again, and turning myself away from the wall and the pool, I reach out my hand and touch my husband's cheek. He leans in and kisses me, gently pulling down the straps of my dress, exposing my naked breasts, then he firmly but gently pushes me down onto the rug. I'm lying down, looking up at the stars and the darkening sky as his fingers caress my nipples. He moves down my body, his tongue softly exploring me, causing the stress and fear to melt like candle wax through me as the flame burns brightly. Then come the fireworks. Sparks move down my body, and I cry out as my insides explode. And in that final, shuddering moment, I know why Chloe envies me, why she wants to be me, because this, this here, now with Tom, is *everything*.

He gently pushes his way into me, and we roll together on the soft rug, half-naked, alone in the silence save for his panting, the gentle lapping of the water and the pool's heartbeat.

Afterward, we lie together for a long time, just holding each other.

"More champagne?" he murmurs. Looking at his handsome face, his strong biceps, his beautiful eyes, I'm filled with such love and gratitude for him.

"I love you, Tom."

"I love you more," he replies, an echo of the early days of our relationship when we had time for us.

I take my glass, and he pours us both more champagne. It fizzes on my tongue, and if moonlight had a taste, this would be it.

After our second glass, we explore the picnic basket, discovering the smoked salmon, crackers, fresh lemons and dill, and ripe, juicy strawberries.

"Let's save some strawberries for Sam, they're his favorite," I say.

"He'd love them for breakfast," Tom agrees, placing five large strawberries onto a napkin, before we go on to devour the rest.

"I hope Sam's okay, hope he hasn't woken up and cried for me. He does that sometimes," I say.

Tom puts a cracker into his mouth and starts chewing, looking at me the same way I'm looking at him. We both know what the other is thinking.

"Shall I go and check on him?" we both say in unison, and laugh.

"I'll go," Tom says, getting up and walking away.

"Don't be long," I say. "I'll miss you."

"I'll miss you more," he replies, and he disappears through the door to go check on our son.

I sit alone in the blueish dark, drinking champagne and thinking how lucky I am. Tom's home, and I feel fearless; even the cruel message scrawled on the wall has lost its potency—if you look at something long enough, you don't see it anymore.

I can even see the beauty in the pool: the thing that's pulled us apart and flooded me with bad memories might still bring us together. Out here it's like another place, just the dark, the eerie light, the flicker of candles, and the constant heartbeat. I'll always be afraid of the pool, but for the first time I think there's a chance I might be able to live with it. Then I hear a crack underfoot, something moving in the bushes.

"Tom, is that you?" I say, smiling, because I know him so well. He won't be able to resist teasing me, and he'll leap out from behind a tree any minute.

"Tom, I know you're there," I say as the door opens slowly, but a small, dark figure emerges.

"Hello, Rachel," she says. "Having a good time?"

FORTY-ONE

"Tom!" I yell in panic as my worst fear materializes in front of me.

"No point calling for Tom, he's too far away, both physically and metaphorically. You really don't know your husband, do you? He's chatting to Iris in the kitchen; he's almost forgotten about you down here."

She's wearing another of her floaty dresses, a yellow one, down to her ankles. She's barefoot, her hair uncombed.

"Go away, Chloe, or I'll call the police!" is all I can muster.

She continues to head toward me, creeping, catlike, then she suddenly stops. "Why are you being so mean to me, Rachel, when all I want to do is protect you?" Her voice sounds different, high-pitched, weird. She's now standing at the far end of the pool, her head to one side, hair messy, dark, mascara-stained eyes.

"I hated seeing you at preschool today," she says. "Why did you lie about the shirt, Rachel?"

I don't respond. My whole body is tense, I can't move, like the picnic rug is holding me down.

She starts to move again, walking to the pool, holding out her arms for balance, tiptoeing around the very edge. One slip and she'll be in the water. My heart is in my mouth. I watch her teetering on the edge, unable to speak.

"Chloe, I don't know what happened with the shirt. I think you brought it back here. I'm confused. I don't want to talk to you. I'm *scared*. Surely you understand that?"

She stops, her head turning slowly in my direction. "Everything I've told you is true. I care about you, Rachel. I used to think I cared about Tom, that you didn't matter. But you *do*, and that's why I told you about him and me."

"Yes, but it isn't *true*, Chloe, and lies hurt people. You've hurt me."

"You've hurt *me*, you picked me up and dropped me like everyone else does. And after you said the terrible things about me today, Jennifer's being weird with me now too." She starts moving again. She's getting closer, behind me now.

I wish Tom would hurry back.

I'm still sitting on the rug, rigid. I can't move. I watch her, tension rising, getting ready to run. She's close now, looking down at me, but the light from the pool is behind her, so I can't see her face.

What if she hurts me now, or worse, then goes up to the house and hurts my family? My throat tightens with fear. How could we have been so stupid? We left ourselves wide open to this. I should have *insisted* to Tom we stay inside tonight.

To my horror, I suddenly realize my dress is pulled up. I immediately pull the dress down over my thighs, make sure the straps are back up. Perhaps I'm subconsciously planning to take flight? Or is this about my dignity in the face of death?

"I miss you," she says.

"I miss you too," I lie. I have to be nice—she's hurt and angry, and if she has a knife or tries to attack me, I won't stand a chance.

She's smaller than I am, but as Rosa said, she's a dirty fighter—she bites and scratches and kicks. I've never had a fight, and I'm no Rosa. I wish she was here now.

Where the hell is Tom?

She makes a sudden movement and I flinch, but she's moving to sit down now next to me.

"Sorry, I didn't mean to frighten you"—she's still talking in the weird voice—"but I couldn't stand by and wonder what he was going to do."

"Who?"

"Tom, of course."

She pulls up closer on the rug. I still can't properly see her face in the candlelit darkness. I'm shaking with fear.

"What you need to realize, Rachel, is that he doesn't love you. He loves your *money*," she announces, matter-of-factly.

I want to tell her to fuck off, that she doesn't know me or my life and this is all based on some weird fantasy she's cooked up in her head. But I *mustn't* do that, I *mustn't* get angry with her, because if I do, it could end in something horrible, and Chloe would probably win.

I can feel the tension in the air. Every sinew in my body is screaming, *Get away from her,* but I can't. She's right next to me, her warm thigh tucked next to mine. How I long to push her away, punch her, run, but I wouldn't dare.

"We had the most amazing time when he first came here," she starts, and even in the dim light I can see her eyes shining at the memory. "We'd sit in the empty rooms of the house with a bottle of wine, or a picnic just like this one." She gestures toward our anniversary picnic. "Tom loves a picnic," she says with a sigh, "then he likes to make love afterward."

This is crazy.

"We were discreet, Rachel." She turns to me. "We didn't go out much. Sometimes we'd head down into Penzance, to a quiet little restaurant and have dinner there. We were never seen together around here, he insisted on that."

She reaches into the napkin that Tom put strawberries in for Sam's breakfast. I want to slap her as she picks out the biggest, ripest strawberry and pushes it into her mouth.

"We couldn't wait for the pool to be finished, and on the first night we just jumped in. We took each other's clothes off and swam naked." She turns to gaze longingly into the pool, reliving the memory of something that never actually happened.

"Tom said he could never do stuff like that with you because you had this insane fear of water." She laughs to herself, like I'm somehow inadequate because I don't hurl myself into water every chance I get.

I say nothing.

Where's Tom? I'm worried about him. Has she already been in the house?

She suddenly turns away from the pool and her naked swim delusions to ask, "You want to know why we broke up, me and your husband?"

My voice has gone. I can't speak, so I just nod.

I'm wondering if I could reach the half-full champagne bottle and at least threaten her with it.

Has she been in the house and hurt Tom or Sam, or both?

She's waiting for me to ask why she and Tom broke up, but I refuse to give credence to her sick fantasy. She believes she is central to everything here, like we're all her toys to play with—even Tom exists only for her pleasure. But now her revenge?

"I used to get upset. I used to make him swear he wouldn't leave me, then one day he said, 'We can't ever live happily ever after together in this house because it's all in my wife's name. She owns the house, and the money is all hers.'"

This, of course, is true. I told Chloe myself that everything is in my name so they couldn't ever live here together. But now

I remember her response to this. *There are ways*, she'd said. My heart is pounding harder now as I see with such clarity what's happening. Chloe's here tonight to get rid of me, because in her warped mind, she thinks that's the only way she can live happily ever after with Tom.

"Tom said if *you* weren't around, we could live here together," she's now saying, confirming my fears. "This was my dream, someone handsome and successful like Tom, a beautiful house with a pool, a little boy. I mean, I was in heaven."

I'm horrified and fascinated by her madness. Her insanity is real, it's brutal, and it tears me in two.

"Tom said the only way we could have all this would be if you had some kind of accident. I couldn't believe what he was saying, but he said you couldn't swim, and no one would question you falling in and drowning. That's why he had the pool restored."

I'm still listening, in awe at her imagination.

"At first I thought about it," she says, as if she's talking to herself, privately recalling her deranged thoughts and plans like I'm not even there. "I didn't know his wife, I'd only seen photos of her in his bedroom," she continues. "Rachel was a picture on a wall; it wouldn't have been hard to push a woman I didn't know into the pool, to pretend it was an accident." She reaches for another strawberry and bites into it. Red droplets land on her pale yellow dress, like blood.

"Tom said you didn't love him, you were unhappy, difficult, always criticizing, so overprotective of Sam you made him fretful and anxious. I thought you were a bad person, so I said I'd do it."

I'm shaking my head. These are just the ramblings of a madwoman, but still I'm finding it hard to listen to.

"But there was a little part of me that wasn't a hundred percent sure," she says, looking directly at me now, trying to re-engage me with this new twist. "So, I came over that first night because I wanted to meet his awful wife, I wanted to see for myself how horrible she was so it would be easier for me to push her in."

"Chloe, enough..." I start, but she's gone back into her own little world again.

"That night I realized that Rachel was human, flesh and blood and warm and friendly and... I couldn't do it. Of course, Tom was furious that I'd turned up unannounced and met with you—he was worried you'd guess there was something between us. But he was even more angry when I told him I couldn't do it, I couldn't kill his wife."

"Chloe, you need help," I start.

Still uncomfortably close, she turns to me, her face in mine. "Let me *finish!*" she hisses. "Why doesn't anybody ever listen to me?"

"If any of this were true, and if you did like me, then why didn't you tell me about this?" It's obvious she doesn't respond well to accusations of madness, so I need to play along until Tom gets back.

I just hope to God he's okay.

She puts her hand on my upper arm—it feels too intimate, and I squirm as she continues to talk. "You wouldn't have believed me, you'd have believed Tom and he'd poison you against me and we wouldn't be friends anymore."

I pull away slightly, but instinctively she grips my arm. "So I didn't tell you about what he wanted me to do, but I tried to keep an eye out, make sure nothing happened. I even thought that you and Tom could stay together, and we could be friends, like you and Rosa are. But he hated when we became friends, even then he kept pressuring me to get rid of you."

Again, more lies, but I'm not going to argue with her. Now isn't the time.

"He was angry with me, said if I really loved him, I'd do it so we could be together. He kept going over and over it, even though

I'd told him no. He said he'd bring you to the pool one night and leave you alone here." She looks around, then turns to face me. "Like now."

My stomach drops. I need to scream or run, but I'm frozen to the spot.

"I was supposed to come here, wait until he'd gone and scare you; then as you tried to get away, I had to push you in."

Is this a threat? Is she about to go through with this so-called plan she's made up in her head?

She's gazing into my face, her eyes dark and unfathomable as she continues to talk. "I told Tom it worked both ways. I said, 'If you loved me enough, you'd get rid of her. Why do I have to do it?' He said because he'd be the main suspect, but no one would suspect me, especially if I made friends with you. All I had to do was push you in, leave you to drown, and once I was sure you'd been under long enough, I had to slip over the wall. We'd stay apart for a few months, then be together for good."

"Chloe, I don't think any of this happened. You *imagined* it," I say gently.

"You don't believe me?" She straightens up, seems genuinely shocked. She's looking around her now, then suddenly seems to see the scrawl on the pool wall.

"What the fuck's *that*?"

"I think you know exactly what it is."

"I don't!" she snaps, then without standing, she begins to shuffle away from me, using her hands. For the first time, it seems that she's scared of me. "You don't think that, do you? You don't think I did it, Rachel? How could you even think . . . ?" She sounds almost tearful.

"Look, Chloe, I know you, you're a kind person, you didn't mean to do it. You might not even realize it was you who wrote that."

"I DIDN'T!"

"Okay, but you said yourself that before you met me and

became a friend, you were prepared to murder me—that's far worse than writing on my wall."

"No, it's not, because as Tom said, I wouldn't *actually* be murdering you. I'd just be pushing you in, and if, as a result of that, you died... then it was your fault for not being able to swim."

"Wow," I say. *She really is insane.*

"It's the only reason I agreed initially, because you were then a stranger who couldn't swim! But as I told him, we didn't *need* for you to die for us to be together. He could just divorce you and we could live in my apartment. That's when I realized he didn't want me—he wants the house, he's sunk all your money into it, and if anything happened to you, I think he'll sell it."

"That's hard to hear," I say, still knowing this is pure fantasy. "So what now, are you going to push me in?" I ask, aware I'm joining her in this unhinged fantasy, but keen to know if I should make a run for it.

"No, of course not. I told you I said no." She stops talking for a moment, then says, "Once he realized I wasn't going to help him, he dumped me. Told me never to come over again, that he'd never loved me, and if I ever told anyone about our affair he'd deny it and I'd look mad." She pauses for a moment. "I've had some depression, a suicide attempt, before. Lost my job, had all kinds of problems at work."

"After a difficult relationship with a former colleague at the bank?" I ask, suddenly feeling a prick of sympathy for this young woman who clearly struggles with her mental health.

"You know about him?"

"Tom told me," I say.

"The bloke chased me for months, then I agreed to sleep with him and he used me until he dumped me. Same old story. But this time I wasn't going to go quietly, and that pissed him off, a bit like now with Tom," she adds in a sneaky aside, letting me know her story hasn't gone away. "So, the rumors started, fueled by all the other beer-swilling married men who belong to their own little infidelity club. It's so easy to make women like me look mad, Rachel."

This feels poignant—perhaps there were gray areas in that relationship for her? She once told me that she can never keep friends or lovers; it starts well, then they tire of her. Those men who rejected her are part of the problem; they are responsible for her current mental health.

"Perhaps I should have told you all this much sooner," she's saying, "but I thought he'd given up on the idea. I even wondered if he'd been testing me: 'Do you love me enough to kill my wife,' you know. But then today I saw him ordering the hamper," she says. "He's seeing someone else, Rachel. I don't know who she is, but I think he was with her before he was with me, he just made me *think* he loved me. He used me, like I've always been used."

"You can't blame someone else for what you did Chloe, you hurt me, you scared me half to death, hanging around the house when Tom was away, leaving stuff on the patio so I'd think we had intruders. Do you know how terrified I was? Have you any idea of the harm you caused me? You stole my son's baby sandals and sent them back to me wrapped in birthday paper, you went into Sam's room at night and kissed him. You are psychotic." Tears filled my eyes, horrified once more at how someone could be capable of such evil.

I expected her to deny this, to rail against what I was saying, but she stayed quiet, looking down, shame stopping her from meeting my eyes.

"I'm sorry, I'm so, so sorry Rachel." She's crying now. "He told me you were a bad person, a bad mother, I thought I was *helping* Sam and Tom, and... I thought he loved me, and this was our chance to be together. I'm sorry I scared you, but he made me do it. He even made me put too much vodka in your drink on that first afternoon we spent together. He wanted everyone to think you were a mess. That's why I called you first thing the next day to apologize. I felt guilty for making you drunk, I *liked* you—but I was in *love* with him." She finally looks up at me, her face a study in a life of pain and rejection. I almost feel sorry for her.

"But all the time it was *her* he loved," she cried, still peddling her own, more acceptable narrative. "Tom was using me to kill you so *they* could be together, and then he'd point the finger at me, the madwoman. I was an idiot, I'd have ended up in prison, you'd be dead, and they'd be living happily ever after."

She reaches out her hand and I recoil. I see the hurt in her eyes, but I don't trust her, and I don't believe her.

"Rachel," she whispers, and I see the crazy in her eyes, she can't hide it anymore. "His plans have changed." She looks around, as if to check no one's listening. "He still wants to be with *her*, he still wants *your* money, and for you to be out of the picture, be careful."

Before she can say any more, I finally hear footsteps.

"Tom, Tom, *help!*" I call, relief flooding through me.

Alarmed, she grabs me, putting her hand firmly over my mouth.

I'm squirming under her, but thank God Tom heard me and he's now running toward us, yelling.

Leaping off me, she runs toward him. "Rachel knows all about your plan to kill her," she's screeching in his face.

He looks at her, terrified, shaking his head in disbelief. "Chloe, are you okay? We can get you some help," he offers, but she hurls herself at him in fury, scratching, kicking, and biting.

I get up, stunned, and run toward them to help him, but by now she's wrapped herself around him like a limpet and they are spinning together as one toward the pool.

There's an almighty splash. I hear her scream, and I'm triggered. My heart's pounding, my vision blurry as they fight in the water.

"Tom!" I'm calling hopelessly, pointlessly. I just want him to be okay; I can see how vicious she is.

"Bastard, murdering bastard!" she's shrieking as she tries to gouge out his eyes.

He stays above water, but she's pushing her hands into his face, scratching and screaming. And then, suddenly, silence.

FORTY-TWO

The clouds have cleared now, and it's cool as I stay by the side of the pool. I am in shock, I can't believe what's happened, and I'm surprised at my emotions. I'm crying as Chloe's body floats in the shimmer of moonlight, and I'm reminded of the day her torn blue dress floated on the pool after her fight with Rosa. I'm filled with a strange sadness that she's now lost her fight.

It's over, no more lies, no more terror every time my phone rings. Chloe's dead, but I have my life back. So why do I feel so conflicted, and more than this, why in these minutes after her death do I feel so *empty*?

"I found her here attacking my wife," Tom is telling the police, who arrived just a few minutes ago. "I tried to stop her, but she started swinging at me, then grabbed the champagne bottle and swung it around my head." I watch silently as two policemen look into the pool and another stares at the message on the wall. It's clear to anyone that this has been coming: Chloe was never far away, watching and waiting.

"... then we both fell into the pool, and she hit me with the bottle," Tom says. It's only then I see the blood trickling down his face, and my mind flashes back to the strawberry droplets on her dress.

"I'm devastated, I can't believe this happened." He's upset and angry and I understand the weird mix of emotions. "I *had* to push her away because she was hitting me with the bottle, but in pushing her away, she must have gone under," he continues, as the officer takes notes. "She can't have been a strong swimmer—she didn't stand a chance. She was so slight. We were only in five feet of water, but it was over her head. I tried to get her out as soon as she went under, but she slipped through my hands, and as I was concussed"—he touches the bleeding wound on his head—"I didn't know what was happening, but my wife saw it all."

"Yes, I did," I confirm eagerly. "Our lives have been plagued by this woman for months. She started with a fixation on my husband, then befriended me. It was terrifying." I go on to tell them what she said to me earlier, and how my husband saved me. Tom's shaking his head as I speak.

"You see, Officer, Chloe Mason mounted a campaign to twist everything that happened during her friendship with my wife. She stalked her, set fires in the garden; she even reported my wife to social services for drinking alcohol. She was *obsessed*, and my wife has been driven mad. If you speak to the parents and some of the teachers at our son's preschool, they'll tell you how badly she affected my wife."

I wish he hadn't offered up Jennifer Radley and her mean girls as witnesses—they're the last people I want vouching for me, and in fact I doubt that they would.

The police sympathize—one of them confides in us that he once had a stalker, and he understands what we've been through. I'm grateful because only someone who's been down that road can know how horrific it is.

I watch them take her away, and as sad as it is for someone to die so young, I'm *glad* Chloe's dead. I hate myself for even thinking it, but I feel like I'm finally free, and my family is safe.

She was gaslighting me, making me doubt myself and my husband. Now she's gone, she can't mess with my head anymore, but as we answer the questions and sign statements, I begin to realize I'm not so sure. Repeating all the lies she told me about my husband and my marriage is causing me to question everything. Is that doubt in the female police officer's eyes as I tell her that the pretty young woman used to work with my husband, she sold him our house, he gave her our keys? That it might be hard to believe, but he didn't even like her, but she was obsessed with him. The look on the woman's face as she hears this is of vague uncertainty, at times disbelief. It reflects my own conflict about what Chloe told me.

And after we've told them everything, and the body's been taken away, Tom and I walk arm in arm back into the house. I'm expecting to feel liberated and without fear now that she isn't in our lives anymore, but it isn't happening. And now I find myself asking: was Chloe so obsessed with me and my husband that she imagined a relationship and lied about everything, or was she telling the truth?

FORTY-THREE

It's nine days since Chloe died. Tom and I are still shaken from what happened that night. She brought thick black clouds of doubt into my world and it will take a long time for me to process what happened. I am conflicted and finding it hard to come to terms with how she died, and the weight of guilt I'll carry with me always. I ask myself all the time if the outcome could have been different, but as Tom says, my life is already filled with what-ifs—it's time to ask, "What now?"

The night Chloe died, Iris heard the screams coming from the pool and called the police. She stayed with Sam while we dealt with the aftermath, and in the days since she's been a great support to us all. She comes round most evenings on her way home from work to see Sam; sometimes she brings a lasagna or chili, for which we are very grateful.

It's Saturday afternoon, and as preschool is closed, Iris is with us. She called in with some paints for Sam, and they are making decorations for his party next week. We'd promised him a fifth birthday party and we don't want him to miss out because of everything that's happened, so he's invited a few friends from preschool.

"Do you have any paper clips and string?" Iris asks brightly, looking up from piles of blue streamers, her long dark hair swinging as she turns her head. I like her—she's great with Sam, and she laughs a lot. We're pretty short on laughter, and I'm glad she's here; so is my son, who adores her.

"I'm sure we have some somewhere. I'll go and have a look, but first, would you guys like some homemade lemonade? I made it fresh this morning."

"Yes, *please*," Iris and Sam chorus.

"Can I have gin in mine?" Tom half jokes as he walks into the kitchen.

"Can I have Jim in mine too?" Sam asks, and we all smile at this.

I pour the lemonade and hand it round, but before I have a chance to go on the hunt for paper clips, the front doorbell rings. It still triggers me, and I glance over at Tom.

"It's okay," he says, smiling reassuringly, and I remember, it can't be *her*.

So I head into the hall, open the door cautiously, and peep out. "Rachel?"

It's Jennifer Radley, on my doorstep with an armful of flowers.

"Hope you don't mind me just turning up like this, but I've been worried about you."

This is a surprise, and I want to ask why on earth she would be worried about someone she barely knows. I don't really understand why she's here; we aren't friends. Perhaps she's here because she's nosey and wants to know what happened, the same way she offered to help out and pick Sam up when I sprained my ankle. It may be that recent events have made me reticent to trust another living soul, but I just know she's here because she wants to poke around in someone else's mess. Jennifer is an ambulance-chasing mean girl who wants a front-row seat to others' misfortunes and scandals, and I'm not in the mood for her.

"How are you all?" she's now saying to my rather surprised face.

"We are good, thanks," I offer, nothing else. I refuse to fill her mouth with information for her to serve up as conversational canapes to the other mums in the playground.

She stands awkwardly on the doorstep, and from my body language she's realized I won't be inviting her in.

She looks around awkwardly. "It must have been so awful. Were you hurt?" she asks.

I shake my head. "I've been told not to talk about what happened," I lie.

"Oh." She's devastated and glances at the expensive bouquet of flowers she brought as a ticket in, no doubt furious that she wasted the money on me.

"I... brought these, hope they cheer you up." She reluctantly plonks them into my arms, knowing once this deed is done she has no more excuse to hang around.

"That's so kind of you, Jennifer, I appreciate it." I dislike her intensely, but there's no reason to be rude, and they are beautiful flowers.

"So, I guess I'll let you get on with your Saturday." She starts to turn, and I'm about to shut the door when Tom appears at my shoulder.

"You okay, Rachel?" he asks gently behind me. "I was getting worried about you..." Then he sees Jennifer, and looking from her to me to the flowers, he says, "Jennifer, hi!"

"I called round... to see how you're all doing," she says.

"That's very kind, thank you." He looks again from me to her. "Well, don't stand on the doorstep. Come in."

She's smiling and nodding and now moving into the hall, and I have this urge to knee him in the groin.

"I was just saying to Rachel how awful it must have been." She sweeps past me and into my kitchen, where Tom is now offering her my lemonade.

"Lovely," she says as I follow them through and put the flowers in water.

I'm used to women falling a little for my husband—he's good-looking and when he wants to, he can be charming. My dad always said, "He could charm the birds off the trees, that one," and I hear him now as Tom hands Jennifer a glass of lemonade. Her fingers almost touch his as she takes the glass, looking into his eyes.

The silence is deafening. I know Tom invited her in thinking I'd keep the conversation going, but neither of us really knows her so we have nothing to say. Still, I try to fill the silence, and what better than to give her some great PR to take back to the mean girls.

"We had some good news this morning, a letter from social services to say they won't be taking the welfare check any further," I announce. "You might recall that Chloe had made a false report?" I say, recalling with some embarrassment how I announced this to the playground while arguing with Chloe.

"Oh, that's good news, isn't it?" Jennifer replies, clearly underwhelmed. Disappointed even?

I glance over at Tom, who gives me an awkward grimace. "Tom doesn't like me talking about it," I say. "He thinks the less it's mentioned, the less people gossip, but I don't believe that, do you?" I ask her, pointedly.

Tom scowls at me while Jennifer takes a sip of her lemonade, then tries to change the subject. "Of all the things to happen to Chloe, drowning was never on my list," she says. "She was such a good swimmer—she swam for the county, did you know?"

Tom and I look at each other. I turn to the flowers and pretend to concentrate on arranging them in the vase.

"She had so many problems," Jennifer's saying, like she's aware of how uncomfortable this is for us. "I knew her at school. What a troubled girl. She stole my boyfriend then blamed me. I was distraught. My parents had to send me to therapy..." She continues in detail about her own experience. I'm relieved that the subject matter is back on Jennifer, and we can relax back into The Jennifer Show.

"I cried and cried, she was so cruel to me."

I'm hoping she drinks the bloody lemonade quickly and goes. Tom's magnanimously invited her in but hasn't a clue what to say, and as she drones on about herself, I know that any minute he's going to wander off and leave her to me.

But just as I'm about to scream, the universe listens; my phone rings and to my deep joy, it's Rosa.

"Sorry, just *have* to take this," I say apologetically, and I march off, leaving Tom to deal with the consequences of letting a vampire in.

"You are bloody psychic," I hiss down the phone as I run upstairs to take her call. "That bitch Jennifer Radley's turned up with an armful of expensive flowers."

"Ugh, how revolting. You told me about her—has she come to feast on the corpse?"

"Something like that. Bloody Tom invited her in. I've left them 'chatting' in the kitchen."

"Oh, that's not like Tom to be friendly?" She sounds almost hurt; she's never seen the charming side of Tom.

"I'm being sarcastic. When I say 'chatting,' she's doing all that while Tom's saying nothing, just standing awkwardly against the fridge. I left her filling him in on her and Chloe's hormonal teenage years."

"That sounds like a teen slasher movie," she replies, and we both laugh at this. Whatever my mood, Rosa can make me laugh about anything. She has this dark, sometimes cruel humor that I need right now, and after just a few minutes, I've forgotten all about Jennifer.

We chat some more, and she says her uncle's calling, so I let her go and wander downstairs, where to my delight there's no sign of Jennifer.

"Did she go?" I ask Iris.

"Think so, can't hear her talking about herself," she says with a cheeky smile.

I wink at her—it seems Iris shares the same opinion as me regarding Mrs. Radley.

"Mummy, did you find the string and paper clips? We *neeed* them!" Sam asks impatiently.

"Oh, I'm so sorry, guys, Mrs. Radley came and then Rosa rang and . . . I'm on it now."

I immediately check the kitchen drawers. I know we have them in abundance but I can't remember where I've put them. So, I wander through to the sitting room, check the drawers in there and then run upstairs to Tom's office, which isn't an office at all, more like a storage room. It's where he keeps his laptop and mountains of papers and financial forms, and I rarely come in here—it's his den and I've been given strict instructions not to tidy it up, says he can't find anything after I've been in here.

I'm surprised he can find anything when I *haven't* tidied, but it's not my problem. *If he wants a messy desk, he shall have one*, I think, looking at the piles of papers and books gathering dust on his antique desk. Tom loves his desk—it cost a fortune, but he says it will appreciate in value and we'll be able to sell it for a fortune one day, like the house—I hope he's right.

I glance over at the window—it's next to Sam's room and though the window's tiny, it's high up and there's a great view of the pool. A perfect rectangle in ridiculous blue, the pink parasols and black sun loungers waiting against turquoise water. I think they'll wait forever; we won't be going down there anytime soon. At least—thanks to Tom's scrubbing—the tiles are now flawless and free of malicious graffiti.

Then, to my surprise, I see him. He's down there, strolling around his precious pool, a drink in one hand, like Kubla Khan gazing on Xanadu. I guess he still has the biggest crush on his pool, and unlike me he's okay revisiting the crime scene as it were. It's good to watch someone you know intimately from afar: the familiarity is erased and you can see them for the first time all over again.

My husband is handsome—he looks good in his blue linen shirt, which complements his summer tan. I need to love him again like I did before this horrible mess happened. I need to stop thinking about what Chloe said and go with what I *know*. Tom has his faults: he spends too much, he loses his temper sometimes, and he can be more materialistic than me, wanting the best of everything. But ultimately, he's a good husband and father, we are happy together most of the time, and he loves me.

Watching him in the evening sunshine, I thank my lucky stars for finding this man quite late in life. He picked me up and fixed me after a very long time of being broken, and then we had Sam, and I was whole again. I hear my little boy laughing and I'm reminded of the task in hand, finding the paper clips and string, so I turn back to the desk, open the first drawer and immediately find a bunch of paper clips. Delighted, I place them on a shelf before trying to find some string, and as I put them down, I look up again for one last glance of Tom by his pool.

But to my surprise, I see Tom's not alone down there anymore; he seems to be talking to someone. He's laughing, and his whole body seems animated, like he's telling a funny story, and then I see Jennifer. She's also laughing, and touching his arm. She didn't go home after all.

FORTY-FOUR

I'm shocked at the ease with which Tom and Jennifer are chatting. He barely spoke to her in the kitchen. Their body language is totally different from the way they were engaging, or not engaging, in the kitchen earlier. Since when are they so comfortable with each other? I tell myself it's nothing to worry about and nothing bad is going to happen.

I watch for a while, and they continue to chat. She has a drink too, and I see he's opened up the pool drinks trolley. I need to go down there, make my presence felt—I am so on edge now, and I know it's partly because I'm recovering from Chloe, but still, it makes me uneasy. I just don't like the way she's standing so close to him. She's far too comfortable, and I need to break it up. I decide to find the string first then go downstairs, and as difficult as it will be to go near the pool, I'll join them.

I go back to the desk and open the next drawer on the off chance there's some string. As I rummage through, I see something shining among the detritus that intrigues me. I pick it up for closer inspection: it's a star key ring with keys attached, and as I look more closely, I see something written on the big silver star that quickens my heart. It says *Chloe*.

I feel a thump in my stomach as I turn the keys over in my hand—these are the spare set of keys to our house. The keys Chloe *insisted* she'd given back to Tom, but he'd insisted she hadn't. But Chloe can't have returned them because she'd have needed keys on the night of the fire, as the only way to get into the back garden is through the house. Unless she climbed a neighbor's wall? She'd had to have them to take the blue plastic sandals from my memory box, and later to get onto the patio and leave the orange towel. And how did she come into the house and steal my shirt, and then return it? She couldn't do any of that without keys.

I remember Rosa suggesting that Chloe might have had the keys copied, but if so, why is her key ring on *this* set?

I pull the drawer right out and find an old mobile phone, pens, a staple gun, and a stack of yellow papers that have been pushed to the back of the drawer. These look like the papers Chloe brought to our home that first night, the reason she stopped by. Tom had taken them from her, referring to the stack of papers as the builders' invoices.

It seemed odd to me at the time that anything from business accounts would be on yellow paper. But I didn't question it and never saw the papers again until now, and as I leaf through them and see they are all blank, I *know* something's not right. The paper is thick, like children's drawing paper—was it something Chloe had in her bag for Emily? Was she *pretending* to deliver something to Tom just to come inside the house? And if so, why did Tom go along with the charade and say these blank sheets of paper were builders' invoices?

I look more closely and find a small plastic wallet Tom's pushed to the back of the drawer. When I open it, I see receipts, lots of them, all kept so he can claim them back as expenses for his tax; nothing unusual about that, but something makes me tip the wallet onto the desk and go through the receipts. One receipt stands out immediately. I recognize the logo: it's a receipt from The Candle Company, for candles bought in Looe just weeks ago. When I'd questioned him about being on the mailing list, he'd said he'd bought a gift for me. I still haven't received that gift—I wonder who he bought it for? Bells are ringing. I'm trying not to hear them, so I continue to go through the receipts. Most are as I expected: for meals he's had when he's been working away and that he needs to claim for, but every now and then I find one for a restaurant not far from here. There are receipts for restaurants in Sidmouth and Dorset, a few in North Devon. I lay them out on the desk, trying to work this out. I was still in Manchester on these dates, and as far as I knew, Tom was here at home, working on the house night and day; rarely did he even go to the pub for a pint. So if he was entertaining clients, or work colleagues, why didn't he tell me?

I feel slightly nauseous. *What has been going on?* There are seven receipts for dinner for two, often with a bottle of champagne, and sometimes an overnight stay. All at the same restaurant in Penzance.

I hear her voice, the high-pitched, anxious whine trying hard to convince me she was telling the truth. *We were discreet, we didn't go out much. Sometimes we'd head down into Penzance, to a lovely, quiet little restaurant and have dinner there.*

Then I find more receipts: a B&B in North Devon, and more recently another even more worrying one, in Cornwall, the day before Chloe died.

I try desperately to come up with an innocent explanation. But however hard I try, I just can't.

I don't know what to think; my head is all over the place. Hotels and restaurants, with dates that are impossible to fathom. It's all too much: the yellow papers, the candles, and now these receipts. I stand over the scraps of paper littering the desk. Have I been stupid? Were the clues here all along? Did Chloe and Tom have an affair? Was Chloe telling the truth the whole time?

FORTY-FIVE

Once downstairs, I head outside to the pool, and as I walk down the garden I hear the tinkle of her laughter and his deeper, calmer tones. I'm not the jealous type, but this time in Cornwall has tested me and made me realize that after all I've been through, I've spent the past few years hiding. I couldn't take any more pain in my life, and I'm now wondering, does that mean I've not faced the truth when it's been right in front of me? Did I find Chloe's stories too hard to take—was it easier to believe she was lying? I don't know the answers to those questions yet. But from now on I'm going to seek the answers, not hide from them, and when I'm confronted by the truth, I intend to face it head on and deal with it.

I push through the door to the pool and enter with a big, beaming smile on my face. Tom and Jennifer are sitting on two sun loungers moved close together, and on seeing me, he immediately stands up, distancing himself from her.

"Jennifer! You're still here?" I say, making a point of looking at my watch.

As we know, Jennifer Radley finds it hard to hide her feelings, and she's clearly disappointed to see me. She shifts awkwardly on the sun lounger, her smile barely causing a crease.

"Actually, I really should go," she says.

"No, stay for another drink; after all, it's *me* you came to see." I pause and look from one to the other. "Isn't it?"

"Yes...I..." She doesn't know where to put herself. She was obviously loving Tom's company, but as soon as I arrived, her light went out.

"So rude of me to bugger off and leave you with Tom. I hope he's been entertaining you?"

Tom is now standing behind the drinks trolley. "I've been waiting for you to join us. I've saved you some." He lifts his cocktail shaker and, grabbing a glass, pours the drink from high.

Jennifer and I watch, mesmerized, as he dresses the glass with curly lemon peel and a tiny lemon flower.

"I have a very talented husband," I say as he hands me the glass. I take a sip. "Wow, Tom, that's *delicious*."

"Sicilian lemon gin. I bought it specially for you. I knew you'd love it." He smiles.

"Aren't you making one for Jennifer?"

"No, I've had one," she says, standing up stiffly.

"Oh, I see, you two started without me?"

Tom gives me a slightly reprimanding look, but I ignore him and sit on the sun lounger Jennifer has just vacated.

"So, I'll be on my way," she says, looking at Tom.

"Hey, good to see you, Jennifer," I say, with a half-hearted wave.

"You have a beautiful home," she says. "Tom's worked so hard on it."

"Yes, he has, we love it here." I smile sweetly.

I watch her leave, escorted by Tom to the house, and wonder not for the first time if I'm becoming insecure, but I put it down to what Rosa calls my post-Chloe paranoia.

I leave it a few minutes but can't stay by the pool alone, so I go back to the house to make sure she's gone.

Tom's in the kitchen, gazing at his phone, which means our

uninvited guest has left the building. I don't want to talk to him just yet. I have a lot of questions for him and I need to gather my thoughts before I start.

I hear Iris and Sam laughing as they run up the stairs. I need a cuddle from my kid right now; I know that will give me the strength to face whatever it is that's waiting for me.

"I'm just making a phone call, Sam. Be back in a minute to read you a story," Iris says.

So I pop into his room, where he's lying in bed with a stack of books, waiting for Iris to return. I smile to myself—poor Iris is going to be here for a while.

"I found what you asked for," I say, brandishing the paper clips as I walk into his room.

"What about the string, Mummy?"

"Sorry, I couldn't find any. I'll get some tomorrow, you can finish the decorations then." I sit on the bed. "Are you okay, sweetie?" I ask. He's had a tough time for a little one. Thinks he's seeing people in his room and waving from the pool. We moved house, he started preschool, made a friend, lost a friend, was introduced to the concept of death, and not just Chloe's. For a while he thought that Emily's dad was buried in her garden, but it was actually sunflower seeds to commemorate him. He died of cancer two years ago, and though Emily is too young to remember him, she has a fascination with death that she passed on to Sam. I feel a constant need to check in on him, reassure him in case his imagination takes over again.

"I'm excited about my party."

"Oh, sweetie, I bet you are, it's going to be great fun." His joy overtakes my fears and anxiety; he gives me hope, and while Sam's here I know everything will be okay. I lie next to him on the bed, kiss his head, and put my arm around him.

"Can Emily come to my party?"

"I'm afraid not, darling. Emily lives in Bristol now with her mummy."

Tom and I have tried to protect him, but kids at preschool have said things to him about someone dying in our pool, and he needs reassurance.

"Is Daddy's friend coming to my party?"

My heart sinks—he's too young to understand what death means, and I have to keep explaining to him that Chloe's not coming back. "You mean Emily's mum... I mean, auntie? I told you, darling, she's in heaven."

"Not *her*!" he replies, impatient at my apparent stupidity.

"Oh, okay. But I don't know who you mean, darling—do you know her name?"

"Mickey Mouse!" he says, and starts laughing.

"If she was a *real* person, she wouldn't be called Mickey Mouse, would she?" I say with a smile.

He laughs at this.

"So, does Daddy's friend have a *real* name?" I ask gently.

"Mickey Mouse!" He nods.

Sam's tired and being typically silly like all four-year-old boys, but I really don't want him to think he's seeing Chloe again, that she's coming to his room to kiss him good night. So I pursue this and try and find out who he thinks this friend is.

"Is Daddy's friend *my* friend too?" I ask.

He shakes his head.

"So this is just *Daddy's* friend?"

"Yes, you know, the lady who goes in your bed with *Daddy*!"

FORTY-SIX

Before I can ask Sam any more questions, Iris appears, bright and smiley as ever.

"Come on, you, let's start our readathon," she says, affectionately.

I thank her, and after giving Sam a final hug and a good night kiss, I head off to the kitchen, where Tom is still gazing at his phone.

"Tom, I'd like to have a talk," I say.

He looks up from his phone, concern on his face. "Okay, darling."

"Iris is with Sam, so we're okay to go and sit on the patio," I say. "I don't want Iris to hear us—or Sam."

"Oh... in that case, shall we have a final drink together by the pool? No one can hear us there."

"It's late and a little chilly," I say.

"I know, but I feel like it's the last of the summer—we should make the most of the evening. It's only six thirty, the night is young," he says, and with a flourish he puts his sweater around my shoulders and grabs my hand. As he leads me down the garden, I have a rising sense of panic. I don't want to go to the pool. I want to stay safely near the house, not down where someone died.

I can only see death in water, but I know if I say anything, he'll think I'm ill again, being hysterical or unreasonable. I tell myself it's a small sacrifice, and if he wants to sit by his pool, then so be it.

"Tom, I feel like there are still some things about what happened with Chloe that I don't understand," I say once we're by the pool. I moved the sun loungers farther away while he poured us a drink and we're now sitting together in the silence.

"Okay, what don't you understand?" He's smiling, caressing my hand.

First, I explain to him about finding the keys in his drawer.

"Well, I didn't put them there—she didn't give them back to me, I *told* you!" He's trying to be patient with me, but I hear the irritation in his voice. "Perhaps she put them in my drawer when she put your shirt back in the laundry?" he offers.

"Yeah, she *could* have," I agree, then go on to tell him about the receipts.

"My expenses," he says with a shrug.

"Dinners for two with champagne?" I ask incredulously.

He lifts his hand from mine, no more gentle caressing; he realizes he needs something more than that to keep me calm. "When a deal's struck, champagne is always ordered. Surely you know that?"

"Is it? That seems slightly decadent."

"Rachel, what exactly are you saying, that I have dinner with another woman?"

"I don't know, but what finance deals were you conducting in Penzance? It's a beautiful place, but it isn't exactly the hub for global finance and commerce, is it?"

"We have clients all over the country—you know that."

"But you never mentioned it. When I was in Manchester, you led me to believe you were just working on the house."

"I was, but I also did a couple of deals. You know how I hate asking you for money, like a child being given pocket money. I just wanted a little financial autonomy, that's all."

"Fair enough, but I just think it's odd you never mentioned that you spent seven evenings in Penzance."

"I'm sorry, I didn't realize we were counting!"

"I found seven receipts."

"Okay, so I didn't tell you where I was every single minute of the day. Perhaps you'd like to put a tracker on me? I'm not sure I know exactly *where* in the city of Manchester you were."

"I couldn't go *anywhere*, I was home with Sam every night." I take a breath. I have to go there. "And talking of Sam, he told me today that Daddy's friend sleeps in our bed," I say.

For a moment, it's like the world stops. The silence is deafening, and I feel like we're both suspended in this make-or-break moment.

"Did something happen when I was away in London doing interviews for that article?" I hear myself ask. It's the only time I've left the house overnight, and I might be overthinking everything, but I have to address this.

Eventually, he sighs and puts his head down. "Oh, Rachel," he says, and I hold my breath, waiting for the confession that will change our lives in seconds. "Sam says all sorts of things—he's always talking about people dying or being buried in the garden. It was Chloe's niece who started all that shit," he says, putting his hand back on mine.

"Yeah, he has an imagination and can get carried away, but he's mentioned 'Daddy's friend' before."

"That doesn't mean *anything*."

"Is he talking about Chloe? Did Sam see you together?"

He's looking at me with such horror now. "No. And I can't believe you'd even ask me that."

"Sorry, I had to."

He seems to consider this. "I understand, it can't be easy for you with me being away, and Chloe spouting her poison." He puts his arm around me. "Rachel," he says softly, all the irritation at my questions now gone. "I was thinking tonight about the last time you and I were here together."

"You mean the night Chloe—"

"Yes, but I don't remember *that*." He's shaking his head, like he might be able to shake her out of it. "Let's not allow her to taint the memory of that night *before* she turned up with her poison."

He starts to kiss me, putting his hand on my knee and pushing it up under my dress.

"I'm sorry, Tom," I say, "I can't. Not now, not here."

"I've been thinking all night about how you lay here in that red dress, your breasts..."

I hear the thumping of the pool—*whoosh thump, whoosh thump*—the eerie blue light coming from the water, just like that night. I'm lying here, where we are now, champagne, my red dress, the way we kissed; it felt good. But now I can't see Tom and me, only Tom and Chloe, in the water together, as they were before, but this time it's different. And that's when I remember. It's all so clear, so terrible, and I've known all along, but like the affairs, I pretended to myself I was mistaken, because I didn't want to lose him.

"Chloe's death wasn't an accident. You murdered her."

FORTY-SEVEN

"You killed Chloe because she'd said too much, and even though I was convinced she was lying, she wasn't giving up. She'd come back to tell me more, to warn me that you were still planning to kill me."

"Oh my God! You really have been messed up by this, haven't you?" he says. "I think we need help for you. I don't think you're fit to look after Sam anymore. I'm going to call a doctor, Rachel, you aren't well at all."

"Chloe told me that you loved her, that you planned to be together," I continue, ignoring his threats. "But for you to get married and live here in this house, happily ever after—I had to have an accident," I hear myself say into the blue darkness.

He's looking at me intently, shaking his head. He seems shocked by this—but is he shocked at what I'm saying, or that Chloe told me?

"Everything is beginning to make sense now. You plowed *all* my inheritance into this house and didn't stop until there was nothing left. I pushed back but not enough. I let you do it because it made you happy and I believed you when you said it was an investment and you had our backs. But all the time, this place was merely somewhere for you to put my money while you worked out what to do with me. My dad was right not to trust you."

"You don't know what you're saying, love." He's trying to sound calm, caring, talking to me like I'm mad. But I can see he's scared. "When we met, you were like this, talking in riddles, imagining things that never happened. I was so worried about you, I thought you might be committed."

"Yeah, but I was never going to be committed to a psychiatric hospital. I was sad and confused, because I was *grieving*!"

"And you're sad and confused again, and still letting Chloe destroy our lives with her lies."

"No, Tom, *you're* destroying our marriage with *your* lies, and the biggest lie happened the night Chloe died."

"You really are confused. You were there, you saw what happened: we fell in the water, it could have been either one of us who drowned. It was an *accident*," he's hissing through gritted teeth.

I'm shaking my head; I can't live with this anymore. "You pushed her underwater. Then you held her head down with both hands until she died."

All the time I'm talking, he's spluttering, trying to speak, but I talk over him.

"Then you made sure she was dead, climbed out of the water, picked up the champagne bottle from the ice bucket and hit yourself over the head."

"That just *isn't* true—you had a panic attack, you were out of it, you have no idea what happened."

I shake my head. "I didn't have a panic attack, I saw it all. I buried it for a while and lied to myself and the police to save you, because I didn't want to lose you. I've lost too many people I love, and I couldn't go through it again. And in truth, I was glad she was dead, and I was grateful to you for killing her, because I got my life and my freedom back. I didn't believe her, I believed you! But now I know a life is worth nothing when it's built on a lie, and

I'm ashamed of myself for going along with you. You *murdered* her, Tom, and I'm just as bad as you because I watched you do it then covered it up with a lie."

He slowly stands up, and I feel the heat of his anger, the fury he must have been containing for a long time. "After everything I've done for you... I saved you, you were a mess. Then your idiot father decided I wasn't good enough—he told me I would never have his money because he didn't trust me. That hurt." He bends down, his face in mine. "It fucking hurt that a senile old man had the audacity to say I wasn't good enough, that I'd blow it all and ruin you."

I'm shocked at this.

"Dad said that?"

"Yes."

I make a move to stand up from the sun lounger, but before I can, he's grabbed me around the throat. Taken by surprise, I can't get my breath, I can't even scream, and he's now lifting me into the air. I catch sight of his face in the darkness, lit only by the pool. It's wet with tears.

I finally catch my breath. "Please, Tom, NO!"

He gives a loud roar that seems to fill the skies, and hurls me into the pool. As I hit the water, the shock numbs me. Trying not to panic, I move my arms, flutter my legs and breathe. But I *can't* breathe, and every time I try to raise my head above the water, he's there. He's standing by the side of the pool, just watching me. I reach out to him, my hands cutting through the water, grasping, and inside I'm screaming. And when I finally sink down into the deep-blue, mosaic-tiled grave, all I see is Toby, his arms open, calling, "Mummy."

My head fills up with water and memories, an old video camera playing a grainy film on a projector in my mind.

Mummy fell asleep, and when she wakes, she can't see Daddy or her little boy in the sea anymore. She can't leave the deck chairs, the picnic, the beach toys, so she stands up, trying to locate them so she can go back to enjoying her rest. Her hand shields her eyes from the sun as she looks out to sea, but there are hundreds of people on the beach and in the water—how will she ever see them? So much splashing and screams of joy today, no one would hear the screams of horror if someone was drowning.

FORTY-EIGHT
ONE WEEK LATER

I ease myself out of bed. It's good to finally be back in my own bedroom; the hospital ward was so noisy and intrusive. After what I've been through I need peace and quiet, and acres of calm.

Gazing into the full-length mirror, I almost can't believe I'm still here, still alive.

When Tom pushed me in the deep end of the pool, he assumed I'd panic, go under the water and drown. Even without Chloe, he was continuing with his plan to kill me, make it look like an accident and play the grieving widower. Soon after, he'd sell the house and walk away a free man with over a million pounds, all my inheritance.

I look at my weakened, battered body and the hand marks around my neck, and though it hurts my throat to cry, I feel it tighten as the tears come.

I remember him watching from above as the water enveloped me, pulling me down under the water, into the dark, silence. I thought I'd died; I believed that was the end for me. But seeing Toby reminded me of Sam, and I knew what I had to do. So, I pushed with all my might and instinct to the surface, thrusting myself up through the deep, dark blue, emerging to gasp my breath. Swimming strongly and confidently through the water, I saw Tom in the distance, climbing over the garden wall, assuming I was already dead.

It had been my dearest wish to move on, overcome my terror and embrace this new life in Cornwall. I'd longed to join Tom and Sam in the pool, spend days on the beach, paddling in the sea—but most of all I'd wanted them to be proud of me, and for my son to know that anything is possible.

I remember that first day, just walking to the pool and sitting there, then stepping in, slowly, cautiously, until the water was up past my knees. My heart was in my mouth, the water was heavy around me like a huge weight pulling me down, and the realization struck me that I was completely alone, there was no one to save me. It had taken every ounce of courage I had, but each morning while Tom was away and Sam was at preschool, I took a step farther, going shoulder-deep, recalling what Sam's teacher Chris had told him about breathing and moving his limbs. I wanted to move my limbs too, but at first sheer terror prevented this. I was frozen to the spot, crying, "I can't, I can't."

But I did, and though my fear was intense, and I was shaking, tears streaming down my cheeks, I finally taught myself to swim. By sitting in on Sam's lessons, and listening to Chris's encouragement, and just watching my little boy splashing and swimming and laughing, I'd overcome my worst fear.

And here I am now. I'm improving, but the damage to my lungs may affect me for life. I was in the water for four minutes—one more minute and it would have been a different story, because at five minutes the brain begins to die, resulting in coma or death. I currently have mild memory loss, and my motor coordination is poor; only time will tell if I'll ever fully recover. But I'm alive, and Sam still has a mummy, which is just as well because his daddy is in prison awaiting trial for the attempted murder of his mummy.

A neighbor I've never met saved me. He heard Tom roaring as he threw me in the pool and called the police.

I've heard a lot of stories about Tom since all this happened—amazing how you can live with someone and not really know them, isn't it? Rosa has been taking Sam to preschool, and she says there are rumors about Tom and Jennifer, lots of flirting in the playground when he was taking or collecting Sam. And on more than one occasion, she drove off with Tom, Sam, and her little boy to the beach—perhaps that's where they taught Sam to swim? *Daddy's friend.*

She apparently also had "sleepovers" with Tom in our bed when I wasn't there, and she was the woman who reported me to social services for having a drink problem. Tom must have given her a set of keys—it seems to be part of his extramarital relationship strategy, as he did the same with Chloe, who was still in his thrall when I first came here. She'd do anything for him, and even after we were friends, in those first few weeks she was still doing his bidding, but she began to value our friendship more than the crumbs she received from Tom. In the end, all Chloe wanted was for someone to respect her, to care about her. She was genuinely my friend and wanted to save me—if only I'd believed her.

I'm still trying to piece everything together. I know Tom's motivation was money, but I had no idea he wanted it *so* much he was prepared to kill me. As I said to Rosa, he had the money anyway while he was married to me, but he was superficial and probably wanted a shiny new wife to go with the new life. He'd obviously fallen for her, even before Chloe came on the scene, but in order to be with Jennifer and keep my money, he had to get rid of me.

That day when I found them sitting together by the pool having a drink, she seemed very much at home, she'd obviously been a regular visitor even before I moved in. Disillusioned by her own marriage, Jennifer Radley no doubt imagined herself living at the house, hosting pool parties, and probably being Mrs. Frazer herself one day. He was arrested at Jennifer's house; he'd climbed over the wall and run all the way there. He said he'd been with her all evening—she was obviously going to be his alibi should there be any questions over my "accident." But by then I was sitting by the pool, wrapped in warm blankets, telling the police how my husband had just tried to kill me.

Knowing the man I loved, the father of my child, wanted me dead is almost too painful to comprehend. I often wondered why my father was so adamant that Tom have no independent control over the inheritance. It angered Tom, and puzzled me, but now I know: my father must have had a glimpse of what Tom was capable of—something I never saw. The restrictions in Dad's will were his way of protecting me, as he always had, and now I know he always will. He's with Toby now, but they walk beside me, and the night Tom tried to kill me, Dad scooped me up and carried me to safety, as he always did, and always will. I will never get over the hurt, and I'll find it hard to trust again, but my father is proof that there are good, kind men out there who hold their loved ones close and protect them fiercely, and forever.

I wasn't sure if I wanted to come back to the house: so many bad memories, and as it turns out, it wasn't the happy home I'd once envisaged. But Sam's here with Rosa, and they make it feel like home. As soon as she found out what had happened, Rosa left her apartment in Manchester and moved in to look after Sam while I recovered in the hospital. Sadly her uncle died, and her aunt was taken into care, but it meant she could care for Sam full-time along with a little help from Iris. Thanks to them, Sam's the one thing I didn't have to worry about while in the hospital, and today I'm home and know I'll have the support of both of them.

"I was so scared we were going to lose you. I love you so much," Rosa said last night when she brought me home from the hospital. Iris had stayed late to babysit Sam while Rosa drove the fifty-mile return journey to the hospital to collect me. I've always valued my friends, but Rosa and now Iris have turned out to be true friends, who were here in my time of need.

Rosa adores the controversial pool and swims there with Sam

every day regardless of the weather. "Perhaps we should change the initials in the tiles," she said the other day.

I'd forgotten that the mosaic was a T, an S, and an R—our initials, our little family. It hit me again how much Tom was prepared to lose just for money. I really never knew him.

My goal now is to join Sam and Rosa in the pool, and even if that means swimming throughout the year, even with snow on the ground, I will do it.

As I proved to myself the night Tom tried to kill me, I'm a good swimmer now. I can swim *very* well, but I want to surprise them, in a good way, though no one's more surprised than me that I can swim. That night when I sank down into the pool, I must have been hallucinating and saw Toby with his arms out. He was calling me, and I longed to go with him, to give myself up to the water and be with my firstborn, but as I held him, he felt like Sam. I knew then it wasn't my time yet, and Toby was telling me to go back and be with his brother because he needed me. That's what had given me the energy and courage to garner every residue of strength I had left and push up through the weight of water. And taking that gasp of air, my first thoughts were of Toby and Sam. I survived with seconds to spare, proof that there's nothing more powerful than a mother's love; even after their child is gone, the love remains.

FORTY-NINE

The police have come to give me an update on the case. They have assured me that Tom will not walk away from court when he's tried later this year, because it turns out he really did intend to kill me. They have a confession, and two female officers gently break it to me that my husband planned my demise soon after my dad died and made me the sole beneficiary of his will.

I can't help it—I cry at this. I had no idea he hadn't loved me for so long.

"He's a psychopath," I say.

"Probably," the officer replies. "You really can't tell—he's a good-looking guy with all the chat. They walk among us," she adds, handing me a tissue.

"He is a piece of work," her colleague remarks, before confirming Chloe's story about his plan to have her push me in the pool.

"After his arrest, during our house search, we found an old phone in his desk drawers," she says. "We're here because our tech unit managed to retrieve some messages, and we wondered if you could shed any light on who he might have been messaging. Whoever it was, we can't find them, but it looks like he had an accomplice who was helping him to gaslight you."

"Yes, and I'd thought it was Chloe."

They look at each other and one says, "Mmm, initially it might have been. He obviously recruited her at the beginning of his campaign, but some of these messages sent recently, refer to Chloe in the third person, and according to the time stamps, messages were still being sent after Chloe had died."

My stomach drops. "So it was someone else and *not* Chloe?"

"It would seem that way; in fact, we don't think Chloe was ever really in the running. Your husband was only with her so he could use her as a scapegoat."

"Yes, he wanted her to kill me so his hands would be clean, and she'd take the rap. He was always encouraging me to call the police about her. He knew that when she did finally kill me as he'd instructed, my calls would be the trail of evidence leading straight to Chloe."

Everything is starting to make sense now, and I know exactly who his real accomplice is. He never loved Chloe, he needed someone stronger, sophisticated, more fitting for his new life, but in order to achieve that, he needed someone like Chloe to do the dirty work. He knew from the time they'd worked together at the bank that she wasn't credible, but she was disposable. Chloe was flaky and vulnerable, and she loved him so much that she'd do anything for him—at first. And if at any point she did change her mind and tell on him, no one would believe her anyway, and he'd just say she was mad. But she *wasn't* mad. Chloe made bad choices and was even prepared to kill for the man she loved. But she *wasn't* mad—or bad, she was simply naïve and desperately seeking love and friendship, the validation of another in her lonely life. But when she finally woke up, and refused to do Tom's bidding, she had to go.

"She always said that men made out some women were mad. Tom did that to her, and he continued to toy with her until her death. And he also wound me up about her—he told me she was dangerous, and perhaps she was, but he was manipulating her—*and* me."

"We have a printout of some of the messages your husband

sent to the other person on his old phone," the officer says, tearing me from my thoughts as I try to process what has happened. She takes out a file, opens it, and hands me three large sheets of paper. "He had named her in his phone as 'Her.'"

I take the papers and begin to read the random texts.

"Some are immediate responses, some days apart," she explains. "We think that the texts stopped when they were together."

I nod, unable to speak, and continue to read.

Tom: I love you. I can't wait to be with you forever.

Her: Me too. I feel guilty, but she's so stressed and anxious. She never got over what happened with her son, and now she can't look after this one. She will turn him into a wreck.

Tom: I know, it breaks me to see my son so weakened by her. She won't even let him in the pool.

Her: We can teach him to swim. Sam will love that.

Tom: I love you. Xxx

Her: I left the towel on the patio.

Tom: Good! Did you make it look like Chloe has been midnight swimming?

Her: Oh yes!

Her: I took the sandals. There are so many things in that memory box. Made me feel sad for her. I don't think I can do this.

Tom: Of course you can. She's unhappy, she never got over it. We'll be doing the kindest thing finally giving her peace.

Her: *I don't know. Hasn't she been through enough? Let's just run away together?*

Her: *I wrote "Drown Bitch" on the tiles in red paint.*

Tom: *Shit. Why did you do that? The tiles will be ruined.*

Her: *Is that all you care about? I thought we decided it had to look real?*

Her: *I called social services, they're looking into it.*

Tom: *Good, if we can discredit her at preschool, with the police and social services, when she has her accident, it will look like she's even madder than she is.*

Her: *I don't think I can go through with this.*

Tom: *Why are you saying this? She's anxious, controlling, she's ruining my life and will go on to ruin his.*

Her: *But, Tom, we aren't killers.*

Tom: *No names.*

Her: *Fuck no names. She's not a bad person. I'm not even sure she's a bad mother, whatever you say. She doesn't let Sam swim because she already lost a child to drowning. That doesn't make her a bad mother.*

Tom: *You can't back out now. What about our plans to sell everything and charter a yacht to take us round the Med? Just me, you, and Sam. Don't break my heart. I'm coming over tomorrow. We can stay in bed for days and I'll convince you. It's the RIGHT thing to do.*

Her: I sent the shirt to C today with a note from your wife to say she's sorry and she'd love to see her wearing it. C will be SO excited. She has a real crush on your wife.

Tom: Yeah, and my wife's gonna be SO pissed off to see her in that shirt.

Her: It's been driving her insane.

Tom: She was convinced C had taken it and she caused a scene at the preschool.

Her: I know! I couldn't believe how well it worked. Anyway, I snuck back into the house when she was asleep and you were playing football with Sam. It's back now in your washing machine.

Tom: Good job! I wondered why she was freaking out. She's white as a sheet.

I finally put down the papers. I can't read every single message—the ones when they're declaring undying love and saying what they'd like to do to each other are just too much.

"I'm sorry to put you through that," the officer says.

"It's fine—if I can help put her behind bars too, I will."

"Who do you think Her might be then—any ideas?"

"Jennifer Radley, a mum from preschool. They seem very close. I reckon she's the one who replaced Chloe, she may even have been in his life *before* Chloe. They may have met when he was alone here in Cornwall working on the house."

"Do you have any . . . proof of them having a relationship?"

"They looked pretty close standing together by the pool the night he attacked me." I stumble slightly on this—it's all still so raw. I can see by their faces I'm not giving them enough concrete evidence to even question her. Then I remember something Iris said. "One of the teachers said she saw Tom and Jennifer driving off together one afternoon."

"Oh, okay, and what's the name of the teacher?"

"Iris Johnson. She's a nice girl, only about thirty. I believe her—she doesn't tell tales."

"Okay, well, we'll need to look into this, but it makes sense that he's been seeing someone locally—we've discovered that when he was supposed to be working away up north, he was actually staying at an address not far from here."

This is another punch in the stomach for me—so he wasn't even being honest about work. No wonder he never seemed to get paid, the consultancy work never existed, presumably all that time he was holed up in some love nest with Jennifer instead. I want to cry again, but I don't allow myself to do that. I need to be strong; I need to make sure he gets the longest sentence possible. As far as I can see, Jennifer Radley is the only person who knows everything, and I bet she would throw him under the bus to save herself. Despite the fact he seems to be protecting her by not naming her, I doubt very much that Jennifer will return the favor.

FIFTY

It's been several days since the two police officers paid a visit. I've called them to find out what's happening, but without a confession from Jennifer, they say they have no evidence to charge her with anything. Unfortunately, I couldn't speak to the officers who came to the house—I had a stroppy male who probably remembers me calling about Chloe, and when I said I was surprised they hadn't got any further, he said, "Thing is, Mrs. Frazer, I don't think having an affair with your husband is a chargeable offense."

So, fed up with their lack of "policing," I've decided to do my own detective work and find evidence of Jennifer lighting fires in my garden.

Rosa says I'm like Miss Marple, that it's a waste of time and I have to get on with my life, but I can't sleep—it's 8 p.m., and I feel well enough to go for a walk. I tell Rosa I'm just going round the block so she won't nag me about inflaming my joints or whatever the medical term is. She's lying on her bed reading, and she nods and smiles. "I can come with you if you like? Iris is here."

"I just feel like some time alone, to walk and think, you know?"

She nods and, blowing me a kiss, goes back to her novel.

Technically I'm not lying to Rosa, because I am walking round the block, to my neighbor, whose garden backs onto mine. I don't know him, but he was the one who called the police on hearing Tom that night, so basically saved my life.

I visit, essentially, to thank him. He's a nice elderly gentleman, and over a cup of tea, some small talk, and a plate of custard creams, I start quizzing him.

"The night before Chloe Mason died and before my husband was arrested, we had a fire in the back garden. My son thought he saw someone out there, and I wondered if the police have already asked *you* if you saw anyone?" I'm determined to find the evidence and wipe that smug smile from Jennifer's face. If I can get her charged with arson, I'll be winning at life.

"No, I haven't even heard from the police. I thought they'd be in touch after what happened," he says.

That figures. I knew that officer wasn't taking me seriously, but then Tom had encouraged me to tell the police *everything*, however small. And I had. And as Tom had hoped, I'd reported some stupid things that I knew were significant but that the police thought were the ramblings of a madwoman. Abandoned orange towel, anyone?

"So, did you see or hear anyone that night?" I continue with my questioning.

"Only the noise of shouting—it sounded terrible, that's why I called the police."

I try not to be too disappointed.

"Thanks so much, Mr. Wilson," I say as I leave the house. "Do let me know if you remember anything, or if anyone you know saw someone hanging around near my house."

"Of course. I'm sorry I can't be more help, dear, but please, call me Lawrence."

He waves me off, and just as I get to the gate, I hear him calling me. "Rachel, I've just realized, I may have something that could help."

He beckons me back inside.

"We had burglars last year, and my son had that CCTV installed. It's state-of-the-art, and he had it mounted high up on a pole. It's motion-sensitive too, I think—my son reckons you can see foxes in neighbors' gardens. I don't know how to use it, but you're welcome to come and have a look." He chuckles. "I'd like to find the fox you're looking for."

"Me too, Lawrence!" I say, going back into his home.

After a frustrating forty-five minutes of blank screen, he calls his son David for technical assistance, and we're soon watching the footage of his garden and some of mine too.

We scroll through for ages, drink ten cups of tea, and are on the second pack of custard creams when we finally see something.

Lawrence's CCTV footage is brutal. It covers the time when Tom moved in, the months when I was in Manchester, and he was alone. I see him with Chloe, naked, swimming and kissing, and my heart breaks all over again.

"Can we just fast-forward to the night of the fire?" I ask, and eventually we find the time and date and there it is. Clear footage of someone running out into the garden and setting the fire. As pleased as I am that we've got it all on tape, I find it hard to watch, like seeing one of the worst nights of your life on film. But as Lawrence points out, as clear as it is, they're wearing all black and have a hood, so you can't actually see their face.

We both sit too close to the screen, our eyes screwed up in an attempt to pick anything out from the footage. Then unexpectedly, the arsonist turns and, presumably without realizing, looks straight into the camera. The face is clear even in the dusk! I explain everything to Lawrence, who writes down names and times on the tape, and calls the police.

Within seconds, I've said goodbye and I'm running home. My lungs are so weak I'm breathless; my leg is in agony, my heart is beating, but I just keep running.

FIFTY-ONE

Home now, I walk up the stairs, across the landing, gasping and pushing through the pain in my chest. I have to see Sam. I *need* to speak to him.

I push open the door, and just seeing him lying there peaceful, clutching his favorite dinosaur, brings tears to my eyes. He's been exposed to so much in his little life. He knows nothing about his father—I've told him Daddy's away working, and so far he's accepted this. I will have to tell him one day, but each step at a time. Iris is trying to protect him at preschool, and can for now prevent him from being exposed to any information, but one day he'll have to be told before he finds out for himself.

"Darling," I whisper as I walk across the dimly lit room.

Instantly he opens his eyes. "Mummy?" he murmurs.

"I just want to ask you something, darling," I say.

He slowly sits up in bed, smiling.

"Darling, remember you told me that Daddy's friend was called Mickey Mouse?"

He nods and gives a little chuckle.

He's waving his dinosaur in the air aggressively; he seems

agitated. Before I can ask any more, Rosa passes his bedroom door, presumably on her way to the bathroom.

She stops in the doorway smiling at me and blowing kisses to Sam, who giggles as he catches them. I notice on her nightshirt is a picture of Mickey Mouse, and my heart feels like it's stopped.

"Sam, is Rosa Daddy's friend?" I whisper when she's gone. "Was she the one in Daddy's bed?"

"Yes, Mummy." He nods vigorously, waving his dinosaur in the air.

A LETTER FROM SUE

Thank you so much for choosing to read *You, Me, Her*.

Like most people, I don't have a swimming pool in my back garden, but last summer I sat there on a warm day, imagining how wonderful it would be. I thought about that beautiful house near the sea with a pool out back, and how family and friends could wander over to swim and splash, and later turn up for drinks as the sun went down over that perfect turquoise rectangle. But being a thriller writer, I wondered what the downside of having a beautiful house with a swimming pool might be. What if you were handed all this, but it wasn't what your heart wanted? And what if the people around you were more flawed than you ever realized?

For me, this book is about realizing your dreams, then paying the price. Because everything has a price, right?

I hope you enjoyed reading *You, Me, Her* as much as I enjoyed writing it, and if you did, I would be so grateful if you could write a review. It doesn't have to be as long as a sentence—every word counts and is very much appreciated. I love to hear what you think, and it makes such a difference helping new readers to discover one of my books for the first time.

I love hearing from my readers—so please get in touch. You can find me on social media.

Thanks so much for reading,

Sue

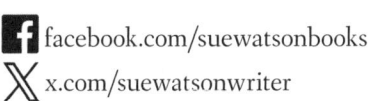

facebook.com/suewatsonbooks
x.com/suewatsonwriter

ACKNOWLEDGMENTS

As always, my huge thanks to the wonderful team at Bookouture, who are amazing, supportive, and expertly transform my ideas into books.

Thanks to my wonderful editor and friend Helen Jenner, who always turns my streams of consciousness into something readable, and hopefully good. Thanks also to DeAndra Lupu, my copyeditor, who provided the final polish and tied up all those loose ends. Thanks also to proofreader Jennifer Davies, and Anna Wallace for a final, final read through.

Much love and appreciation to my friend and beta reader Harolyn Grant, who finds so much in my writing from timelines to dialogue to plot holes. This time she even dragged her brother into the read—big thanks to him too! A special thank you to Su Biela, an amazing beta reader who always finds the vital bits I miss and saves me from falling down plot holes. Huge thanks as always to Sarah Hardy, for being a great publicist and for doing one of her excellent and insightful first reads.

One of the joys of being an author is meeting and getting to know readers and reviewers, all of whom are incredibly friendly and so supportive. So to every single one of you who read, review, and shout about my books—a great big thank you!